Scottish Borders

3 4144 0098 1427 4

GERRI _____ After deci_____ up literat_____ Bristol. _____ in Spain, Thailand, Canada and the United States. She has worked as a cleaner, ice-cream seller, sandwich-maker, pottery sponger, editor and nanny, and is now a professor of creative writing at the University of Alaska, Fairbanks. She is married to fantasy writer, Ian C. Esslemont.

I0626346

# DEAD OF WINTER

ALSO BY GERRI BRIGHTWELL

NOVELS

*Cold Country* (2003)
*The Dark Lantern* (2008)

GERRI BRIGHTWELL

# DEAD OF WINTER

SALT

CROMER

PUBLISHED BY SALT PUBLISHING 2016

2 4 6 8 10 9 7 5 3 1

Copyright © Gerri Brightwell 2016

Gerri Brightwell has asserted her right under the Copyright, Designs
and Patents Act 1988 to be identified as the author of this work.

*This book is sold subject to the condition that it shall not, by way of
trade or otherwise, be lent, resold, hired out, or otherwise circulated
without the publisher's prior consent in any form of binding or cover
other than that in which it is published and without a similar condition
including this condition being imposed on the subsequent publisher.*

This book is a work of fiction. Any references to historical events, real
people or real places are used fictitiously. Other names, characters, places
and events are products of the author's imagination, and any resemblance to
actual events or places or persons, living or dead, is entirely coincidental.

First published in Great Britain in 2016 by
Salt Publishing Ltd
12 Norwich Road, Cromer, Norfolk NR27 0AX United Kingdom

www.saltpublishing.com

Salt Publishing Limited Reg. No. 5293401

A CIP catalogue record for this book is available from the British Library

ISBN 978 1 78463 049 2 (Paperback edition)
ISBN 978 1 78463 054 6 (Electronic edition)

Typeset in Neacademia by Salt Publishing

Printed and bound in Great Britain by Clays Ltd, St Ives plc

Salt Publishing Limited is committed to responsible forest management.
This book is made from Forest Stewardship Council™ certified paper.

*For Cam and my boys, Conor, Ross and Callum.*
*Thank you for making life so much fun.*

| SCOTTISH BORDERS LIBRARY SERVICES | |
|---|---|
| 009814274 | |
| Bertrams | 23/03/2016 |
| | £8.99 |
| | |

# DEAD OF WINTER

SCOTTISH BORDERS COUNCIL

INFORMATION SERVICE

F ISHER STOPS AT the lights. It's going on four p.m. and the town's got that deep undersea feel he hates. Beyond the windshield, shapes swim out of the darkness: a lit-up city bus heaving itself through the intersection, a busted-up Chevy bouncing in slo-mo over a snow berm, a cop car trailing it silent as a shark. Headlights catch frost clinging thick as algae to a fence. Across the road a row of buildings squats against the cold. Neon flashes red and pink and green. Hot girls. Cold beer. Small splashes of color against the sub-arctic night.

Fifty-seven below when Fisher reached the airport to drop off his fare and the ice fog's settling in. Already the streetlights are blurred and past the intersection it's real bad, like a stirred-up sea. Here traffic making the turn vanishes: red taillights hang for a moment, then shrink and wink out like they've gone forever.

It gets you, that kind of cold. It seeps into your soul. It doesn't help that the news is on and Fisher has it turned way up over the rush of warm air from the vents. A suicide bombing in Iraq, the cops here in town looking for a missing state trooper, a pile-up on this very road a few miles away where it leads to the army base and the ground's low and the fog can get real bad. Two people dead, three injured. Fisher's hands tighten on the steering wheel. He thinks of twisted metal and severed limbs, of heads dented and broken. He wonders, when will it be my turn to be snuffed out? Those people, minding their own business, driving to the store or to pick up the kids, and now they're dead. No warning, just gone.

He thinks what he'd leave behind. Not much: a dingy trailer beside his hardly-built house, a sulky, troubled teenage daughter, an ex-wife who's reinvented herself right out of remembering she loved him once upon a time. I'm not a has-been, he thinks, I'm a never-was, a two-hundred-and-forty-pound sad sack, a Class A freaking loser.

He takes a breath and lets his eyes close. Now that he's wrapped in his own darkness, the ache in his head swells and its echo starts up in his cheeks, only that pain's sharper and more insistent. This is the root of his misery. The cold's squeezed all the moisture out of the air, and it's so dry it's making his sinuses smart, as though the front of his head has been scraped out with a knife. He needs something to dull it: Christ, maybe he should call Grisby, get himself some Vicodin, because the pain's bad enough to leave him swimming inside himself, to make the day feel cursed, to make him wish he'd called in sick and watched TV until it was time to go to bed again.

Two hours left of his shift, unless he quits early. Two hours of driving through ice fog and the ache in his head. But hell, the cold means money. People stranded by dead batteries. People who won't be waiting for the bus. Fuck, he can do it.

Staring out the windshield, he can't remember who his fare is. He stops himself glancing in the mirror. A game he has: who's he driving now? He pictures himself pulling up at the airport, the surly guy he was dropping off shoving a twenty at him. Someone coming across the sidewalk, a spidery silhouette, and now he's got it: a lanky woman in a long coat and skirt pulling a small case on wheels. Longish hair. A thin, sour face, a beaky nose. Now he looks in the mirror: her face's bonier than he remembered, her eyes deeper set, but that sour expression's there all right, as though she can't believe her stinking luck at finding herself in Alaska, and not in one of the beautiful parts but the undramatic, deep-frozen Interior, and to cap it all, she's being driven to her hotel in a turd-brown Bear Cab with a cartoon grizzly painted on the side, for fuck's sake. Who came up with that? Maybe she thinks Fisher did.

No hat, a thin scarf, her wool coat some Lower Forty-Eight designer's idea of winter wear. She must have thought January in Alaska wasn't anything to bother herself about because, hell, she's from Minnesota or Michigan where their winters beat all. Fifty-fucking-seven below. No wonder she looks pissed and closed in on herself as she stares out the window. She has her case perched beside her like it's a pet. No other luggage— Fisher'd have pegged her as being in town for a conference or a job interview, except she's headed to the Valu-Inn. A dump of a place. Maybe she doesn't know that. Or perhaps by now she's decided the whole town's a dump. One time he drove a young Scottish woman from the university to a hotel downtown. It was summer and he asked what she thought of the place. She said she'd expected it to be like Sweden, but instead it looked junky and half-derelict, and he'd laughed and said she was seeing it on a good day, too, then had driven fast because he wanted to be shut of her.

Fisher drives this route so often he can pretty much guess how much longer the red will last: long enough for him to reach into the glove compartment, snatch out his bottle of ibuprofen, snap off the lid with his teeth—not enough time to take off his gloves, he thinks—and tip two onto his tongue and wash them down with his half-cold coffee. He's almost right, but the light changes as he's lifting the cup. The pickup to his left surges into the intersection on a cloud of exhaust and he can't see a damned thing, but he finishes the motion of bringing the cup to his lips—the coffee's colder than he thought, disgusting, in fact—and he tips the cup too far. Coffee dribbles around his mouth and he swallows quickly, wipes his chin with his glove. From his pocket his phone rings. He ignores it and steps too hard on the gas. Over the bleat of the phone comes the rush of tires spinning and the slight slip of the cab's rear shimmying.

"Fuck it," he says under his breath and eases up until the tires grip and the gleaming road hauls itself beneath them. The cab bounces over the bumps of ice and its frozen metal groans like a ship going down: at least, like a ship going down in the movies. Then there's a flash of headlights from vehicles waiting at the intersection, the blankness of the fog closing in, and his phone stops ringing.

# 2

H OW OFTEN DOES Fisher's phone ring in the next two hours? Later, when he counts, he'll come up with four times: he'll remember that it rang in the supermarket parking lot as he was helping a skinny old guy into the backseat and settling his groceries beside him; that it rang as he was nosing the cab through the fog downtown with a smug, overweight teenager in the back ferociously chewing gum until he let out a stiff laugh and caught Fisher's eye in the mirror and said, "Bear Cabs—dude, how the hell did you come up with that? You should dress up in a bear suit. Wouldn't that be crazy?"; that it rang again while he was on the expressway getting a lecture from a bland-faced, bristle-haired old woman about not wearing his seatbelt, and trying to tell her no cab driver does, it's too risky, and that it rang again while he was trying to pull out from a stop sign into the thick of the five-thirty traffic by Fat Al's Pizza.

All those times his phone rings, and he doesn't pull it out and check his messages. There's something about the cold air peeling in off the cab's windows and the raw pain pulsing through his head that makes him think, *Fuck you all, fucking leave me alone*, because, really, who could be calling? Someone he gave his card to, someone wanting a ride when he hasn't had any dead time all afternoon. Could be Sally wanting to talk, but that thing they had is over because who needs a girlfriend who's got a husband she forgot to mention on the first few dates? Could be his step-mother wanting something—she always wants something—or Grisby saying let's meet at the Klondike for a

5

drink, when all Fisher wants is to go home and sit in front of the TV with his dog. Maybe it's his daughter: but no, Bree's off to Anchorage with her mom for a couple of days, or should be unless she's fucked things up again. She has a way of doing that.

It's close to six before the idea of all those missed calls needles him and he pulls over outside the Gas-N-Go. Over the radio comes Reggie's scratchy voice telling him he's got a fare wants a no-smoking cab over at the movie theater. Fisher tells Reggie he needs to look at a clock because his shift's about over, but Reggie barks back that he's not far away, is he? And hell, doesn't he want the money?

Reggie's always seething, like it's the only way he knows how to be. Two new cab companies have started up and all he could think to do was paint that ridiculous smiling bear logo on all the Bear Cab vehicles. Who wants a beaten-up taxi with a smiling bear on the door when they can take a sleek white City Cab? Reggie calls them Shitty Cabs, but hell, even their drivers look sleek, not fat-butted men wearied by life, or hard-bitten women with hard-set mouths, or ex-cons who can't do much except drive, and who've been known to take a fare to the airport then come back and rob their house. At least, that's how it was before the cops wised up and now the cabbie's the first person they suspect.

The movie theater's only a few minutes away, and this far up Airport Road the fog's cleared a little. Still, the streetlights have a grimy halo around them, and the blacktop a sleek crystalline look. The cab lurches over the lip of snow into the movie-theater parking lot with its dying-ship groan and Fisher pulls up close to the row of glass doors. Someone hurries out. A man in a green parka and a fur hat, with squarish glasses too big for his thin face, and a peering, mousy look about him. Grisby, like a freaking vision summoned up by the gnawing ache in Fisher's head.

6

He stoops to look through the window and Fisher lowers the glass a little. He calls out, "It's OK, it's me. Get in."

Grisby gets in beside Fisher and taps him on the knee. "Hey man, I called you, I dunno, a hundred times. Why didn't you pick up?"

"Been busy," he says. "Fuck, busy like you wouldn't believe."

"What's the point in having a freaking phone if you don't use it? I mean, that's the whole idea, right? You have it with you so if someone needs you, they can call and there you'll be. Like the freaking cavalry. Had to call Bear Cabs and ask for a no-smoking and hope it'd be you. Fuck it."

"What happened to your car? You lose it again?"

Grisby pushes back his hat a little. The bulk of the fur makes his face look small and pale beneath it, as though he's hiding. And maybe he is. He says, "No, I didn't lose it. Shit, it won't start."

"You turned it off when it's fifty-seven below and went to watch a movie?"

"Christ no—something wrong with the starter. Either that, or the spark plugs. Fuck, I dunno." He sniffs and wipes away the moisture the cold's left beaded on the stubble beneath his nose. His glasses have misted up from the sudden heat and he pulls them off and rubs the lenses with the fingers of his glove. "Just get me out of here."

Fisher swings the cab round and the headlights slip over the exhaust blooming from parked cars. Just before the access road he slows. "Where to?"

"How about that place does the Hawaiian burgers?"

"That's right here." Fisher nods out the window at the bright lights of the restaurant just ahead on the corner. It's always like this. There's something not right with the way Grisby's wired, like he's permanently lost and always will be.

Grisby pushes his glasses back on and stares about him. He

7

rubs his chin and his glove grates over his stubble. It looks like he hasn't shaved in a few days, and that means trouble. "Well shit," he says, "someplace else then. Wherever."

"C'mon, Grisby."

"I've just spent the whole freaking afternoon watching dumb-ass movies. Give me a break."

"Tessa mad at you again, is that it? You worried she's going to come find you? Shit, who needs a girlfriend he's scared of?"

"Shut it, Fisher. I just need a place to hole up for a day or two, that's all."

At first Fisher doesn't say a word. Grisby's going to leave the shower running and the water tank'll run dry, or so well-and-fucking-truly lose the TV remote that they'll never find it, or spill his beer on the sofa and not say a word until Fisher's sat down in it, or forget to let the dog out while Fisher's working and poor Pax'll piss all over the carpet. That's what he did over Thanksgiving when Tessa threw him out of her place, then came looking for him and tried to kick in the door. But what can you do? Grisby showed up with all the fixings for dinner—for the Thanksgiving dinner he was supposed to be sharing with Tessa—plus Vicodin in one pocket and Percocet in the other, and a bottle of bourbon to wash it all down. Man, oh man.

Fisher lets his breath out between his teeth then steers the cab onto the access road. "OK, but I don't want Tessa coming round looking for you again. She's a piece of work. And you still haven't fixed the dent in my door."

"Don't be like that, man. Your trailer's a piece of crap and you're worrying about a dent in your door? Besides, who the hell helped you get the foundation in for your house? Who you going to call to help you unload lumber this summer? Hey?"

Fisher slows for a stop sign then glances over his shoulder as he changes lane. A gas station across the way, a small Mexican restaurant, a hair salon, and it might just as well be two in the

8

morning for the whole strip looks deserted. He pulls up at the lights with the turn signal clicking away and his hands off the wheel. He picks up the radio and tells Reggie, "Nine. Fare to Safeway on Airport and Dawson. Then I'm coming in."

Reggie's voice crackles back at him, "Switch to channel two, Fisher."

Fisher jabs the button, says, "What the hell?"

"Better not be one of your flaky friends you're giving a ride to who's gonna light up in the cab, Fisher, or puke on the seats, or sell painkillers to a real-life goddamn paying fare. You got that?"

On the palm of Fisher's glove the handset looks small, a shrunken head with hard slits across its surface. He says, "What is it with you, Reggie? You wanted me to take this fare." Then he jams the thing back into its holder.

Beside him Grisby's tapping his glove against his knee and his knee's jerking to a crazy beat that's got nothing to do with the Eagles' number coming through the radio. Then he bursts out with, "You're like Captain freaking Kirk in this thing, cruising along nice and warm. But just look out the window—it's some blasted alien planet, and you're the hero, man, carrying me away."

"Why's she mad at you this time?" He glances at Grisby, and Grisby drops his smile.

"Nah," he says, "we're cool. I've got some guy says I owe him for the Vicodin he bought off me. Says it was Tylenol and now he wants his money back. Three hundred bucks."

"That's a lot for Tylenol."

"Wasn't Tylenol, man. I know the difference. He even has the freaking nerve to show me the bottle and tip out these freaking Tylenols like it's proof or something, and he tells me he wants his three hundred bucks back. Can you believe it? He's switched them out then he shows up at my place and threatens

9

me with a crowbar. How the hell did he find out where I live?"

Fisher doesn't even look at him. Christ, Grisby can do a deal with a guy and not recognize him ten minutes later. You'd think he wouldn't be surprised by the bad luck that brings down on him, but he is. Fisher lets his eyes close for a moment, lets the gentle darkness behind his lids wash around him, but behind it all his head's throbbing. He says, "My sinuses are acting up—what you got?"

Grisby's head swivels toward him. "For real?" He sighs, then pulls off one glove and digs in his parka pocket. He holds up a small plastic bottle. "Give you these for what I paid for them—what d'you say? Thirty bucks a pop."

"Vicodin?"

"Only the best, man."

Fisher nods. "OK, OK." Up ahead, the supermarket stands out bright against the night and he pulls into the parking lot, holds out his hand for the bottle. "You wait here until I've dropped off the cab, OK? Reggie sees you, he's gonna freak."

Grisby stares out the window. The moon's half-full and hanging low in the sky, a world away from this frozen town. "No way, man." He turns back to Fisher, the plastic bottle tight in his hand. "No way, I mean, what you want me to do? Go stare at fresh produce for an hour? Check out the low-fat low-sugar wheat-freaking-free organic breakfast cereals? And what if it slips your mind to come get me?"

Fisher leans on the wheel. "D'you get banned from there too?" He sighs, though Grisby doesn't answer. "Fuck it." He steps on the gas and steers the cab back toward the main road. "When we get down there, go warm up my car. Don't come in, understand?"

"Whatever lights your wick, Captain, sure thing," and he does a mock salute.

# 3

HERE'S THE THING about Grisby: he's twitchy as a squirrel, and with good reason. He's a lost soul, a menace to himself, a stranger in his hometown, a permanent accident-waiting-to-happen. If he drives downtown for a drink at the Klondike he'll come out and get lost looking for his car and have to call Fisher to come fetch him; if Fisher isn't wearing his bulky old ex-pipeline worker's parka and his red wool hat, most likely Grisby'll walk right past him. He doesn't recognize faces. He recognizes people by their clothes, their glasses, their limp, and if you take that away it's like he's never seen them before, never mind that he's just spent six hours working his shift with them in the kitchen of the Great Alaska Pancake House, or used to date them, or is dating them right now. It's nothing personal. It's just that something's not right in his head.

No wonder he gets jumpy—he can't tell which Safeway manager threw him out for selling Percocet in the bathrooms last month, or which teenage freaking asshole pulled a gun on him when he showed up with the Vicodin the little fucker wanted. For one memorable week, six years ago now, he was a driver for Bear Cabs, except he got lost driving a fare down the one and only road that leads from the airport, then couldn't find the Sheraton, the largest, tallest, most visible hotel in the whole of downtown. Fisher thought he was new in town and took pity on him. He's a sucker for lost causes. That week he spent his shifts driving around with his phone pressed against his ear giving Grisby directions, but that only worked some of the time because if Grisby couldn't tell which street he was

II

on, there was no hope of saving him from himself. Then when Grisby offered a fare something for his headache, Reggie got to hear about it and Grisby was history.

Grisby makes a fine short-order cook, though: all that nervousness gets funneled down his arms into his twitchy hands, and those hands snatch and tilt and twist, ladling out pancake batter, flicking over bacon, scooping up scrambled eggs like he was born to it. And when the rush's over, he sits on the plastic garbage can in the backroom and pops something to calm himself, and sucks down a can of cola, then another, the bulb of bone at the corner of his jaw bulging as he widens his mouth and the corrugated tube of his throat flexing as he swallows. He's got the pared-down, thin-skinned look of a much older man, someone worn down by constant vigilance because hell, the way he's so twitchy you'd think the world was out to get him. And who's to say it's not when it gets all of us in the end?

## 4

T HE ROAD OUT to Fisher's place has a precipitous turn where it curves back on itself. It's easy to misjudge, especially in the dark with a little Vicodin buzz on, so Fisher slows way down. On both sides the road drops off where gold was clawed from the ground by titanic dredges, holes as broad and deep as the foundations for skyscrapers. Across one of them the road barrels out then switches direction a full ninety degrees, then switches again to climb the hill past Goldpanner Trail and Paydirt Road, Grubstake Street and Hardluck Alley, then Luckystrike Drive where Fisher turns. Here the road straightens out and he holds the wheel with his knees while he fumbles the plastic bottle open and tips a second Vicodin into his mouth. The pill's dry and sticks to his throat, and he almost gags before he gets it down.

In the tunnel of his car's headlights birches bend under the snow frozen onto their branches. "Next year," Grisby's saying, "I'm gonna move to Hawaii. No more of this bullcrap, winter lasting eight months and a cold that freezes your balls off. I'll get me a job in one of those resort hotels, and when my shift's done, I'll be down on the beach catching waves. You too, man— why not? That's the way life should be."

Fisher knows it's nothing but talk. That's the thing between the two of them, this kind of shooting the shit because, hell, what hope is there that either of them is suddenly going to break through to a better life and be a better person to match it? But this evening the words spin around Fisher's head like midges. He pictures it—Grisby on a surfboard with his pigeon chest, his too-big glasses, his bone-thin arms. He pictures himself with his flabby belly white as a fish flesh, his tree-trunk legs, his gnarled toes with their yellowed nails, the thick slope of his shoulders, his big face with its uneven skin and eyes that, even to him, always look too small, designed for another face altogether. The trouble with Hawaii, he thinks, is that Grisby'll still be Grisby, and he'll still be him.

"Fuck Hawaii," he says. "That's just a different load of bull-crap." The car lurches and creaks. The road here's just snow packed down on top of dirt, and that snow's been molded into an uneven track with a ridge in the center high enough to scrape the underside of his car. On either side run grooves where tires have passed hundreds of times, and at the bend sits a hollow where each summer rain washes away the earth, but now, in the heart of winter, every vehicle tilts and jerks.

Grisby says, "Wait 'til that freaking second Vicodin kicks in, man, and feel the love, because you don't mean it. You just can't imagine Hawaii right now, that's all. All this dark and cold," and he waves a hand toward the windshield, "it makes you forget it's not like this everywhere. Right now—right this freaking goddamn minute—people are lying on beaches and thinking, *Fuck, it's so hot and sunny, what'll I do with myself?* Imagine it, Fisher. That's what I call a happy problem. That's what we need—happy problems instead of our freaking sad-ass problems, like: Did I plug in my car? Did my heater go out? Am I gonna die because I locked my keys inside my car and it's fifty-seven below? That's what bullcrap is."

Ever since Grisby's dad died and his bitch of a step-mom moved to Hawaii, it's been like this. A window has opened up in Grisby's head and he can't stop himself looking through it at another world, and bringing every conversation around to Hawaii, like he's talked himself into believing it's in reach, or could be before long. But where the hell would Grisby get the money to move there? When Grisby needed a new pair of snow boots he had to buy a pair of beaten-up, scuffed-up white bunny boots at the Salvation Army, that's how bad things are. His dad left everything to his wife, never mind that she hates Grisby with a steady loathing and always has. She didn't even tell him she was leaving town. Grisby only found out when he went round to fetch some of his dad's ashes and a woman with red-dyed hair and bad breath opened the door and even Grisby knew she wasn't his step-mom. He thought he'd got the wrong house until she said, "Last owner sold up and left after her husband died, month ago now. Place was a right mess, if you don't mind me saying." She'd cleaned up so good she'd dumped the ashes into the old outhouse at the back of the property, and telling Fisher about it over a beer Grisby had cried, like he'd forgotten there'd been no room for him in his dad's rotten heart.

Through the trees a flash as Fisher's headlights catch his trailer. Three years ago, when the price of heating oil skyrocketed, he covered it in foil-sided insulation. Now it gleams like a relic from the space program that fell out of orbit and landed intact. Behind it, barely visible, the outer walls of his unbuilt house rise like a stockade. He's known people driven by the endless light of Interior summers to put up a house in four months: walls, a roof, windows and doors, enough to live in and spend the winter sheet-rocking the inside. How come in six years he's gotten almost nowhere? He recognizes this thought: it meets him every time his car pitches up the last few yards of the driveway.

Grisby's still going. "Man, you can pick them in your garden. Juicy and warm—"

"Yeah yeah, I get it," says Fisher. He turns off the engine. "Hawaii's paradise. Right."

"Your problem," and Grisby swivels to face him, "is you don't have any imagination. That's what's gonna get you away from here. If you can't imagine someplace else, you're never gonna *be* someplace else. Know what I mean? Look at what you're working on—your house, for fuck's sake. Every fucker in Alaska wants a house in the hills with a great goddamn view, and to build it with his own hands and all that shit. And for what? So you can look out at all the freaking snow? And all the hills covered in snow? And the mountains covered in snow? Really? What's that all about?"

Everything's quiet except for the ping and snap of metal cooling too fast, and they sit there, staring through the darkness at the snow. Already the heat inside the car is leaking away and their exhaled breath hangs in the air like jellyfish, at least until Fisher huffs and rubs his face with both hands. There's a raw stinging behind his left cheek, and another above his eyes. Soon the second Vicodin will have eased those pains away and he'll sink into his armchair and stare at the TV with his dog by his feet and let his thoughts drift off like balloons. Hell, he won't even care if Grisby yanks on the cord for the blinds so hard that the whole damn thing comes off the wall, or uses his towel and leaves it on the bathroom floor, won't care until tomorrow, and anyway, he can always call in sick. What the hell's it matter? Soon there won't even be a Bear Cabs. That thought slides across his mind. Fewer cabs than last year. Drivers jumping ship to other companies, though only Ella got hired by City Cabs. Reggie won't admit there's a problem. Him and his freak of a son working dispatch now that Jordie's gone. Fisher should leave too. Get out while the going's good, but hell, not yet. Not yet.

It comes quickly, that second flood of Vicodin, like dawn breaking inside his head and turning everything golden and beautiful. He was rooting in the snow for the end of the power cord to plug in his car and now he straightens up with it in his hand, ice against his lips where his parka collar's zipped up past his mouth and he doesn't care. Everything about the night is sharp and lovely: the air so dry it freezes the moisture right out of his breath; the stars quivering in the darkness. He sees them through the porthole of his hood with its thin fur tendrils covered in frost waving slightly, and he might as well be a sea creature looking out from the center of an anemone, and this the ocean floor he's lumbering across with the cord in his hand, back to the dark shape of the car.

By the time he's shoved the plastic plug onto the metal prongs and the orange glow of the idiot light's blinked on, his fingers are numb inside his gloves. Everything's slowed down a little. He sees himself tread through the snow toward his trailer and pull his keys from his pocket. He sees the keys slip through his fingers, and himself stooping to pluck them out of the snow. On the front steps his boots thud and squeak and the sounds travel right through him, like he's no more than the wooden steps, a thing made of rigid parts pinned together, then he pushes the key into the lock and feels the sweet click as it gives. From behind him comes the slam of a car door then Grisby's right there, jumping from foot to foot, saying, "Fuck it's cold, man oh man."

Enough ice has built up on the doorstep that Fisher has to shoulder the door open. His shoulder should hurt but it doesn't. Instead all he notices is the curl of fog rolling across his carpet and vanishing against the far wall where his DVDs are stacked. In here the air's swampingly warm and layered with smells: the pizza he ate last night, the bathroom that needs cleaning, the clothes and bedsheets that need washing, and over it all the woolly stink of dog.

"Paxson?" Fisher calls. "Pax? Come on, boy." From the bedroom doorway comes a stiff-legged dog the color of old snow. He has sad eyes and bent ears, and pushes the bony dome of his head against Fisher's shins.

Grisby treads across the carpet with his boots on, leaving

lenses of compressed snow behind him. In an instant the TV's spitting out sound and light. Local news and Grisby snorts. "Christ," he says, "look at that backdrop. Looks like it's made of cardboard. If she sneezes it's gonna fall over. And that hair! Man, someone take her hairspray away from her, *please*," and he snorts again. Floating on the screen beside the newsreader's head, a photograph of a young man with hair so blond it's almost white. Where his collar should be hang the words *Missing trooper.*

Grisby calls out, "Some cop doesn't show up to work and he's *missing*? Man, they're short on news. And the cops themselves can't find him? Christ, we're in Interior freaking Alaska—there aren't that many places to look." He lets himself drop into the recliner and kicks out the footrest, says, "Ah, who gives a fuck," and switches to CNN.

On the screen a photo flashes up of a girl in pigtails and a pink T-shirt, then there's footage of her parents and an old guy who's a friend of the family who's crying and shields his face from the camera. Grisby calls out, "What is it today? Nothing real happening, so it's all about cops and little girls who've *disappeared*? Wanna know what I think?" and he half turns to Fisher. "That old nutball did it." He gestures toward the screen with the remote because there's the old guy again, caught by the camera with his face wrinkled in sadness and his head hung low. "Look at him. Who lets some old perv babysit their kid? And he's the last one to see her? Freaking cops need their heads examined if they can't work that one out." Along the bottom of the screen runs BREAKING NEWS, and Grisby settles himself into the recliner, calls out, "Hey man, got a beer?"

Fisher scratches Pax behind the ears until the dog lets out a chesty rumble. A cloying stink rises off him, and a gluey thread of saliva dangles from his mouth. One day before long, Fisher thinks, he's going to come home and call out, "Paxson!" and the dog won't come. He'll keep calling his name as he crosses to the bedroom, a way of warding off what he knows he's going to find: his dog dead and stiff at the foot of his mattress with his eyes gone dull. What a job it'll be to wrap him in a blanket and carry him outside. Not to bury him, not unless it's summer and the ground's thawed—but to where, then? He doesn't know. But he's had that picture in his head for weeks now, him in his parka with the dog in his arms, has tasted the pain of being left so utterly alone that his soul will ache. What was Paxson to begin with but a way of filling the emptiness left when Janice moved out and took Breehan with her? A stupid thing, to get a dog when he had to give up the house and find a place of his own to live, but wasn't that him all over? Besides, there was a strange comfort to be found in looking through ads with their *No Dogs* or *No Pets* or *Extra Deposit for Pets*, proof of what he'd just discovered, that the world didn't want him.

Pax's bowl is still half full. Not a good sign. He isn't even whining to go out and he's been in here since morning. Fisher flips on the outside light and wrenches open the door. Pax ducks his head against the cold and Fisher grabs him by the collar and hauls him through the doorway. He stands by the closed door listening for the sound of the snow creaking under the dog's feet so he can let him back in. It doesn't take long. Twenty seconds, maybe. Barely long enough for Pax to have gotten down the steps. Either Pax has already pissed on the bedroom carpet, or he's going to, Fisher thinks. The thought feels far away, a possibility not a problem. Nothing's a problem when you've taken a couple of Vicodin.

"Hey man," Grisby calls out again, "where's that beer?" With Grisby here everything feels thrown out of its usual orbit. Grisby snaps his fingers at Pax to make him lie down, and the dog wants to, but he won't: there's his blanket folded up by the recliner, but it's Fisher he wants to sit by, and Fisher's busy hanging his parka on a hook by the door, and even when he's finished he doesn't sit down but tosses a beer to Grisby and opens one for himself. Then Fisher leans against the small table where he eats his meals and lets the cool fizz of the beer wash over his tongue. If it wasn't for the Vicodin, he'd be all on edge, he's sure. That's the way it goes when his sinuses are bothering him, as though he's slightly out of sync with the world. Instead he feels poured full of honey.

Only now does Grisby pluck off that ridiculous fur hat he wears. Without it his head looks fragile and misshapen, long and narrow as a bean. His hair's thick and dark and flattened like it's been licked down, and his face is lit by the colors of the TV because he's tilted slightly forward, away from the backward lean of the chair. He lifts his beer and takes a swig, wipes his hand over his lips. "Christ," he says, "look at me—what a sucker. It's that freaking music that makes it sound like something's about to happen and all that *breaking news* crap. Nothing's going on. They don't know shit." He aims the remote like a man shooting another man down and blinks the TV through one channel after another until he settles on cartoons.

Fisher, meanwhile, feels his empty stomach coiling up. He pulls on his gloves, steps back into his boots and out into the clench of the frozen air. From under the trailer he drags a cooler and roots around in it, loads his arms, then treads back up the stairs with the snow crackling beneath his soles. He dumps the burritos he's brought in onto the table, where they rattle and slide like old bones. One clatters to the floor and Pax looks up. Even the plastic they're wrapped in is so cold it's brittle.

He rips open the plastic and piles the burritos onto a plate, then pushes the plate into the microwave. He stands with his hand over the buttons. Ten minutes, he thinks. Except those things are frozen solid. Twelve, maybe?

From a box by the window he plucks a tissue and blows his

nose, blows so hard that his cheeks smart and air wheezes back into his head and blood stains the tissue. He should have picked up some Sudafed, he thinks now, some Afrin too, because, hell, the Vicodin just makes you feel better. What's he supposed to do? Get enough from Grisby for tomorrow, too? Or spend another shift peering through the fog inside his head at the fog that's settled over the town, carrying the ache in his face with him everywhere he goes until the cold lets up? And maybe even then he'll still feel lousy. Just after Thanksgiving he got so bad he went to the clinic. Put it all on his credit card—one hundred and seventy-five dollars for the consultation, sixty dollars for the antibiotics and some spray that had the raw smell of geraniums and he couldn't bear to use, and he's still paying it off, Christ Almighty.

He lets himself sink onto the sofa, although here the chilled air from the window drifts down over him. It touches the back of his neck and he shivers. The plastic he taped up over the glass is ripped from a few weeks ago when Grisby tossed him a beer and missed, and he's out of tape to fix it. Buy tape, he tells himself, buy milk, buy some fucking cheese and some fucking healthy apples. He closes his eyes and the Vicodin makes the whole idea of the supermarket float gently away, and he listens to the squeaky voice of a cartoon character, the rattle of fake gunfire, the soaring of the music, and he imagines some hero zooming off into the sky.

He could fall asleep, except for that cold creeping in around him. There's a throw over the arm of the sofa and he wraps it around himself, right up to his neck. Pax lays his snout in the dip between Fisher's knees. Fisher rubs his thumb over the smoothness between the dog's eyes, tells him over a yawn, "You're a good boy."

No wonder when a bleating starts up Fisher doesn't move. His phone. Fuck it. Let it ring. Grisby calls out, "Don't tell me you're not gonna get that. I mean, Christ! What is it with you?"

But he does let it ring. He's not going to shove away Pax's snout, or get up from under the warmth of the throw, or focus his attention on anything in particular, not until the microwave pings and all he has to do is load those burritos onto plates, and find some napkins, and fill his belly.

Which is what he does.

In the end he won't pull his phone out of his parka pocket until Grisby's shut himself into the bathroom, and that's an hour and a half from now. Then he'll sit on the edge of the sofa and stare at the small screen. He'll notice that the battery is almost drained and think to himself he needs to plug it in. He'll check for messages and find seven, four of them from Grisby, one from his step-mother Ada, and two from his ex's landline. He'll feel a small twinge of worry, and only then will he play his messages, staring at the TV with the phone held hard against his ear.

By then it'll be too late, because this is what he'll hear: *Dad? Are you there? Brian's going fucking ape-shit. Can you pick up? Please? I can't deal with this. You've gotta* [voice becomes indistinct] *and get outta here. Just come and get me, OK? OK?*

The next message is from Ada. He doesn't even listen to it. He scrolls down, finds another message from Bree then listens to her voice all stretched and hollow. *Dad? Goddamit, pick up! What a fucking mess. I don't know what I've done. You got to get me out of here. I've* [voice becomes indistinct] *had no idea* [voice becomes indistinct]. *You're gonna come get me, right? Please, Dad?*

He's on his feet without knowing it. The softness that the Vicodin gave to the world drops away and instead his head feels thick and unwieldy. The dog's staring up at him from his blanket, tail thumping the floor. Fisher still has the phone against his ear, though it's telling him he has no more new messages and to press four to review existing messages, and five to—he holds it away from his head and stares at it.

Bree didn't make it down to Anchorage, then, and Brian—Mr Step-Dad, Mr Control Freak, Mr Tight Ass—has gone ape-shit. But then, these last few months his temper's been humming like a taut wire. No freaking wonder. He's a man who dresses in dark blue button-up shirts like he's in uniform, and keeps his hair cropped short, and so totally lacks a sense of humor you can't trust him. He's a man who has a room downstairs he calls his den but in truth is his gun room where he opens the lockers one at a time, and takes apart his handguns and rifles and shotguns, and oils them, and even—Fisher's seen this with his own eyes—sits with one of them cradled on his lap while he watches his big-ass flat-screen TV from his armchair. He favors movies like *The Deerhunter*, and *Platoon*, grim movies about soldiers that are full of tragedy and downplayed heroics and he sits through them with his face as unchanging as a photograph.

Bree calls him Major Jerkoff, but only when Fisher takes her out. They'll be lining up for a movie or eating pizza and she'll say something like, *Major Jerkoff's got Mom pissed off. Missed two appointments with clients 'cos he was out with his buds playing soldier* or *Major Jerkoff says I can't come home 'til five as he and his buds are having a Strategic Meeting*, and she'll laugh. Major Jerkoff and his buds who stockpile guns and ammo, who bitch about the feds, and about paying taxes, or don't pay them at all. What a joke. Except Bree's eyes have a slippery haunted look these days, and when Fisher drops her off, her mom comes to the door looking gaunt with worry.

Fisher rubs the screen of his phone with his thumb. He needs to think, but his thoughts are all over the place. Grisby's coming out of the bathroom. Beneath his zipped-up blue fleece the hem of his T-shirt shows, and the sag of his too-big jeans over his skinny ass. "Hey man," he says, "what's up?"

"It's Breehan. She wants me to come get her."

But Grisby just sits in the recliner and tilts his head into his hand. "What she do this time?"

"Not that kind of trouble. Says her step-dad's gone ape-shit." Fisher turns away.

"Hell, you know how she is, Fisher. Come on, man, don't let her do this to you. Just stay here and chill."

Fisher stares at the phone sitting in his hand, as if it's going to tell him something he doesn't know. Like what to do. Like whether put on his coat and drive all the way out there when, chances are, Grisby's right. Could be Bree's pissed at her mom for not taking her to Anchorage and came home buzzed and Brian's mad at her. It'd be just like her to do something dumb, like the time she slapped another girl in the face at school, or was caught smoking pot when she was supposed to be in detention, or scraped the hell out of a teacher's car with her keys, or so he said, because it turned out no one actually saw her do it.

Could be Bree's mad because Jan canceled the trip to Anchorage—really, who's fool enough to drive all that way in this kind of cold? Fisher'll get over there and Jan will tell him something like *Get out of here, Mikey, it's none of your concern,* and if he objects, she'll fix him with her eye and say, *For Chrissakes—you had your chance to be a real parent and you blew it. You can't start now,* and Brian will rub that stupid attempt at a beard he's grown this winter and say, *Mike, it's all under control. Breehan knows the consequences of her behavior. Why don't you just go on home?* and that will irritate the hell out of Fisher, and before you know it, Jan will be shouting in his face and he'll be shouting back, and Brian will have that tight-jawed look he gets when he's about to get real nasty in that quiet way he has. Meanwhile Breehan will have slunk off to her room. Maybe that's the reason she called him: so that everyone'll forget why they're mad at her.

But Christ. Her voice was all choked up. Since when does Bree cry? She's not the type and never was. From the day she was born she's had an iron will and an anger that turns inward. It scares Fisher. When she was small, if he told her off she'd hide and inflict an injury on herself—biting the inside of her cheeks until they bled, scraping at the skin of her forearms with her nails—or onto whatever was around: the wallpaper, the loose back of the sofa, the carpet whose tufts could be plucked out only by someone very determined and with great patience. If Fisher tried to get her to come out she'd stare wildly at him and not look away, just like an animal would if you cornered it.

Grisby turns up the TV. Some cop show. "Tell me you're not gonna go out there. You know what? She's got you wrapped around her little finger. No wonder she's such a headcase."

"Shit, I think something's wrong."

"Something's always wrong. Hell, I don't blame the kid, but it's just too freaking sad to see you jump whenever she calls, and she only ever calls when she's got herself in trouble. Know what I mean?"

Fisher closes his fingers around his phone. How easy it would be to slip it back in his pocket, and whatever made Breehan call him will fade away as though it never happened, and nothing will be any different because he sat here in the warmth of his trailer instead of getting into his parka and boots, and warming the car, and driving the ten miles out to Janice and Brian's place.

His fingers are tight around the phone. He stares at the screen for a moment, then his finger is jabbing at it, dialing the landline. Maybe Janice'll pick up and be pissed that it's only him, not a client or one of her friends, or maybe he'll get Brian telling him everything's fine and why wouldn't it be? It rings and rings. No answering machine. Heck, they were going to have their landline disconnected until they took away Breehan's cell phone and couldn't leave her with no way to make a call if they were out. Even they wouldn't do that.

He calls again, and at the other end the phone rings and rings.

It's close to eight. Could be everything's quiet over there. Bree upstairs in her room: sent there for the rest of the night for whatever she did that pissed off Brian. Jan's at the table with a forkful of pasta lifted above her plate and her mouth pulled to one side because she's hungry and hasn't eaten all day, has been showing houses to clients, is plain worn out. And Brian? Down in his den with a gun in his lap and his face blue in the flickering light of some movie.

The phone's still ringing. Ten times, he thinks. He's been counting without realizing it.

Something's not right. Bree was frightened. He licks his lips and feels where the skin's turned hard. Brian's not the type to go ape-shit. He's a buttoned-up, held-in, clamped-down kind of guy, and isn't that what's scary about him? Because you can't help thinking that one day all that rage will come surging out? What if one day is today?

Fisher pulls on his parka. He doesn't have to go up and knock on the door, he tells himself. No, he'll just drive over and take a look. See whether anyone's home. If Bree's waiting, she'll wave at him from her window or come running out to meet him.

Grisby's watching. "Oh, for crap's sake," he says, and puts down the remote. "You're such a sucker."

26

5

I N THE DARK and cold the air seems thicker, pushing back against Fisher's car so that it strains even on the flat stretch beyond Denby Hill. Fisher's gripping the wheel too hard and he knows it. He tells himself he's driving like an amateur: letting the car jolt over the dips and humps of frost heave, over-correcting on the bends, stepping too hard on the brakes, even though it's fifty-seven below and the ice has lost its slickness. Beside him, Grisby has finally shut up. Under his breath he's whistling some half-assed tune that slinks along the edge of recognition, annoying as a fly caught behind glass, and he sways with the uneven motion of the car—lets himself sway, maybe, to make a point about Fisher's driving—and every now and then he shakes his head in its ridiculous fur hat, as though the two of them are still arguing.

Fisher didn't ask him to come along. What the hell does Grisby have to gripe about? If he'd wanted, he could have been sitting in Fisher's recliner watching the end of the cop show with a beer in his hand and a bowl of chips on his knees. But there's this about Grisby: he doesn't like being on his own. You can't even leave him in your living room and shut the door without him getting just a little freaked out. Maybe he thinks he won't recognize you when you come back in, or maybe he thinks you're abandoning him and he'll never find his way back to town, let alone his apartment.

Two miles of the road spooling out flat from under the car's hood and now it slopes upward again. Before long the headlights catch the only thing out here that isn't white or black: the red of a stop sign mottled with snow. Fisher brakes and glances left and right, only to see Grisby lean forward too, his head blocking Fisher's view and his whistling suddenly louder. All's darkness except for the glare of Fisher's headlights off the snowbank across the intersection, and Fisher sends the car barrelling to the right. Only there's something on the road. Something huge. Tall legs the color of spruce bark scissor away. A moose. He swerves, cursing, and it takes off between the trees.

They're almost at the house when Fisher recognizes the tune Grisby's been whistling: the theme from *Hawaii Five-o*.

# 6

FISHER PULLS UP at the bottom of the driveway. Through the trees the house is drunk with light. Each window is a luminous rectangle, no blinds pulled down, no curtains drawn except for the butt-ugly living-room curtains. In itself this is strange. He was going to park here where the road and driveway meet, beneath the sign that says *Trespassers will be Shot, Survivors will be Shot Again*, but now, making an awkward turn and the car lurching through softer snow, he steps on the gas and sends the car careening to the top of the driveway.

He thinks: Any moment now, someone's going to look out the window to see who's here. He thinks: There's no need to get out of the car, no need at all.

Beside him, Grisby's stopped whistling. He says, "Fuck, some kinda private party going on," and sniggers.

For a moment Fisher doesn't understand. Then he hears it: above the rumble of the engine, a heartbeat of bass pulsing through the fragile skin of the windows. Someone's got the music turned way up. *Breehan*, he thinks. Then, *Shit*. He flings open the door and rushes across the snow. Threading through the air comes the whine of an electric guitar and raw-throated singing.

Already the inside of his nose is tickling where the hairs have frozen stiff, and his eyelashes stick with frost where his breath catches them. The Vicodin must be wearing off, because where the cold seeps into his head the delicate membranes throb like something inside him is trying to get out.

The house is built like a boat at dock, jutting out from the hillside in three floors, the v-shaped deck above him its prow. There's a door right next to the double doors of the garage and he knocks with his glove on, presses his thumb hard on the doorbell glowing green, knocks again. He waits. The next time he pushes the doorbell he tilts his head close to the wood. Over the angry rush of the music he hears the bell trilling upstairs.

From behind him comes the crunch of Grisby's boots over the snow. "This is weird," Fisher says. The cold rushes in around his teeth and over his tongue. "She must be home. Christ."

"That kid of yours. What d'you wanna bet she called you out here for nothing? She's forgotten whatever the hell bug she had up her butt earlier and now she's having herself a little party." He reaches past Fisher and turns the doorknob. The door swings open and out belches warm air smelling of floor cleaner. The music's clearer now: Led Zep. For fuck's sake, thinks Fisher, since when did Bree listen to anything that old?

Above the bench along the hallway hang coats and jackets, and beneath it sit boots and shoes and slippers all lined up the way Brian likes. It's impossible to tell who's here and who's not when there are always enough clothes and boots for a dozen people. To the left, a doorway into Brian's den. The lights are off and the door half closed.

Fisher makes his way to the stairs. You're supposed to take off your boots so you don't tread snow or mud or whatever other filth you've brought in with you onto the pale carpet. He's walked up these stairs in his boots only to have Brian bark at him, "You're gonna ruin the carpet. Put on a pair of slippers, that's what they're there for." Which makes him *forget* the next time too. Just to piss Brian off, to see whether this time he can wind him up far enough for him to lose it. But it's never worked out that way. Brian's stood at the turn in the stairs glaring at him, even come down the stairs with his hands balled up and snapped, "Slippers—you know the drill." Fisher hates the things: cork-soled, felt-topped, clunky and ugly like it's Brian's mission to humiliate you. Brian's own slippers are black leather and sleek, like boots for someone who doesn't want to wear boots inside for fear of ruining his carpets and the resale value of his house.

"Come on," Fisher tells Grisby, and off they go, up the stairs in their boots, Fisher craning his head as he comes around the turn and peers through the banisters. The music swamps him as he stands just short of the top. He can barely see for trying to think through the noise. The sound system: where is it? Here's the living room with its leather sofa, and its coffee table of magazines, all pristine like no one actually reads them, and its framed reproductions of old maps of Alaska, and its large black and white photograph of a man in a leather cap beside a bi-plane out on a frozen river. The shit-brown velvet drapes across the windows to the deck are drawn tight, for once, and it feels too warm in here. There's a wood stove over by the stairs to the next floor, a small flat-screen TV, and speakers the size of shoe boxes bracketed high on the walls. The amplifier's not where it used to be. Fisher scans the room, finally spots a small black box on the open shelves between the living room and the kitchen. He walks toward it half-crouched, like he's cowed by the force of the music, then pushes the first button he sees. And just like that, like a balloon ripped apart, the noise is gone.

Only now does Fisher feel a twinge of fear. He calls out, "It's me, Mike. Anyone home? Brian? Jan?" His ears sing in the silence. "Got a call from Bree asking me to come over, so—here I am. You there, Bree?"

Grisby rolls his eyes. It's strange to see him standing on the pale carpet in his huge, white bunny boots and green parka and ridiculous fur hat, like someone from an uglier world who doesn't belong here. Like him, for that matter. Except Grisby's clueless that he doesn't belong here. He's stuffed his gloves in his pockets and now his hand goes to a small camera at the end of the kitchen counter, weighing it, smoothing its surface as though he means to pocket it. "Hey," says Fisher, "put that down. Don't mess with their stuff."

Grisby shrugs. He slides the camera back onto the counter then pats it once with his fingers, like a promise that he won't forget it.

Already the warmth is making Fisher sweat. He plucks off his hat and calls out, "Bree? Bree, it's Dad. Where are you, sweet pea?" Silence. "I came, like you asked me to."

He pulls off his gloves. His hands are damp and he wipes them down his parka, then sniffs and looks about him. The heat's making his nose run, but he won't blow it, not yet, not into this odd silence.

Over by the stairs the wood stove ticks quietly, and he can't help himself, he opens its door and glances inside. The embers flush with the rush of air, but the fire's almost out. No one's fed it for hours. And really, he thinks, the music could have been going for hours, too. No easier thing than to set an album to replay, or to shuffle songs, to make the house pulse with life when no one's home. *Bree*, he thinks. Did Janice and Brian take off for the evening and she got pissed enough to crank up the music? Is she lying on her bed with her earphones on? Or has she gone out too? A friend could have come and picked her up, and any moment now Brian and Janice might walk in the door, and here he'll be in their house, wearing his boots on their precious carpet. He glances over his shoulder, even goes over to the kitchen window and glances outside. Nothing but darkness and the glow of someone's porch light way off through the trees.

He comes back to the woodstove and peers up the stairs to the next floor. He tries to feel his way into the silence. Is it thin and innocent, nothing but the sound of a house left empty? Or is it thick with expectation? Is someone lying in bed upstairs, too buzzed to care about the doorbell ringing, or the music stopping, or the voices calling out from downstairs? Who could that someone be except Breehan? Still, dread pinches at Fisher's stomach.

He glances back. Grisby's opening drawers in the kitchen and he wants to tell him to cut it out, but all of a sudden he doesn't want to raise his voice. Taking a breath he starts up the stairs. His knees strain and his forehead's cool with sweat. Under his boots the thick carpet gives unpleasantly, and the only sound is the slight thud of his feet and the hiss of his bare hand along the banister. How easy to imagine Brian coming upon him and asking what the hell he's doing sneaking around his house, or Janice opening a door and seeing him there, and smacking him across the face as she's done a few times before, years ago now. No wonder Fisher's head swings this way and that, snatching at the creak of a floorboard, the drip of a faucet, the huff of his own breath.

On Breehan's door there's a blotchy black and white poster of two men, one in glasses, one bearded, both sullen. Beneath them, *Dead Beats* in uneven capitals. An ugly thing and meant to be, he's sure. He nudges the door open. This is a room that sneers back at you: the walls covered with posters, the lightbulb giving off an eerie pinkish glow that turns the purple bedsheets lurid. Everywhere, clothes: piled by the bathroom door, by the open closet, spilling from drawers. Jeans, socks, thongs, a black bra, a pink bra, wrinkled T-shirts like shrugged-off skin. Over it all floats a smell that's earthy and metallic. Where does Fisher recognize it from? He can't say. It doesn't fit here; for all that, it seems part of the mess.

He treads over some magazines spread-eagled over the carpet and lays a hand on the bed. The sheets are cold. What did he expect? He even gets down on his knees and peers underneath. A few years ago she'd have been hiding there, or in the closet. But she's fifteen now. He has to remind himself of that.

He doesn't bother with the bathroom: the light's off, the air still. He wants to escape that smell and he pulls the bedroom door closed behind him. A noise. From a doorway at the end of the corridor. Fear swells up inside him, and his voice cracks as he calls out, "Anyone home? Jan? That you in there?"

A humming sound. A whispering. He's not breathing. His whole self's straining forward to listen. "Jan?" His voice is quieter this time.

He comes down the corridor with arms held out and feet high and slow like a deep-sea diver crossing the ocean floor. In the room off to the left a light's on. The office. He's shivering now and his hand's a long way away as it reaches up and nudges the door open. An empty chair. A computer screen. The ceiling light glaring off the windows. No one here. No one staring back at him. On the desk a fax machine hums as it prints a message, and a sheet of paper whispers over another. Who the hell still uses a fax machine? "Fuck," he says, so lightly he barely hears it.

The window glints like dark water. He stands and looks out. Someone's left the light on down on the deck, he can see the railing and the flower boxes on it, thick with snow now. Beyond lies the terraced yard Jan's so proud of, and a view of the valley and the jagged teeth of the far-off mountains, not that you can see any of that tonight. You pay for a view in this town, that's the way it goes. And Jan and Brian can look out at those mountains while they work their butts off to pay for the privilege, sitting up here making appointments for property viewings, arranging open houses, closing deals. To think that when he was married to her, Janice was overweight and worked the cash register at the supermarket. What had Brian seen in her that he could reshape? Because she's not the woman she was—the same wide-eyed look, the same stolid way of standing,

34

but she's lost fifty pounds and the indolence he'd loved about her. Now she's all tailored pant suits and nervous energy, her fingers tapping countertops, or dancing fast across the screen of her phone, or snatching up her car keys because there are properties to show and clients to meet, and, for Chrissakes, she can't eat without her phone ringing.

Under the brightness of the overhead light, small eyes of green and red flicker from the silvery surfaces of routers and CPUs, of gadgets Fisher doesn't even know the use of. He lets his hands rest on the back of a desk chair and it swivels, knocks against the pull-out tray for the keyboard, snaps the computer to life. Fisher leans close and covers the mouse with his hand. An excitement leaps in his chest. One click of that mouse and a dialog box pops up, demanding a password. He tries JANICE. He tries PATRIOT and NRA and MILITIA and 2ND AMNDMT. Brian's a jerk but he's careful. He wouldn't be that obvious.

What did Fisher want to find, anyway? Dirty pictures? Incriminating emails? Something he could hold against that jerk, that's for sure, even if he never let on that he'd dug up his secrets.

He turns away. On the wall, a rack with keys hanging from it. On the desk, a pot of pencils—how he hates those things. *Armstrong Realty* in blocky white letters on apple red. He's found them in his car, in his trailer, even one in his cab. He takes pleasure snapping them in half and throwing them in the trash. By the desk stands a printer on a small table. Next to it, two filing cabinets spotted with fridge magnets: most are shaped like houses with the A of Armstrong Realty making the point of the roof: there's also a blue circle with *Jansson's Title Services*; a metallic key-shaped magnet saying *Realti-Key*; a bland square thing that says *Northern Sewage and Septic*; and a cartoon grizzly holding a rifle, of all the dumb things, and

35

*Arctic Gun and Supply* haloing its head. As dumb as a bear painted on a cab, for fuck's sake.

He stands in the doorway and looks down the corridor. What's he doing here? Breehan's long gone, and Janice and Brian are out. Is this revenge? Poking around the house when they're not here? It's not like that, he tells himself, but that's a half-truth. In the years since Jan remarried, he's never been free to roam around in her new life. On the other side of the corridor stands the door to the master bedroom and he hesitates, rubs his lips with one rough finger, then walks softly toward it in his boots, though there's no need for that when the carpet's thick and pale as fresh snow.

He eases the door open. The lights are off, but a bluish glow jerks over the walls and the pale sheets of the bed. He calls, "Jan? Is that you?" but even before the words have vanished onto the air he knows the flat-screen TV on the wall is playing to no one. It's on mute and a music video's quick cuts make it twitch from long-legged women slow-stepping down a staircase to a man tumbling from a window, and tumbling again, his wide-open mouth filling the frame. How odd that this room exudes a quiet all its own, as though everything from the bedcovers thrown wide to the painting of birch trees on the far wall to the stand for necklaces on the bureau is holding its breath.

He's been in this room once before, when Janice showed him around, a realtor showing off her new home, her new life, her step up from the life she'd shared with him. But then the room was stark and barely lived in. Tonight there are pink panties draped over the edge of the laundry basket, and on the bedside table a glass and a bottle of Laphroaig, mostly empty. Brian's nothing if not a man of expensive tastes, even when he's just getting buzzed like any other poor fucker. Fisher steps closer. In the shadow of the bottle sits a tiny enamel box that he flips open. In it, a couple of circular white pills scored across the center like shirt buttons. He touches them with the end of his finger. Percocet? he wonders. Or something out of that league entirely? Grisby would know. But then, Grisby would find a way to slip them into his pocket.

He could turn this room inside out. He could root through the drawers, he could get down on his hands and knees and search under the bed. Is he so desperate to dig up their secrets? This isn't just about Brian. This is about why the hell Jan married a mean-mouthed tight-ass like Brian, and why she's stayed married to him when underneath the guy's boiling with rage—it's there in his eyes, and in the clamped-down way he talks these days, and if Jan can't see it, she's fooling herself. She hasn't left him, though, has she? Not the way she left Fisher, taking off to an apartment she'd already rented without a word to him, taking their baby daughter, their car, so that when Fisher got home from work, the place reeked of an emptiness he's never gotten over.

He pushes his hands into the small pockets at the waist of his parka, the pockets that lead through to the warmth of his body, and sighs. He's already weighed down by tiredness and the ache in his head—what good would it do to poke around in this room? Other people's secrets lodge inside you like shrapnel. Be better than that, he tells himself, you can do it, then his mouth pulls into an uneven smile. That's what Jan used to tell him: *Be better than that.* Only, he couldn't.

Suddenly it's easy. He's sick of the whole thing, anyway: of creeping around Janice and Brian's house, of searching for Bree when it's clear she's gone. He turns on his heel and starts back down the corridor.

What stops him just before the stairs? That smell, that slight stain on the air as he comes close to Bree's doorway. He rests one hand on the cool wood of the newel post as though he means to go downstairs. But he doesn't. That smell nags at him. Where does he know it from? He wheels around with his lips tucked tight against his teeth in irritation at himself, and pushes Bree's door open again.

At first he simply stands in the doorway. What more is there to see than the mess of clothes, the posters on the wall, the photo of Bree from when her hair was long and pretty and Jan had taken her to Vegas, the small TV on the bookcase, the books leaning every which way, the desk littered with gum wrappers and pencils, the pencil sharpeners, the erasers, the used tissues crumpled into untidy blossoms and dropped around the garbage can? He steps toward the window and peers into the darkness. Nothing beyond the glass except the night. He rubs his face with both hands.

He's closer to the bathroom now and the smell unfolds itself. It makes him think of the woods, of the one time his dad took him moose hunting and the whole filthy business of butchering an animal too big to drag back to the truck intact. With one finger he touches the bathroom door. It groans and swings open a few inches, allowing in just enough light to suggest something uneven about the shadows, something that makes Fisher's heart squeeze in his chest.

The air reeks and he wants to retch. One hand goes up over his mouth with his finger and thumb pinching his nose. His throat's so tight his breath drags noisily in, out. Then, forcing his shoulders forward and with one arm raised, though who knows against what, he flips on the bathroom light.

Red, sprayed across the tiles, the shower curtain, the toilet, the towel hanging from the rack. Slumped against the wall beneath it, Brian. Naked. In the side of his head there's a glistening crater, and his open eyes have a dry look to them, as though they've been staring at the washbasin for hours.

Fisher tips himself over the toilet and vomits.

## 7

Fisher has to bellow Grisby's name a half dozen times before he comes upstairs, and when he does there's something furtive about him, something about the jerk-jerks of his head and the way his hands keep retreating to his pockets. Fisher snaps, "What the fuck—didn't you hear me?" and Grisby snaps back, "Hey man, what the fucking fuck—you don't have to be like that." He slides his hand over the edge of the desk then looks about him as though he's just noticed the smell. "What the hell's that stink?"

Fisher can barely speak. He swallows against the taste of vomit in his mouth and lets himself down on Bree's bed. It squeaks under his weight. "In the bathroom," he says at last. "Christ—it's fucking awful."

When Grisby comes out he's dangling the black L of a gun from one finger. "Guess Mister Deadguy won't miss his piece now," he says, "and I know someone who'll buy it. This baby's gonna boost my Hawaii fund."

"Fuck it, Grisby, put it back," and Fisher stares down at his boots on the carpet. His fingers grab hold of his hair and pull until it hurts.

"Two birds with one stone. Guess we know why your little girl didn't wanna hang around waiting for you to show up. Mom and step-daddy are away so she has a little fun, only things don't go the way she wants with this guy, you know, maybe he—"

Fisher raises his head. "Don't be a moron—that's Brian. That's her step-dad."

Grisby lets out a strange whoop. "Holy shit. Naked in her

bathroom, oh man, what sort of a twisted place is this?" He slaps his leg. "This is bad—fucking *bad*. Well I guess we know why she called you and not the cops. Man!"

"Shut the fuck up. Get it? Shut the fuck up!"

"They'll just send her to juvie. It's not like it's going to completely ruin her life. Hell, maybe they'll believe it was self-defense and let her off. Won't be hard—something bad must've been going down if he was naked in there." Grisby steps back with one hand up in surrender. "Don't look at me like that. I'm just telling it like I see it."

"You're seeing it all wrong," Fisher bellows, then his voice catches. He lets his head sink and he closes himself into the darkness of his folded arms. His breath heaves in and out, over and over, as though this is just the way of the world, that one man should be sitting on his daughter's bed breathing while another—a stupid, self-righteous, uptight shit, but still—lies naked and dead a few yards away in her bathroom.

Grisby's got it all wrong, he tells himself. All wrong. But he can't help hearing Bree's voice all tangled up saying, *Brian's going fucking ape-shit*, and *What a fucking mess. I don't know what I've done.* So where's Jan? Did she head down to Anchorage on her own? Brian would have been here with Bree, buzzed and naked. Why hadn't she just locked the door against him? Had he shown her the gun to scare her? Christ. Fisher shakes his head to clear it, shakes it again though it hurts like hell.

"It wasn't like that," he says at last. "It couldn't have been."

For once Grisby doesn't say anything, just looks at him from under the edge of his fur hat, his eyes big behind their glasses, then turns away.

Fisher says, "How the fuck does this make any sense, really?" His voice creaks and fades, and it's all he can do to add, "Goddamnit."

He wishes he hadn't taken that Vicodin. The calm that it

sent through him earlier has drained away and his thoughts can't quite fit themselves together. He tells himself, if only his head were clear he'd understand everything and know what to do. He remembers the times his phone rang and how easy it would have been to slip it out of his pocket and say, "Yup?" Bree would have been on the other end, all frantic, true, but he could have asked what the hell was going on and she'd have told him, and none of this would have happened.

Only, it's too late for that.

Grisby's got the gun clenched under his arm and he's skipping those quick hands of his over everything. They tap-tap their way along the edge of Bree's desk, and lift papers, and fast-touch earbuds that turn out to be attached to nothing, sniffing out what might be hidden beneath slippery magazines and flaccid T-shirts, until Fisher hisses at him, "Just stop with that, OK? We need to think."

"Think? I've already done my thinking. There's some sweet stuff in this place that Mr Step-Dad's not gonna miss." Grisby's face is a little shiny, and no wonder when he's still got his hat on and his parka zipped up.

Fisher kneads his knuckles into his eyes so hard the lids pop and smack. "Oh great: so it's going to look like a burglary that went wrong, and you're going to be the dumb-shit who did it and have a murder hanging over you too?"

"But just think—it won't be Bree they're looking for. Everybody wins."

"Everybody wins?" he says quietly, and looks up at Grisby. "It'll be you they're looking for, and me too. Christ." He sniffs. His nose is stuffed up. He yanks a tissue from his pocket and blows hard. That's a mistake because the smells from the bathroom—the blood, the sour smells of vomit and urine—are sharper now. Familiar, too, making him think of buckets of soapy water and scouring brushes and bleach, because years ago he cleaned up messes as bad as this at the motel his dad and Ada run. A woman murdered by her boyfriend, and after the police left Ada sent Fisher along to fix up the room. Perhaps that's why the idea comes to him. "We'll get rid of him and take care of this mess. There'll be no reason for the cops to look for Bree. No body, no murder, no murder suspect, nothing but a guy who's taken off and not told anyone."

Grisby's mouth pulls wide. He lifts both hands, the gun swinging from one of them. "Whoa now, I can't be cleaning up that shit."

"But you want to take that gun and sell it? And whatever the hell you've got in your pockets? Think about it: stuff from a house where a guy's been found shot dead? Oh yeah, real smart." Grisby's looking past him, but Fisher sees his jaw tighten.

"Christ, man, fucking Christ."

"We'll take him out someplace and dump him."

"That's your brilliant idea? Come breakup, those fuckheads who like hunting and fishing and crap are gonna be out. Someone's gonna find him."

"That's months away. For now, what I need is time to find Breehan before she digs herself in any worse." He forces himself to his feet. How far away the carpet is, how insubstantial this house, with its windows looking out onto the darkness. A dumb idea, to think that such a place could keep anyone safe.

# 8

To wrap a body takes thirty-five minutes and a blue tarp (large and without holes or tears), duct tape (most of a roll to do the job properly), plastic sheeting (if you have it) or, in a pinch, newspaper to lay in the trunk of your car to catch fluids that might leak out, and rope—don't forget the rope, because without it you'll have nothing to grab hold of when you drag that body to your car, and from your car to its final resting place; rope, properly tied, will give you a handle of sorts to pull with, especially if you think to tie it into loops or, better yet, to cover those loops with rags to prevent the rope biting through your gloves because, if you didn't know already, you'll soon find out what *dead weight* means.

To clean away the evidence of someone dying from a gunshot wound in a bathroom takes three times as long as wrapping the body, and a lot more equipment. If you've had experience as a housekeeper, cleaning motel rooms, for example, you'll know instinctively what you need: rubber gloves, buckets of soapy water, a scrubbing brush, bleach to rub into grouting where blood has stained it, spackle to fill in the hole in the wall left by the bullet (unless it has, by a miracle, lodged in the body), paper towels to wipe down mirrors and tiles, a washing machine to launder towels and the bathmat. It helps if you haven't vomited into the toilet. If you have, count on an extra five minutes to scrub it clean, and you'll want to do that: who knows if vomit contains DNA to identify you, but you'll worry that it does.

Lastly, you'll need to take a break, however hard that is at a time like this, and come back up to that room with fresh eyes that will catch the tiny red flecks that would otherwise give the game away, the white chip that looks like a sliver of bone, the gray smear down by the baseboard heater that you think might be brain but could be something more innocuous. You'll worry that the place is too clean—cleaner than the rest of the house, for Chrissakes!—but you'll tell yourself that's just too bad, and really, who's going to notice?

To occupy yourself while the washing's on—bathmat, towels, perhaps even your own clothes (it's hard to avoid getting blood on them, after all, but in the end maybe you can't bring yourself to sit around in your underwear in this place)—watch the TV (something mindless but not violent or it'll remind you of what you've been doing and you won't be able to finish the soda you took from the fridge without thinking, and that's another thing to remember, as you'll need to wipe the empty can clean of prints or take it with you, which reminds you that you mustn't forget the bags of garbage with their bloodied paper towels and rags you've set by the stairs).

Best of all, bring a friend you can count on. Not one more interested in rooting through the bathroom cabinets, or hunting for the keys to the gun lockers in the den, and looking over the desktop computers and laptops and flat-screen TVs, the jewelry, the watch left on the nightstand. Not one who can't mop a floor, or who disappears downstairs and tries every key he can find on the gun lockers, never mind that he's supposed to load the towels and bathmat into the dryer when the washer's finished. And when all that's done, don't forget to pack a bag with clothes, and a shaving kit, and even the poor dead sucker's wallet and passport, to write on the bag's label his name and the address of some hotel you invent down in Denver, because this guy's leaving town. Permanently.

44

## 9

THERE'S A PLACE Fisher has in mind a couple of miles south of the center of town: a stretch of river just downstream from the power plant where, even in the heart of winter, steam drifts lazily from black gashes of open water, and the ice is rotten and treacherous.

He drives hunched like an old man. Beside him, Grisby's bobbing his head to an old Bachman-Turner Overdrive song on the radio and sipping coffee as though nothing the hell's the matter, as though the car hasn't been stiff with the silence between them since they pulled out of the driveway.

What is it with Grisby? Fisher thinks. He kept carrying more stuff out to the car, like they were emptying the place— boxes bristling with guns, for crying out loud, two laptops piled together like a sandwich, a box of electronics with wires trailing out of it. He filled the back seat and was going to start on the trunk until Fisher asked where the fuck he thought they were going to put the body. *We could always come back for it,* Grisby said, then added, *Hell, OK, OK.* Fisher walked away, back into the house. One last check in Bree's bathroom in case he'd missed something. And what was Grisby doing downstairs? Making coffee and pouring it into two travel mugs he'd found in the dishwasher. Now he's sipping his coffee like there's nothing wrong with any of this, driving along with a dead guy in the trunk and the backseat crammed with his stuff, and Fisher can't bear it: he lowers the window and tosses his travel mug out, plucks Grisby's from his hand and throws it out too.

Grisby blurts, "Hey, for fuck's sake—"

"Fucking evidence, isn't it?"

"Man, you're letting this get to you," and Grisby turns up the radio.

It's close to eleven at night and fifty-four below. A little warmer, not that you can feel it. The DJ says: *Stay safe, you guys out there, we're still in the deep freeze, and it don't take much to slip over the edge.* Behind his voice, the chords of a Steely Dan number start up, then the music takes over. The song pulses out, wrapping itself around Fisher like the world means something, like there's some plan to it. Within seconds the music crackles and yawns, and when it comes back it's all twisted around by the cold, and Fisher's just a guy driving through the night who's gotten in over his head.

How hard it is to drive as though it's just him and Grisby heading to the south of town, for a drink at the Lucky Fox, perhaps, or to pick up some beers at the convenience store. This is the time of night when the cops wait like wolves, hungry and ready to strike. Fisher's not in his cab; that would give him a little slack with the cops because, hell, cabbies drive home drunks and druggies and put up with their shit. No, in a sorry-ass dented-up Mazda all it takes is a bend you should have braked harder for, a wobble as you correct, and they're onto you, no matter that a moment ago the world was nothing more than the glazed road and the silvery gleam of streetlights. A pair of headlights will bear down on you, glaring off your mirrors and licking round the inside of your car until—your heart can hardly bear it—they twitch with red and blue and you have to pull over.

What would Fisher say? Ever since he eased the car down Jan and Brian's driveway he's been putting together explanations: that he's helping his friend here move into a new apartment, which is why the car's crammed with stuff. Except it's eleven at night. The cop's gonna ask, *Couldn't do it during the day, huhn?* and he'll say *Nah, we're on different shifts this week,* and he'll look at Grisby, and if there's a pause before Grisby remembers to agree, the cop will linger. Can he search the car? He'll need a reason to, but how the fuck will he not see what's on the back seat? A box of guns, a couple of laptops, stuff piled so high it blocks most of the back window. Sure, Officer, he'd say, we're on an innocent mission here, and his heart pinches in panic at the thought of it. Maybe he and Grisby stink of bleach. Maybe a dead-man reek will ooze out from the trunk—how long would it take for a body to freeze back there? Hell, maybe Brian'll go stiff with rigor mortis and the way they folded him into the trunk will be their undoing, because how the fuck are they going to get him out?

How easy it is to set his mind winging around and around like this. But before long it settles again and probes the delicate wound of his real dread: Is it possible that his daughter's done this? That she's killed a man? He tells himself no, it wasn't her, that carrying away what's left of Brian is all for nothing, a fool's errand, that someone else shot him, one of his gun-nut buddies, or Jan—because where's she? Did she drive down to Anchorage on her own in this merciless cold? Why would she, unless she shot Brian first?

No, he thinks. Bree said Brian was going ape-shit. She said she didn't know what she'd done. Now somewhere out in this frozen land she's hiding, and so afraid that she's lost all sense of what she should and shouldn't do.

He tries playing through what happened: Brian naked and buzzed, watching TV in the bedroom, and somehow Bree pisses him off. Maybe she was whining about being left here when Jan was supposed to take her to Anchorage, or maybe she wanted to go out and he told her no. So he goes ape-shit because he's buzzed, and they argue, and he pulls out a gun. Hell, he always has a gun around. He follows Bree to her room, and she's so scared and he's so buzzed that she gets it away from him and

47

shoots him. No, thinks Fisher, there was something else. Was Brian jerking off in his room, and when she disturbed him he came on to her? Is that what happened? A hot surge of hate slides up his throat.

What keeps coming back to him is that Janice's car wasn't in the garage, that she took off for Anchorage and left Bree behind. Wasn't there something to make her suspicious about Brian? No clue that maybe he had a thing for her daughter? And even if she couldn't see it, wasn't it enough that he was so hard on Bree? No wonder she didn't fit in at school. All those rules, taking away her phone, shutting her off from her friends, not letting her go anywhere, perhaps not even down to Anchorage with her mom. What kind of man does that? A man with a thing for his step-daughter, that's who.

He lays this idea of Brian—Brian the molester, the rapist—over the man he knew, tries to push it down so that it snaps into place, but it won't, and he realizes he's driving without paying much mind to the road for all that he's bent over the wheel and his hands are aching from holding it tight, and he brakes, cursing, because there's the bridge, and there's the goddamn turn already.

## 10

TO REACH THE low bluff just beyond the bridge, Fisher has to take one snow-packed road, then another. Of all the shitty luck, just as he makes the second turn, headlights sweep out of the darkness. In an instant, he's snapped off his own lights. Grisby lets out, "Fuck, that's stupid—now they know we're up to something."

The vehicle comes at them steadily. Soon it's so close its lights dazzle off the ice built up around the edges of the windshield. A pickup, the chassis high on outsized wheels, and just as it seems about to pull up next to them, its engine roars and it's off in a storm of exhaust. Fisher watches until its taillights have vanished. The car's barely moving. It crawls along until the snow widens into a turn-out, and here Fisher pulls up and lets out his breath in one long sigh.

Even with the moon long gone the night's not all darkness. In winter it never is. The snow catches the faint light of the stars and turns the color of old jeans. Fisher doesn't bother with his flashlight. Safer not to, he thinks, but jams it into his pocket just in case. The trunk's hinges groan and from its gaping mouth comes a whiff of something foul.

Grisby comes crunching across the snow and stands beside him. He mutters, "Fuck, man. I've got a thousand other things I'd rather be doing right now."

Fisher steels himself and reaches in. He grabs the rope tied around the tarp and uses his own weight to hoist the body, feels gravity pulling back and hisses at Grisby, "Help me, for fuck's sake." Between them they haul one half of the body over the lip of the trunk, but when it tips forward Grisby lets go and jumps back. The tarp snags and rips, and the thing slumps onto the edge of the trunk like a wet blanket over a clothesline. Something cracks. Fisher's stomach clenches at the thought of what they're doing. Why's this part so hard when dragging the body down the stairs and across the living room, and all the way out to the car was easy? Even getting it into the trunk hadn't been that bad. Adrenalin, he thinks, he'd been driven by adrenalin, and now he feels worn out and sickened by it all.

He leans into the trunk and feeds his gloved fingers through the rope where it's tied around the legs. With one heave he lifts those legs and the body slumps forward and nearly takes him with it. He has to let go and it flops onto the snow with a wheezy thud.

The guardrail's only a few yards away, but the snow's softer here and their boots sink as they drag the body between them. In their wake they leave two sets of tracks with a smooth depression running between them, and the sight of it makes Fisher swear under his breath.

On the other side of the guardrail lies a ledge, then a steep slope bristling with bushes and twiggy willow. Below, a long, flat crust of ice that doesn't reach the shore. The open water's dark and greasy and from it lift tufts of vapor. Fisher thought it would feel safe here—a forgotten place, except by a few old guys who sit on the bank in the summer and fish for grayling, but there's the bridge with its lights, and a car humming along it, and another. Beyond, like a magnificent city seen from far off, the red and white lights of the power plant hang in the sky.

Fisher can hardly bear to touch the tarp again—the thought of what's inside, the ridiculously loud crackling it makes because the plastic's frozen. It doesn't help that now they have to get the body over the guardrail, and that means wrapping their arms around it. Fisher feels the round mass of the skull against his shoulder and has to swallow so he doesn't throw up. Grisby's staggering under the weight of the legs, and the sharp edge of the guardrail sings against the ropes and the woven plastic. But then the body's up and going over, it's tipping and falling, and it lands in the soft snow of the ledge. Silence, then from it comes a breathy groan.

Grisby staggers back. "Holy freaking fuck, he's still alive."

Fisher can't feel his fingers. The cold's everywhere, eating its way into him, and he lets himself shiver hard. "No way. There was a hole in his head, you saw it."

"Did you check? I mean, fuck—did you?"

"I just scrubbed his brains off a bathroom wall."

Grisby's laughing into his gloves, an awful chittering sound, then he's bending over, saying "Oh Christ, oh Christ, fuck fuck fuck."

"Come on, Grisby,"

But Grisby's not listening. He's walking back to where the car's rumbling and its exhaust curling out, his boots slipping in the lumpy snow and his arms hugged over his chest. There's the flash of the dome light and Grisby's face gaunt under his hat, then the door slams shut and takes the light with it. Grisby vanishes.

Fisher leans against the guardrail. The cold burns through to his thighs.

He thinks, we could drive him into town. We could dump him at the hospital, and who's to know what happened?

He thinks, who am I kidding?

He thinks, we could leave him here: he's dying anyway.

More than anything he wants to take off after Grisby and close himself into the warm shell of the car, to drive headlong across town and hide in his trailer so that all of this will fall away and be forgotten. But fuck it, if Brian's alive, won't he have recognized him? And if by some unimaginable miracle he survives—

Fear's sinking its teeth into him and he can't shake it loose. He's so afraid that he takes his flashlight from his pocket and turns it on. The cold's been sucking away at the batteries and the beam's flimsy. He shines it at the guardrail then forces himself after it: over the metal edge, onto the ledge on the other side. The snow has an icy crust, but beneath it's perilously soft and he stumbles, the light swooping wildly as his arms flail, and when he falls he falls against the body. It rolls away down the slope. He hears it crashing through bushes, and when he looks up it's come to rest against a spindly spruce. He thinks, fuck, that could have been me. In the back of his throat, a vile sour taste. He swallows against it and forces himself to his feet, so gingerly he's scarcely moving. More than anything he wants to take hold of the guardrail and heave himself back over it to safety. But how can he? Come sunrise, a blue tarp caught on the riverbank is going to catch the eye of everyone driving across the bridge.

"Fuck," he says, "fucking goddamn fuck." Snow's got into his parka and his gloves, has come in over the tops of his boots so that cold fingers of it creep over his skin. He makes himself turn sideways, slowly, to dig in one boot then the next, taking his time as though a sickening griping wasn't stirring his guts. He slips twice and drops his flashlight. He paws it out of the snow and slides a little, has to sit down to save himself. He's so close to the edge that it pulls at him, and the effort of resisting leaves him dizzy. It doesn't help that his flashlight's shining out over the treacly water. He knows how it goes: it's not the cold of the river that kills you, at least, not the way you'd think—the shock of it makes you gasp, and your lungs fill, and like that it's all over because you've been dragged beneath the ice. Your body sinks to the bottom where you molder into the mud come spring.

It doesn't bear thinking about it. Not when you're about to send another man to this fate.

The snow beneath Fisher's butt has curved to his shape, cradling him even as it soaks the warmth right out of him. He's so cold and scared he's shaking. It's all he can do to swing the flashlight toward the tarp. Even in that sad light it's a ridiculous crayon blue, the rope a cheery yellow, the silver duct tape gleaming. The beam's shrinking and he cups the flashlight close to his face and breathes on it a few times, then he shines it where he imagines Brian's broken head must be.

"Brian?" he says. How thin and insincere his voice sounds. "Look, hey, we thought you were dead. I mean, you'd been shot in the head, right?" He lets out a flat laugh and his breath hangs ghostly along the beam of the flashlight. "You're dying anyway, you know that. Besides, I have to think of Bree. And I mean, what the fuck was going on? You, naked in her bathroom? Because if I find out you were coming on to her, I'll come back and shoot you myself all over again," and he lets out another laugh.

His upper lip's cold where his breath has condensed on it and tried to freeze. He wipes it away with the back of his glove and the light jumps around. "Seriously, Brian, you always were an uptight shit, but when you lost it, did it have to be with Bree? I mean, for fuck's sake, she's just a kid!"

The dying beam of his flashlight is drawing in like a tongue, and the darkness steps closer. He leans forward and strains his hearing toward this thing lying just past the twin mounds of his knees. He waits. He watches it. A movement, a shift in the shape of a bulge, and he blurts, "Fucking hell!" and is about to crab-walk his way back up the slope as fast as he can when he realizes. The flickering flashlight. The play of shadows. The tarp hasn't moved. Still, he'd do anything rather than touch that cursed thing again.

Be better than that, he tells himself, but he doesn't move. He makes himself think about Bree and what her life might become if he's too afraid to finish this job. A trial, he thinks, her story in the paper. Even if they let her off, the stink of what she did will cling to her for years, for the rest of her life most likely. That mightn't even be the worst of it. What's it like to run and know you're being hunted? What does that do to you? And what might it make you do, especially if you're Bree?

He forces out one hand to grab the rope and heaves, heaves, to swing Brian's legs past the thin spruce trunk, but he can't do it. His lungs are aching from the effort, his knees numb where his pants and longjohns are pulled tight across the bone. He scoots closer to the tree and tucks both arms under the tarp. He feels the bend of knees over his right arm and his belly clenches. Then he cries out and hefts those legs with all his might. The body comes loose and rolls madly through the snow, then it sails out over the edge, suspended for a moment, and crashes into the water.

As for Fisher, his arms are windmilling against gravity. The flashlight flips end over end in a perfect, short parabola then embeds itself in the snow. All the while Fisher wills himself backward, backward, can't find his balance, can't find anything to hold on to except air until—just when he's got the iron taste of death in his mouth, so sure is he that he's going over the edge too—one hand closes around the spruce, and its top flexes like a fishing pole as he drags himself back toward the safety of the slope.

He crawls up the incline because he doesn't trust himself to stand. His hands are numb and his feet, his knees, his face, and he's almost sobbing, is saying to himself, "Fuck oh fuck," because he's carrying with him the thought of what he's done. Hasn't he just killed a man? A dying man, it's true, but nonetheless one alive enough to sigh and groan? Those sounds haunt him all the way up to the guardrail, and over it, and across the packed snow toward the car.

The air's so warm inside that he can scarcely breathe. He rests his head against the steering wheel and feels himself trembling. Grisby's fiddling with the radio. He says, "Christ—how long can it take to throw a dead guy in the river?" and "Man, I thought you'd fallen in with him."

"Nearly did," Fisher says. "He got stuck against a tree and I had to go down after him. Fuck," and he rubs his face. "Maybe he was a shit, but I just threw him in the river to die."

Grisby rocks forward and grins. "Nah," he says, "he was dead. Dead as a freaking dodo."

"We heard him."

"Yeah, fuck, I nearly pissed my pants. But hey, remember that summer I worked as a cleaner at the funeral home? One day I'm mopping the floor around this body they've got laid out with a sheet over it, and suddenly I hear this groan and the body sits up. It's some old guy and his eyes are rolled up in his head and his arms are doing the zombie-reach thing, and bubbles are coming out his mouth. Man, I pissed myself, I actually did."

"So he wasn't dead."

"Fucking gases, man. They build up and do weird stuff. The guys there thought it was a huge freaking joke when I came running out with my pants all wet. Man, I quit and never went back. Too goddamn freaky for me, know what I mean?"

Fisher's face aches from the inside where the sore tissue of his sinuses is coming alive again in the warm air. He says, "You couldn't have told me earlier? For fuck's sake!"

"Didn't think about it until just now." He sniffs. "I was as scared shitless as you."

"Except you didn't have to throw him in the river."

Fisher has one hand bunched into a fist. He imagines it

smacking into Grisby's cheek, bone cracking against bone. He might have done it, too, but Grisby turns to him and says, "Your idea. I was just going along with it. And hey—you checked he got sucked under, right?"

Fisher's foot's a clumsy frozen thing in his boot, but he forces it down on the gas pedal until the engine's shrieking, as though that will make what he sees inside his head disappear: the sun coming up late-morning with its glassy golden glow, and the blue of the tarp lit up where it's come to rest against the ice, held fast by the current.

Grisby says, "Well—did you?"

"Did you? Or were you sitting here in the warm, thinking about how much you're gonna get for Brian's stuff?" and he jerks his thumb over his shoulder at the boxes piled in the back seat. "You think you need to check, go check. I'll wait for you." He sits pressing the gas pedal until it's clear—as they both knew—that Grisby's going nowhere, then they take off over the rutted snow, back to the highway.

Grisby switches stations until he finds some nerve-jangling rock, then he sits back and yawns. Fisher is perched forward to see the road because ice has shrunk the windshield to a port-hole: his breath and Grisby's, frozen onto the glass. He jacks up the heat and turns the vents to melt it. He can't see far enough to drive safely, but he doesn't give a shit right now. He steps hard on the gas and soon the car's gobbling up the blacktop like it's being hauled in by the pull of the headlights, like there's no way anything more could go wrong tonight. But all Fisher can think about is everything they've screwed up: if they didn't want Brian found, why didn't they wrap him in white sheets, for crap's sake, instead of a blue tarp? And then there's all the stuff loaded into the backseat—the black bag he packed with Brian's razor and underwear, his pants and shirts, his toothbrush, even a book, for fuck's sake. He should have thrown the bag in after him—why didn't he think of that? Then there's the electronics and guns and God-knows-what that Grisby's loaded into boxes. If Grisby's not careful, that stuff's going to show up in the wrong places and the shit's going to hit the heater. And since when has Grisby been careful?

Beside him Grisby's bobbing his head. Over the whine of a guitar played punishingly fast Grisby shouts, "You know how it is: you wake up and the day's just an ordinary day, and then something happens and it goes all crazy, like you're in a movie or something, and by the time it's over—"

"This one's not over."

Grisby leans toward him. "Near as dammit, Fisher. How about you drop me at my place? It's not far, right?" He peers into the night beyond the car as though he has any idea where they are.

"Thought you needed to lie low."

"Yeah, well," and he licks his lips, "reckon it's late enough for me to go home."

Fisher checks his mirror then steers the car over onto the slip road. "You can't sell that stuff. You have to sit on it until this all blows over."

"Ah, c'mon, don't start. I helped you out, didn't I? Huhn?"

"If someone puts two and two together, it's—"

"Listen, I know what I'm doing. OK? So drop it." He slumps back against the seat. "You're turning into a real tight-ass. I mean, the thing with the travel mugs—c'mon. No one's even gonna be looking for him. He's left town, right?"

"We can't screw up. It's not just us: it's Bree, too."

"Yeah, well, she got us into this." He huffs his breath out his nose. "Hell, if she keeps her mouth shut, what are people gonna think except that some shitbag husband took off while his wife was away? Maybe your ex won't do a thing; hell, she's rid of him and she didn't even have to clean up the mess. She comes back and he's gone, that bathroom's cleaner than it's even been. What's not to like?"

"For fuck's sake—"

"Hey, it's not like we killed him. We just found him with his brains blown out."

Fisher swallows his saliva because he can't help but think of that house, and Brian slumped against the wall with that hole in his head, and what they've missed that could lead the cops right to them. But anyway, dumping a body's not a crime is it? Or maybe it is, but it's not like he killed Brian. All he did was dispose of what was left of him, and that from the best of motives. Plus he was careful: those yellow gloves, all that washing, all that scrubbing, the bags of trash he's carried away and that it'll be easy enough to get rid of. But the rest of the stuff, it's like a bomb waiting to go off. Fuck, why did he agree to let Grisby take it? Stupid, he tells himself, stupid stupid stupid. He takes a breath and says, "I can't let you take that stuff, I just can't, not yet. It's too risky."

Grisby's head swings toward him. That narrow chin, that too-long nose, that grubby look of stubble on his cheeks. "You're being a jerk."

"You know it's too risky."

Grisby lifts his hands in surrender. "Well, fine then. You win. You take it all home. You hide it away in that *huge* trailer, and you make sure no one accidentally comes across it, and you get rid of it, OK? OK?"

Fisher's about to say OK, *fine*, but nothing comes out his mouth. He imagines it: all that stuff in his trailer, and Jan coming round because she wants to know where the hell Bree is, and isn't she with him? She'd recognize that stuff right away. So, he'd have to take it to the transfer station—but even at fifty-four below there are guys who hang around and go through your trash, who'll drag it from the dumpster and fight over it. There must be other places: holes he could dig, except the ground's frozen; or the river again, except some of that stuff might float, and he's biting his tongue, because there has to be some way to get rid of it. Hell, he could take it back to the house, couldn't he? But the thought of going back there . . . no, he can't do it.

He lets out a sigh. He's so tired, so very tired, and his head's throbbing. All he wants is to sleep, because in the morning he's going to have to search for Bree. "OK," he says, "OK then, you take it, and Brian's travel bag."

"No way, that was your idea. You take it."

They fight all the way back to Grisby's apartment before finally the silence of the parking lot, and all the windows looking out across it, makes them shut up. Fisher even helps Grisby carry the stuff up to his door, and dumps the bags of trash in the building's dumpsters, and comes back up to say goodbye. Grisby doesn't ask him in, and he's glad. He climbs back behind the wheel and drives off, so fast his car almost catches up to the darkness just beyond its headlights.

## 11

O F COURSE, THERE'S the bag. The almost-new black wheel-along bag that Fisher packed for Brian's trip into the great beyond and that Grisby refused to take. All the way home Fisher senses it in the back seat like one of those sullen fares who clamp their mouth shut and stare anywhere but at his eyes in the mirror, as though it's his damn fault they have to pay him for a ride home.

First thing he does when he pulls up outside his trailer is wheel around in his seat and stare at the bag, like he's trying to catch it out because this is a horror movie and the thing's alive and out to get him. But there it sits like a stout black-coated torso, with its white label gleaming in its plastic pocket, and there's a smugness about it, as though it knows he planned to get rid of it and was too chicken. There were dumpsters in town, but someone would spot a brand-new bag in a dumpster and haul it out. He could have tossed it outside one of the crackhouses where he's dropped off fares—but in those streets someone's sure to be watching, they always are. On a lonely stretch of road then—except a truck came hurtling up behind him just as he slowed on the highway home, and it occurred to him how many people take this route, and how soon the bag would be found. He thought of the pits at the bottom of his hill where gold was once dug out of the earth. Too close to home. Like leaving it on his own goddamn doorstep.

So here's the bag still in the backseat with that stupid label where he wrote Brian's name and the address of that made-up hotel in Denver. Christ, what was he thinking? He can't remember. To throw it in after Brian? To leave it someplace where it'd be found in a few days? With his handwriting on the label?

Now he wonders what else he's done that's so freaking dumb. He lets his head tilt back against the headrest. One in the morning and he's hollowed out. His thoughts freefall through the emptiness in his skull with nothing to run up against, no sense, no logic, nothing except exhaustion and—he feels it again now—a lurking anger. At Brian for being naked and dead in his daughter's bathroom, at Grisby for being such a shithead and insisting on taking Brian's stuff, at himself for not having thought it all through more clearly and somehow stopped it, all of it. Why didn't he answer his phone when he could have? Then none of this would have happened. Something milder and quieter would have filled its place in the great sequence of events tipping through the universe, and by now he'd be asleep and untroubled by what he didn't know, that by picking up his phone he'd saved himself from this mire of worry and fear.

Already the cold's swamping the car. With each breath the air's a little sharper until, in how long—two minutes? three?— the inside of his nose is smarting, and the aches in his head and his cheeks are pulsing like they've got a life of their own. The Vicodin wore off long ago. He could go inside and take more, but right now shouldn't he be searching for Bree? Isn't he the only one who can save her from what she's done? But where the hell to look at this time of night? He has no idea.

That's me all over, he thinks, and pulls his keys from the ignition. No fucking imagination. No fucking ideas.

He heaves Brian's bag across the snow and up the steps to his door. He's careful twisting the key in the lock because what could be worse than snapping it off on a night like this? A moment later the key turns and he steps into the warmth of his trailer. He unzips his parka and calls his dog, and when Pax comes limping across the carpet and sniffs at Brian's bag, he pushes the dog's head away and stares at the bag, saying over and over "Jesus fucking Christ" until Pax looks up at him with his tail mournfully beating the air.

## 12

FISHER JERKS OUT of a nightmare that twists away like a shark into the deep. There's Pax snoring beside his bed, there's the green light of his alarm: 3:02. He doesn't want to fall asleep again and fights being pulled under by staring into the darkness. Pax snuffles as he dreams. The refrigerator whirrs, a comforting sound. Then the shadows congeal. They have form. There's a shape standing by the window with something off about the tilt of its head, and Fisher catches the stink of blood.

He sits up. He's awake for real now and his T-shirt's sticking to his chest. Who knew you could dream smells?

At six, when he should haul himself out of bed and belly up to the toilet to take a piss, and make himself coffee, and head into town for his shift, he snatches up his cell phone and calls in sick. Reggie curses at him, but hey, Reggie can go fuck himself.

Too early to go out looking for Bree. Too early to do anything but sleep, and he pulls the covers up around his head.

☙

It's still dark when Fisher's woken by a hammering on his door. Pax struggles to his feet and lets out a throaty volley of barks. Fisher rolls over. His alarm says 8:03. He'd meant to get up an hour ago, and now he remembers why. He needs to look for Bree. He needs to be on guard in this strange new world where Bree's shot Brian, and Brian's dead and been dumped in the river.

Bree: he has to tell her he's taken care of things and she

doesn't need to hide, that in fact it'd be better not to. She must have holed up with a friend. He knows a few names and faces: Frisbee with his curtain of dark hair across his face, Jen with her sulky lips and too-small nose, Tomas who's tall and lanky and restless, Logan—all he can picture of that kid is his green baseball cap. But where do these kids live? How the hell can he find them?

He rolls over. The sheets are cold through his longjohns. His head's clogged and heavy, and his breath whistles through his nose like someone trying out a tune. He pulls a tissue from the box by his bed and blows his nose hard enough to drag up a hurt deep behind his eyes, then he blows again and drops the tissue into the pile on the carpet.

Whoever's at the door hasn't given up. Another rat-tat-tat of knocks and Pax barks back, then glances through the darkness at Fisher. For a moment he thinks: it's Bree. Then his insides turn to liquid—Christ, it could be the cops. He tells himself that's impossible, but his body won't believe him and his legs tremble as he hoists them over the edge of his bed. The edge of the mattress digs into his thighs and the room's chill makes him shiver hard. "Fuck," he says to himself, "fuck fuck fuck." Pax pushes his nose against his hand. It's warm and dry as leather. Pax lifts a paw and his claws scratch down Fisher's shin. Is he urging Fisher to his feet? He gently pushes the dog away and hauls on his jeans.

From the living room he catches the low lurching grumble of a badly tuned engine. The light spilling through the curtain's a ghastly white. Headlights. His asshole grows tight and damp with fear. He waits for the light to pulse red and blue and red again in that Christmas-tree effect the cops favor these days. Is that how they come for people? With their colored lights giving them away? Maybe that's just for traffic stops. Besides, surely they'd be cleverer than that if they thought he was a murderer.

64

He pads across to the window in his bare feet. His guts have curdled, his hand's jerky, but he pulls back the edge of the curtain and rubs at the ice on the glass until he's melted a hole. On his steps someone's waiting, head tilted toward his door, hand raised to knock again.

The sight of that person makes him think: Brian. A zombie-Brian with decaying skin and gelid eyes and nothing in his head except vengeance.

But if Brian's come back for him, Brian's found himself a parka and a pickup that he's left running in the driveway.

Grisby? he thinks. Maybe he's borrowed a vehicle, because that's not the ridiculous VW Rabbit he drives. But why would he have come out here at this time of the morning when he should be at work? No, he thinks, not Grisby. Grisby's busy at the diner and will be until two, and those boxes of electronics and guns and God-knows-what-else stacked by his door will stay there, safe for the time being.

Fisher's breath freezes on the glass and he rubs it again. Whoever's come for him isn't tall. For one heady moment he's sure it's Breehan and, like a jerk, here he is leaving her knocking and knocking on his door. He's just about to let her in when he hears, "Mikey—I know you're in there. For pity's sake, open up before I freeze to death."

A raw voice. Ada. His step-mother. Christ. Fisher lets out a breath he didn't know he was holding. He thinks: of course, fear can do strange things to you. Breehan went to the motel, never mind that she hates Ada and Ada hates her back. Why didn't he think of that before? And now here's Ada because she wants Bree off her hands. "Coming," he shouts. "Give me a moment."

His T-shirt doesn't quite cover the bulge of his belly. He's not going to open the door with his gut slumping over the top of his jeans, because she'll say something acid, she just can't let an opportunity pass.

Her voice comes through the door again. "What d'you think—it's Hawaii out here? Let me in."

"Coming," he yells, but he's digging through the jackets and coats hanging behind the door until he finds a fleece. He shrugs himself into it and snaps on the lights, and the whole time she's talking, saying things like, "You can't treat people like this, Mikey, how many times do I have to tell you?" and "Have you got someone in there? Is that it?"

The lock's so frosted up and cold it burns his fingers. He swings open the door and ice fog rolls across the carpet like a cheap movie effect, bringing Ada with it.

He opens his mouth to ask, "Breehan?" but he doesn't even get the first sound out because Ada's saying, "Eight o'clock—right? I said I'd come fetch you. You went and forgot, didn't you? Didn't even bother to set your alarm. Most people are up by now, you know that? Most people are on their way to work already."

A twinge of recollection: at the weekend Ada called and asked him to come with her to the hardware store Thursday morning. He'd said yes, probably, could tell her for sure when he had his schedule for the week, then the whole memory of it had slipped away.

"You were gonna call," he says. "I didn't know my shifts."

"Honestly, Mikey—I did call, yesterday evening. I told you to call back if you couldn't make it, and you didn't. Now I'm thinking you didn't even check your messages. What's up with you?"

"For Christssakes, you can't just take it for granted I can come—and as it turns out, I can't. I've got stuff to take care of this morning, urgent stuff."

She's unzipping her parka, but she pauses. "Oh yeah? What sort of urgent stuff?" Her eyes are hard on his and he can't think of a single thing to say that won't sound lame.

She takes off her parka and dumps it on the armchair, then looks back at him with her mouth twisted to one side. "Like I thought," she says and walks over to the kitchen in her boots, like there's nothing wrong with treading snow across someone else's carpet, especially not your stepson's and especially because, as she's told him pretty much every time she's been here, it's so filthy she can't bear the thought of standing on it in her socks.

The snow boots exaggerate the thinness of her legs, but in truth she's a stick of a woman and proud of it. That must be why she wears tight white pants and a close-fitting fire-truck-red sweater whose v-neck shows off the wrinkled skin above her breasts. Around her neck gleams a gold chain and a cross stuck with diamonds, real ones but small as grit. Her lipstick's the same red as her sweater, her hair so blonde it's almost white. It's been pulled back in a pony-tail and her bangs teased and sprayed into a froth over her forehead, like she's still twenty-something and can get away with dressing like a cheerleader. You'd think after all these years Fisher'd be used to the sight of her, but he isn't. She's all wrong, as wrong as the motel she runs with his dad with its phony antique clock in the reception area, and its vases of silk flowers, the cheap prints of Denali on the wall, the warm stink of her cigarettes beneath the fake-vanilla scent of air-freshener and, worst of all, the cheery Hi *there* she croaks out to guests. Every time he sets foot in the place he wants to tell her, you're not fooling anyone.

But maybe she knows that and wants her hardness to shine out like a warning. That's what occurred to Fisher when he was twelve and his dad led her into the kitchen and left her standing by the sink as he helped himself to a beer from the fridge. He took a swig and wiped his lips on his wrist before he told Fisher, "This is your new mom. You be good to her, you hear?" Fisher glanced over at her. She was leaning against the sink tapping her cigarette ash into the drain. Her low-cut sweater was a sour-apple green and her yellow pants so tight they showed the fleshy crease of her crotch.

Maybe she caught him looking, because as soon as his dad sat in front of the TV in the living room she came close, so close that the soft skin above her breasts was only inches from his nose. "Have a good look, I know what boys are like," she said, "but don't go getting ideas." She let her smoke snake out of her nostrils. "I don't like sneaks or pervs. You want kicks, don't get them by spying on me and your dad, or you'll be out on your ear before you can say *jerking off*. Got it? I'm not your mom. I'm not the maid, or the cook, or the nurse. You want something, go get it yourself. You see something needs taking care of, you take care of it. If you're not happy, you shut up or you leave. This is my home now, and don't you forget it."

Within a few days the photos of his mom that had stood on the TV were gone. Fisher found them in the trash. He took them from their frames and carried them inside and hid them at the back of his closet. This is what he understood about what had happened to his mom: she'd been out late one night and hadn't come home. Someone had called the cops because by a small lake up at the university a car had been found and a woman a few yards away, her head and chest in the water. A single shot to the head, her body dumped, and no one ever arrested for it. Four months later, his dad married Ada.

Now here she is popping the carafe from his coffee-machine and filling it at the sink like she owns the place. "Go wash your face, Mikey, and hurry up about it. I had to leave your dad handling the desk on his own, and he's as crabby as you in the morning."

Fisher hasn't moved. "I told you—I can't do it, not today."

Over her shoulder she says, "You knew I was gonna call— why couldn't you check your messages? You do it on purpose, don't you?" Then her voice stops and her face hardens. She's peering past him. Without looking he knows what she's spotted. Brian's bag. Standing a few feet away against the wall. "So that's how it is—you've got someone staying." She sets down the carafe and looks around, as though there might be other signs of a visitor that she's overlooked.

"Fuck, no," he says. "No one's here except me."

"You can stop with that language. If you couldn't make it this morning, you should've let me know. It's only common human decency—or is that beyond you? And now you're too busy to help out because something better's come up. You're off somewhere and you couldn't care less about leaving me in the lurch, like it's not worth a second thought when I organized my day around you coming with me."

"No, it's not like that. I'm not off anywhere. Christ, I just have stuff to take care of. We can do this another day."

"Maybe you can. I have a business to run." She empties the carafe into the machine and slaps down the lid. She wipes her hands down her sweater as she comes across the carpet. "My, what a nice bag," she says. "It's not you at all."

It's not until she tilts her head at an odd angle that he looks down at the bag too. Stark against its black side, the luggage label in its plastic pouch. Ada's stooping toward it when Fisher snatches at the handle and the handle telescopes out, making the bag totter. "Christ," he hisses, "it's just a bag, all right?" and he drags it behind him, squeaking on its tiny wheels, pitching and tipping, into the bedroom. He rips off the tag. BRIAN ARM-STRONG written in clear black capitals and then The Marriott Arbor, 1570 City Road, Denver CO. The Marriott Arbor, for fuck's sake. How did he come up with that? He tucks it into his jeans pocket then shoves the bag into the closet.

His hands are damp. His heart's throwing itself against his ribs like it wants to burst out. Christ, he thinks, one small thing and she's onto it. He sits on the edge of the bed and presses his fists against his cheeks. Did she see the name? Was she close enough?

When he looks down, Pax is watching him from the floor. What sad eyes—and how unlike him not to come see who's here. Fisher cups the dog's head with his hand. "You poor old boy," he says. "Not feeling so good, are you?" Pax lets out a snuffling yawn and sits up to push his muzzle into Fisher's palm. But soon even that's too much effort, and he sinks onto his paws with his soft belly across Fisher's feet.

Fisher thinks, I have to get rid of her. He thinks, Where the hell can Breehan be? How can I find her friends? But maybe she's been smarter than that. Could be she took off with one of Brian's credit cards. If she's got money there are any number of places she could have hidden away; could have bought herself a flight to the Lower Forty-Eight, to Canada, even. He wonders if she has a passport. How could he not know?

Before long the smell of coffee has forced its way through the trailer and when Fisher comes out of the bathroom, unshaven but washed and hair wetted down at least, Ada's at the kitchen table with a mug in front of her. She puts a cigarette between her lips and takes a lighter from her pocket.

"Not in here," he tells her.

"You're not going to make me smoke outside at fifty below, Mikey. Forget that." She holds a flame to her cigarette and lets the smoke flare from her nostrils, then she takes a sip of the coffee and makes a face. "No milk, no cream—not even creamer. You need to get yourself together. I don't know how you can live like this. Look at you: forty-three and on your own. One glance says it all, believe me. You need a shave, you need to lose a hundred pounds, you need decent clothes that fit you. Who wants a guy who doesn't take care of himself, huhn? I'd run a mile, I tell you." She taps a few flakes of ash from her cigarette into a beer can she must have dug out of the trash and takes another drag.

He bites his teeth together and pours himself some coffee. In the thin electric light he can see the bottom of the mug through it, knows before he takes a sip how bad it's going to be: the flavor of the coffee floating tenuously over the hard taste of boiled water. Ada's coffee. Miserly coffee, hardly worth the effort of drinking.

She sits with her elbows raised, as though she can't bear to rest them on his table with its crumbs and stains. To make her point, she scratches one red nail at something caked onto the wood and exhales more smoke through her nose, her lips compressed so he'll knows she's disgusted.

He says, more loudly than he intended, "I'll come with you some other morning, but today's just not gonna work. Sorry you had a wasted trip. And put out that goddamn cigarette, you know it's bad for my sinuses."

"Sorry?" she spits back. "Sorry?" She gets to her feet, her skin looking creased as crumpled tissue in this light, her eyes bright and hard. "You listen, Mikey. I don't want excuses. You need to learn a little responsibility. I haven't got time to drive all the way out here only to find out you've got better things to do than help me like you promised." She steps so close that the smoke trailing from her cigarette drifts into his face. He shifts his head, but it's too late because the smoke's found its way inside him, prickling the soft flesh of his sinuses until it swells. He presses his fingers against his nose to stifle a sneeze.

"I told you," he says, "something's come up that I have to take care of. Besides," and he steps away, "why don't you ask Lyle? That's what you pay him for."

"Don't start in on that. This isn't about Lyle, it's about you."

"Got better things to do, has he? What's it this time? Another doctor's appointment? Or frozen pipes and he's waiting

71

for the plumber? A great handyman he's turned out to be. If he wasn't your nephew you'd have fired him long ago." He pushes his fists into his pockets and looms over her. "I told you I'd help out when I could. That's the best I can do. Now, you need to leave because I've got to get going." He even starts toward the door, as though there's any hope she'll follow.

When he glances back she's got her arm crooked to hold her cigarette close to the red gash of her mouth. "Well, aren't you the assertive one," she says quietly. She purses her lips and sucks hard on the cigarette. "Eager to get rid of me, aren't you? And why would that be?" Smoke gathers about her head and she waves it away. "Wouldn't be something to do with that bag, would it? Maybe I should go take a closer look. Where'd you hide it? Under your bed, or in your closet?"

"Fuck you."

"You never were much good at secrets, Mikey. What's it this time?"

He stares back at her and the world shrinks, painfully. He tells himself not to say anything, but the silence wraps itself around him until he's trapped and he hears himself tell her, "Just doing someone a favor."

When she smiles he knows he's lost. "Sure you are," she says, "just looking after someone else's bag. That's a big favor all right," and she touches the stiff froth of hair above her forehead. "I can pretend I didn't see it. Is that what you want? Huhn? Now, hurry up and get your coat on, I'm already running late." Then she drops her cigarette into the beer can, where it hisses.

## 13

IT GNAWS AT Fisher, the time wasted going to the hardware store when Bree's out there somewhere, maybe scared out of her mind. He turns off the car radio when the news starts, turns it on again with the volume way up. A local guy threatened with jail time after a court appearance over unpaid taxes when he cursed out the judge. Air quality in town dangerous thanks to the inversion. Nothing about a body being found, but then, what's he thinking? Sunrise isn't for another couple of hours, and even in the tepid pre-dawn light, who's going to think a tarp caught in the river is anything worth taking the trouble to pull out?

He follows the blink-bliiiink of Ada's brakelights, because she drives with one foot on the brake and the other on the gas and won't be told not to. This morning the sight of those lights needles him because it's Ada all over, driving like she doesn't give a shit about anyone else, swerving between a semi and a square box of a car like she has every right to, never mind that the semi brakes and lets out a blast of horn. Ada always has to have her own way. She had to hire Lyle as the motel handyman, though she must've known Lyle's a useless fuckwit who can't put up a towel rack straight, and besides, he always has better things to do than work. Two years of that crap: Lyle getting paid and Ada calling Fisher to fix dripping taps and holes in walls because Lyle's too busy, or his truck's in the shop, or he's off moose-hunting, or dip-netting down in Chitina, always something, but she forgives him because he wanted to see Alaska and she promised him a job if he moved here.

Of all things, Fisher told her to go ahead and hire her goddamn nephew. That was when he thought it'd get Ada off his back, before he knew Lyle and his creepy, sideways way of looking at you, or the snaky charm he turns on for Ada. And she falls for it. Now here she is, tailgating some poor fucker in a sedan through the ice fog, and veering into the slow lane to pass him when the turn to the hardware store's coming up, and she swerves out in front of a cop—a cop!—to make the turn in time. Fisher wills the cop to pull her over—that'll teach her!—but the cop doesn't do a thing.

Just as well. Has Fisher forgotten? She's a spiteful woman. She probably thinks he stole Brian's bag and would have found a way to mention it to the cop. *So sorry, Officer, I'm all upset. You see, my step-son—well, I was just over at his trailer and noticed some property I'm sure isn't his, and he acted kinda strange...*

The thought of it so riles him up that his jaw tightens and his teeth hurt. He pulls up behind her so hard that his car skids a little. He's close enough to see her outline through the back window of the pickup, and to focus his hate on the narrow shape of her head with its ridiculous handle of a pony tail sticking out, when she turns to watch the traffic rush by.

Something catches his eye. He glances to his right. The cop, staring at him. Fear rushes through him like cold water. Does it show on his face? He turns away—too quickly? Maybe. He looks out the windshield at his headlights glaring off the strawberry red of Ada's truck and won't let himself move until, he realizes, that's going to look suspicious, because who sits behind the wheel without moving? So he reaches down to the radio and presses the channel buttons just for something to do. When he looks back up, the lane beside him is empty. Up ahead the bloody eyes of taillights are vanishing into the ice fog.

His T-shirt's sticking to his armpits. His bowels ache, like he needs to take a dump, right now. He closes his eyes. Get a grip, he tells himself. Be better than that.

After all, Ada's spiteful, she's heartless, but she's not stupid. She needs him. Isn't that why she didn't put up a fight when he refused to let her drive him into town? And when he refuses to do more than unload the supplies into the motel lobby, what's she going to do? She's like a parasite: if it kills its host, it's done for. She'll be mad at him, but she's got something she can hold over him. That bag: oh yeah, she'll remind him she knows he's hidden it, but she won't push too hard, not yet, or it'll all be over. And by the time she does make her move, he'll have gotten rid of it and there won't be a thing she can do.

The green left-turn arrow lights up. The exhaust from Ada's pickup floods over his windshield and he follows the angry gleam of her taillights through the intersection and into the parking lot of the hardware store.

## 14

H ERE ARE THE jobs that Fisher has done at the Alaska Travel-Inn since his dad and Ada bought it: unplugged bathroom drains thick with hair, washed vomit off walls, broken open the doors of rooms in which drunk or dead guests were lying in bed and had been for two or three days, hauled reeking mattresses into the pickup to dump at the transfer station, dug bullets out of walls and filled the holes with spackle once the police had finished looking the place over, steam-cleaned the carpet of a room in which a young man had hanged himself (Dotty the cleaner wouldn't set foot over the threshold, and no wonder, the stink of piss and shit was gagging), picked up syringes from under beds, replaced mirrors that had been smashed or scratched with obscenities, unblocked toilets clogged with diapers, or turds so big you'd think they'd been left by a different, massive species. That's not all. He's replaced carpets and windows, painted walls, grouted tiles, rewired shot wiring, and learned how to install toilets and washbasins, because there's only so much they can take before they crack irreparably.

You'd think that Fisher, with all the skills he's picked up, would set himself up as a handyman, like the guy he's seen driving around town with Stan the Handy-Man painted on the side of his van. And he did, years ago, when he was married to Janice. But now every time he sees that van he thinks, *Poor fucker*, because being handy is about the worst thing you can imagine. All the shit comes your way. Worse than that, your friends and family call you up to fix things, and replace things, and unblock things, then look betrayed when you hand them a bill. Other people, the ones you don't know, forget to tell you they've poured Drano down the bathtub and when you pump it out it's all over you, or they watch over your shoulder then say something like, *Hell, I coulda done that myself* or *Christ Almighty, fifty dollars when it only took fifteen minutes?* No wonder he went back to driving.

Ada and his dad have never paid Fisher. Before he moved out, he could see the logic of it: he was earning his keep. After he moved out—well, by then his dad was in a wheelchair and could barely walk because he'd grown so huge, his legs like sides of beef, his belly a great balloon balanced on his lap. After a whole week of one job after another at the motel and Ada cooking Fisher and Jan dinner to say thank you, Jan handed Ada the bill for all that work. Ada tore it to pieces right there and then, and Jan balled up her napkin, threw it onto her plate of spaghetti, and told Fisher if he ever set foot in the motel again she'd leave him.

What could he do? To make up for doing unpaid jobs for Ada on the quiet, he took extra work so that he and Jan could pay their rent, and their health insurance, and afford all the things they needed for the baby when Janice got pregnant, and in the end Jan still left and Ada never has a good word to say about him.

As for Lyle, you'd think the sun shone out of his ass, which is funny because he was doing time for assault and petty larceny before he came north. Not that Ada ever mentioned it. Sometimes there are advantages to being a cabbie. Over the years, a number of ex-cons have driven for Bear Cabs, hard-mouthed guys, soul-chilling bastards, some of them. But there've been those who've felt friendly toward Fisher, who've sat with him on a quiet mid-morning until a call came through, who'd say kind of off-handed, *That guy working at your folks' motel? I knew him inside down in Seattle and he's one mean mother-fucker. You tell your folks to watch their backs, OK?*

Sometimes Fisher wonders if Lyle has it so easy because Ada's scared of him. She damn well should be, he thinks.

❧

The hardware store's squintingly bright. It's a world within a world, its ceiling so high and its shelves piled with sleek white toilets still in their packaging, and bathtubs stacked on their sides like massive handholds, and way up beneath the roof a small bird darting between the beams and singing out for others of its kind.

Ada's waiting for him with a low, long cart. Not that she's going to push it. She steps away and gives him a nod. "See if you can at least keep up with me driving that thing." She turns on her heel and takes off across the store. Fisher has to wrestle it along on stiff wheels that want to turn forever left.

This place depresses him at the best of times. All those rolls of flooring made to look like tiling, the cheap-as-shit towel rings—maybe it'd be different if he was picking up material for his barely-begun house, but what this place makes him think of is hours wasted at the motel. Fitting stain-resistant rug to replace carpeting so foul no steam-cleaning can save it. Prying off smashed shower tiles. Replacing washbasins cracked open like tea cups, or doors staved in like meringues, or having Ada pull her lips to one side at the sight of the grouting he's just finished then telling him it's not neat enough and for Chrissakes, can't he do a better job covering up the hole in the wall?

At least there's this about shopping here with Ada: there's no dallying around while she makes up her mind. She's bought the same paint so many times she can point out the shade to Fisher, and tell him how many cans, knows to buy turps and masking tape, and which pattern of linoleum for the bathrooms. Then she quick-walks down the aisle toward the checkout while Fisher struggles to load a roll of flooring onto the cart. Already he's sweating. He heaves that cart along on its wheels that twitch and veer to the side, leaning his whole weight against it, his shoulder straining from the effort. Halfway down the aisle he snatches off his hat and wipes his face with it, then crams it into his pocket. Ada's gone, standing in line most likely. The cart handle's warm and greasy, and he rubs his hands down his coat to rid himself of the feel of it. A young man walks past him in a red apron tied so slackly it's hardly tied at all, his pants low and loose, his heels scraping along the concrete floor. It takes Fisher only a moment, then it hits him: Frisbee. Bree's friend Frisbee, working here, and Fisher calls out, "Hey!"

Maybe the guy doesn't hear him. He doesn't stop, and Fisher abandons the cart and runs after him, calling out, "You're Frisbee, aren't you? Wait up," and only then does the guy turn around.

His hair's a flat black and falls across one eye. The other gazes at Fisher with a steady look that could mean anything from distaste to loathing. Even for someone who lives in the sub-arctic, his skin's an uncanny white, his lips as lifeless as the edges of a pie crust waiting to be pinched closed.

The name tag pinned to his apron says, "I'm Wayne and I can help!"

Now they're face-to-face, Fisher's courage fails him. His voice shrinks down his throat. "My daughter, Bree: you know her, don't you?"

The guy seems to think it over then touches his hair with the flat of one hand. "You her dad?"

Fisher nods.

"Yeah, think I've seen you pick her up a couple times. Something like that." Then he waits, and it must seem like Fisher's about to say something, the way he licks his lips and takes in a breath. But he doesn't say a word and Frisbee nods a couple of times as though something's passed between them, then says, "Catch you later, dude," and walks away.

Fisher follows him. "Have you seen her? Since yesterday?" Frisbee turns and his eye narrows just enough to make Fisher rush on: "She's taken off. She left a couple messages saying she wanted me to come get her, but I don't know where she is."

Frisbee's mouth twists to one side. "Her mom's taken her down to Anchorage, you know, before school starts back up. Didn't she tell you?"

"She didn't go, and now I can't find her."

Frisbee tilts his head a little. "Well, I can't help you, dude. I thought she was out of town."

"I just want to know who she could be staying with. You know, close friends."

Frisbee's face hardens. "No idea," he says, and he strides away down the aisle.

Fisher hurries after him saying, "Listen: when she called she sounded real scared. I need to know she's OK."

Eventually Frisbee slows down. "Hey, she'll get hold of you when she wants, right?"

"Her step-dad—he was going ape-shit over something. That's what she said."

Frisbee stops. "Now there's a real jerk," and he lets out a half-laugh. "But I guess you know that, huhn?"

Fisher nods back at him. "First class jerk, yeah. So I need to find her, because this wasn't like he'd just grounded her or something. It sounded way worse than that, and now she's taken off."

Frisbee's face closes in on itself and he turns toward the display of blinds at the end of the aisle. "Of course," he says, "these are gonna last you. Worth the extra cost if you ask me."

A man in a red apron, his head as bare and shiny as a wet pebble, calls out to Fisher, "That your cart back there, sir?"

"Sure is."

He strides up to them and gives Fisher a wide smile. "Wayne here looking after you, is he? Let me know if you need anything else, all right?" then he claps Frisbee on the shoulder and hurries off.

Fisher and Frisbee bend their heads toward the slats of vinyl until the guy's out of sight. Frisbee says, "Her ex is working at the Stop-n-Go on Airport."

Fisher nods like he knew Bree had an ex. "The one opposite the movie theater?"

"Yeah. He'll know—they're still pretty close. Maybe she's staying with him," and he shrugs. "Used to work the morning shift, maybe still does. Guess he could be there right now."

"OK," says Fisher, "and hey, thanks." He takes off at a half-run, the cart left at an angle across the aisle and his red hat close by, dropped and lost for good.

❦

He doesn't give Ada a second thought. Maybe she spots him rushing off and thinks he's headed to the bathroom, or maybe she's looking the wrong way and doesn't see him barge out through the automatic doors and into that savage cold where he checks his pockets for his hat. Gone. No way is he going back for it. Instead he pulls up his hood and takes off across the parking lot.

On the highway the traffic's heavy, but Fisher's heart's full of hope. He dips and swerves around other vehicles with the heater on high and the radio blaring. Even the ache in his head hardly bothers him.

When his phone rings he snatches it out of his pocket and checks who's calling. Ada. He chucks it onto the seat beside him and follows a City Cab through the ice fog, all the way to Airport.

## 15

E VEN IF YOU were blind and walked into a convenience store without knowing it—how that could happen,
Fisher hasn't worked out—you'd recognize it by its odors: the
muddiness of coffee left warming too long, the hot grease of
wieners rolling beneath a heating lamp, the sugariness of candies
and pastries, the bright translucent scent of floor cleaner. On
a January morning this far north, when the outside world is
frozen and dark and smells only of poorly combusted fuel,
stepping into a convenience store is like stepping into spring:
the onslaught of aromas, the packages colorful as flowers, the
dispensers and signs all reds and blues, the buttery quality of
the electric light, that delicious warmth that engulfs you. It's
no wonder Fisher stands just inside the entrance and rubs his
cold head—of all the days to lose his hat—and blinks at it all
before remembering himself and heading for the coffee pots by
the checkout.

He doesn't let himself look at the cashiers, not yet. Instead
he pours coffee into a cardboard cup and peels open a small
container of cream that spits droplets over his fingers, and only
when he's emptied a couple of sachets of sugar into it and stirred
it with a plastic stick does he glance up, as casually as he can.
Two young men behind the counter. One of them's in his late
twenties, he'd guess, and with a beaky, hard look about him,
his skin with the slight grayness of perpetual exhaustion, a
tattoo showing above his collar, his ear a curtain rod of silver
rings, and his hair shorn close to his head. The other's tall and
overweight, a droop-faced sack of a boy with flushed cheeks

and dark hair brushed forward toward to his eyebrows and a re-signed look about him. Christ, thinks Fisher, one of these guys is Bree's ex? He takes a sip of his coffee, all creamy and sweet, then fixes a lid over the rim. He looks about him. Over by the back wall a guy's loading bottles into a fridge, a curly-haired, narrow-shouldered kid with a rawness about his cheeks where he must only recently have begun shaving. Bingo, he thinks.

Fisher carries his coffee over to him. "Hey," he says, "I think you can help me—you know Bree Fisher, right?"

The kid looks up and the skin between his eyes puckers. "Who?"

"Bree Fisher. My daughter. Are you the one she used to date?"

The kid's face flares a livid red and he pulls two bottles of orange juice out of the box at his knees, holding them deftly between his fingers, then shoving them into their slot in the fridge. "No," he says, and he's already turned away, "not me."

There's something so *Fuck you* in the way he goes back to stocking the fridge that Fisher leans closer. "I'm her dad and she called me to come pick her up last night. By the time I got there she'd gone and now I don't know where she is."

"Can't help you."

"I'm just looking for her, that's all."

The kid looks up at him with watery eyes. "Man, I've never heard of Bree Whatever-the-Fuck—let me alone, why don't you, before I call the shift manager over?"

Fisher lifts his free hand. "Whoa there," he says, "I'm just looking for my daughter, is all. No need to freak out on me."

"Freak out on you?" the kid says. "Fuck, who the hell—"

But Fisher's walking away. His coffee slops around in the cup and the cup's uncomfortably hot. Christ, he thinks, he should have slipped one of those cardboard belts onto it, but really—who needs coffee so hot you have to shield yourself from it?

Just before the checkout there's a stand of plastic-wrapped pastries. He bends to look at them, bear claws and danishes and cinnamon buns all wet-looking from too much glaze. You'd think he was having a hard time deciding what to eat, dithering, changing his mind, picking up a bearclaw and weighing it in his hand. But the whole time his eyes are darting up to the clerks working back-to-back at the checkout, from the fat teenager with his meaty hands that pick up bottles of soda and chocolate bars so slowly, so deliberately, you'd think he'd never seen such things before, to the guy behind him whose hands fly, whose fingers stab at the cash register like he's working to music playing inside his head. The moment the second guy's finished with his customer and called out a flat *Have a good one*, he leans over the newspaper spread on the counter in front of him.

The newspaper. Fisher can't help himself. He wheels around until he's spotted the pile of papers like a truncated pillar by the counter, feels a surge of panic as he hauls himself closer to read the headline. What's it going to be? CABBIE CAUGHT UP IN MURDER PLOT? Or POLICE HUNTING TEEN KILLER? Which would make his blood run colder? He couldn't say.

The headline doesn't make sense. His thoughts twist on one word: SLAIN. But the photo beneath it is of a young blond man. Not Brian. No, a cop, smiling, in his uniform. MISSING TROOPER FOUND SLAIN.

Fisher lets out his breath, even bends forward in relief, as though all that's kept him upright is fear.

The fat kid's looking at him and Fisher grabs up the paper and has to decide: Which guy? The fat one? Or the guy with the earrings and the worn-out look? If he wasn't such a dumb-ass, he'd have asked Frisbee the guy's name. Only he didn't. He pretended he knew Bree had been dating someone, like he was the sort of dad who'd be cool about it, the sort of dad a daughter could really talk to.

The fat kid calls out, "Ready, sir?"

Fisher pretends not to hear. He tucks the newspaper under his arm and walks back through the short aisles, and lets his eyes run over the bars of chocolate, and the bags of hard candies, and when he's worked his way across the store, he turns back to the checkout where the second guy's hunched over his paper.

Fisher slides his cup and a bearclaw onto a small patch of empty counter, but he has nowhere to put the newspaper except on the paper the guy's reading. The guy looks up in annoyance, then turns to the cash register and sends his fingers darting over the buttons. He's still looking at the screen when he calls out, "Four forty-eight, need a bag?"

"No bag." Fisher digs in his wallet for a five. He doesn't lay it on the counter but holds it, and doesn't let go when the guy tries to take it. "Hey," Fisher says, "I think you know Bree Fisher. Is that right?"

Only now does the guy look into his face. His eyes are a curious even gray like they've been punched out of tin, and tiny dark hairs show on the soft skin just above his cheeks. The hair gives him a grubby look, as though he's rubbed soot into his face and not managed to wash it off. One hand rests on the plastic wrapper of the bearclaw, the other's still holding the five, but he's stopped dead. "Bree Fisher?" He shakes his head. "Never heard of her."

Fisher lets the guy take the five and ring it up in the cash register, and dump his change onto the stippled rubber mat by the take-a-penny dish. He's already put the pastry and news-paper into a bag, and now he adds the receipt. He passes the bag to Fisher, says, "Have a good one," then busies himself squirting cleaner from a bottle onto the screen of the reg-ister, and wiping it with a cloth in quick sleek movements, never mind that Fisher's still standing on the other side of the counter.

Fisher lets him spray and wipe and spray again, and only when the fat guy turns round and says to his co-worker, "Hey," with a nod at Fisher, does he stop and lean straight-armed onto the counter. In one hand the cloth is balled, the other's a fist. The floor behind the counter must be raised because he looms over Fisher. "Anything else I can help you with, sir?"

Fisher's top lip's cool with sweat and he rubs it with one finger. "Bree's in trouble. I need to find her."

"Like I said, never heard of her."

Fisher glances at the fat kid, says, "I heard her ex works here. Bree Fisher—d'you know her?"

The fat kid says, "Nope," and folds his hands over his belly. He leans back against the counter, like he's settling in for a show.

"But one of you—at least, that's what—"

The leaner guy tilts forward onto his fists. "You need to leave, right now. Get it?"

There's such menace coiled into his voice that Fisher steps back, the bag swinging ridiculously from his wrist, but he doesn't leave. That menace holds him there, for what can it mean except that the guy's lying? "Just tell me," he says, "is she all right?"

"D'you have a hearing problem, huhn? I said you needed to get out of here."

There's just the counter between them, and the guy perches farther forward, taut as a cat, like he means to leap over it and come at Fisher. Fisher's ears are singing and he knows he's afraid. This is what it's like to work the nightshift and have some fare pull a knife on you, or having to go into some guy's apartment and take his TV or his hunting knife as collateral, and the whole time his hate's washing out from where he's

87

watching you, like it's your fault he can't pay his fare.

You don't let the fear take over. You push back at it. Fisher notices that his fingers are burning on the cup and a muscle beside his eye's twitching. He swallows to loosen his throat, says, "I'm just asking for your help, that's all."

"Finding someone who doesn't want you to find them? What kind of a creep are you?"

But there's something too worked-up about his voice, like he doesn't quite believe what he's saying. Fisher sets his coffee on the counter. "I'm her dad. Last night she left me a message saying to come get her because she was in trouble. By the time I got there she'd gone and now I'm real worried."

The guy's eyes shift, then he ducks his head. The light flashes off the earrings corrugating his ear. Over his shoulder he says to the fat kid, "I'm taking my break, Josh. Don't fuck up this time."

## 16

I N OTHER TOWNS, in other seasons, Fisher and the guy
would have stood out back by the dumpsters and the guy
would have smoked his cigarette there, tapping the ash onto the
broken concrete and staring up at con trails burrowing across
the sky. As it is, once the guy's snatched up his cigarettes from
under the counter, there's nowhere to go except out to Fisher's
car.

Fisher's left it running. Even with the rush of cold air when
they get in and sit side by side, staring out the windshield at the
blank brick wall of the store, the sudden warmth is cloying. It
doesn't help that the guy puts a cigarette between his lips and
slides a lighter out of the pack.

Fisher wants to say, "Hey! Don't smoke in my car."

He wants to tell this guy, "I've got bad sinuses, c'mon
now."

Instead, rather than piss him off, he watches the flame show
up the creases in his face. He has the wizened look you see on
malnourished infants, skin in folds, the eyes a little too big.
How old is he? Twenty-five? Thirty? How the hell did Bree get
mixed up with someone his age?

The guy snaps out the lighter and sends twin plumes of
smoke rushing from his nostrils. In an instant the car's clouded
with it. Fisher digs a tissue from his parka pocket and holds it
against his nose, as though that's going to do any good. The
guy turns to him. "She came over last night."

"What time?"

"I dunno—maybe around seven. She wouldn't come in, just

stood in the arctic entryway saying she needed to borrow whatever money I could lend her."

"And did you? How much?"

He gives a lazy shrug. "A hundred. All I could spare and hey, since we split, you know—what the hell, I still care and all, but it's not like we're together."

"She tell you where she was headed? Was it Anchorage?"

"How the hell would I know?" and he shoots Fisher a sullen look. "She didn't say much. She was freaked out about something, I could see that. I wasn't going to push her." He taps the ash off his cigarette and onto his jeans. He rubs it in with the ends of his fingers, then glances out the side window.

"That's it? She wanted money and you gave it to her? C'mon, she must've said something."

"Yeah," and his voice is dull, "she said she was getting out of town for a while. Soon as I gave her the money, she took off."

"Took off? You mean, she was driving?"

He holds the cigarette to the dark hole of his mouth and draws the smoke deep into his lungs. "Fuck yeah—her step-dad's Highlander. If he was pissed at her, he must've been pissed as hell when she took it. But I guess that's the least of his worries now," and he gives a short laugh.

A tickle of panic catches Fisher in the throat. Bree—did she tell this guy what she'd done? That she'd left Brian shot dead on her bathroom floor? Why not? Because how can you keep something like that held down inside you? Those calls he hadn't picked up—shit. And so she told this guy instead, and now he's pretending he doesn't know Brian's dead, like he can't trust Fisher.

Fisher mashes the tissue in his hand. "What exactly did she tell you?"

"I said already: she was freaked out. Scared, even." He turns to Fisher. "You ever held a mouse? Know how they tremble all the time like they're scared half to death? That's how she was—like she couldn't stop trembling. It's no fucking wonder, when her step-dad's mixed up in some serious shit."

Those words hang in the air. Fisher thinks, Serious shit? Militia serious shit? Or the kind of serious shit that leaves you naked and dead on your step-daughter's bathroom floor? He doesn't look at the guy when he says, "You mean the militia?"

"You need to read the paper. That missing cop showed up dead at their place. Your ex came home late last night and found him. Can't blame Bree for taking off like she did. Fuck," and he lets out a half-laugh.

It takes a moment for what the guy's said to catch up with Fisher. Then the inside of the car's too small. It's a fragile space run through with invisible wires wrapping around his head and he can't think, can't move, hears his own breath sawing through the narrow openings of his nostrils, has to open his mouth and heave in a lungful of air, never mind that it's curdled with smoke. Then he curls forward like he's been knocked hard in the belly.

The guy's saying, "It's all in the paper."

A pickup pulls in beside them and Fisher flinches. Just a pickup and a woman in a sweatshirt trotting hunch-shouldered into the store. Ridiculously, Fisher holds onto the steering wheel. The plastic's worn and beyond it the light from the store catches the dust on the dashboard, the crack in the windshield running like forked lightning from left to right.

Before long, Fisher thinks, his life will have come to a halt. Hiding evidence of a murder—that's one thing. But now there's a dead cop caught up in this mess, and how's he going to explain he didn't have anything to do with that? Christ, he could go down for years. He imagines himself in an orange jumpsuit, and the dreariness of being locked into a cell for so many days they add up to decades, and everything he meant to do—saving

Bree, building his house, making something of his life before it's too late—it's all gone to hell.

The guy's saying, "He's got himself into some serious shit all right, him and his sovereign citizen buddies. Sovereign citizens, my ass—bunch of motherfuckers who like playing with guns. All that crap about being ready to defend Alaska—from what? Huhn? Goddamn Canadians gonna storm the border? You know what it's all about, really? Their jackass leader not wanting to pay his fucking taxes. He gets together a bunch of shit-for-brains guys and tells them they're the Alaska Citizens Guard, and they're all sovereign citizens and they have to protect each other when the feds show up. Which means protecting him. Fuck. That stash of weapons the cops found at the ice park last week? That was them. Now they've killed a trooper, and Bree's caught up in it just when it could all turn real bad." He lowers the window just enough to push out what's left of his cigarette.

"She was supposed to be going down to Anchorage with her mom."

Without his cigarette the guy's hands fall into his lap and stay there like dead things. He must feel it too, because he reaches into his pocket and pulls out the pack. He lights another and sucks on it hard. "The way I see it, they're having a meeting at Brian's place—you know, what the fuck to do now that the cops are onto them and a bunch of their weapons have been found. They think they're on their own because your ex and Bree are off to Anchortown. Then this cop shows up snooping around, and they're such fuckheads one of them shoots him: Brian, that's who. But Bree's home. She fucked things up with her mom and has been laying low. She hears the shot and comes down. Brian sees her and knows he's really in the shit, they're all in the shit because they can't have a witness. Somehow she gets out of there. Or maybe Brian doesn't see her—she sneaks down to the garage and takes off in his car. Either way, she's going to be scared shitless because she knows too much, and she knows they'll be after her." He lifts his cigarette, takes another drag.

Fisher closes his eyes. It's too much. All of it coming at him, and he's trying to make it fit. "She said Brian was going ape-shit."

"So he did see her. Fuck. And now he's looking for her. Shit, this is not good."

Fisher opens his eyes. There's the cracked windshield, and beyond it frost thick as moss on the store wall by the doorway. He says, "No, that's not right—" Shut up, another part of him says, shut the fuck up. The guy's watching, but Fisher can't look back at him. He had the words on his tongue: *No, that's not right, Brian's dead.* Except he needs to forget finding Brian slumped against the bathroom wall, and wrapping him in the tarp, and rolling him into the river, like none of that happened. But how the hell do you make yourself forget something like that?

The guy's still looking at him and Fisher licks his lips. He says, "Maybe, but he's her step-dad. Christ, I don't know, I really don't," and those words are just filling the space between them while he's sifting through what might have happened, and what he can say without giving himself away. One thing makes sense: Brian shot the cop, and Bree saw him, and he wanted to shut her up, so she shot him first. One thing doesn't fit: Brian was naked. Why'd he be naked in her bathroom?

This is how he felt at school in math class. Not the simple stuff of calculation—that was just a matter of being careful—but the problems that sat in front of you like a solid slippery mass that you glanced off no matter which way you came at them. Sometimes he'd imagine that his life depended on solving one of those problems and feel himself getting sweaty as he sat there with his pencil between his fingers. And in a way his life did depend on it. What happens if you don't make it to college? If you don't even go to technical school because you think you're too dumb? You drive a cab for a living and consider yourself lucky, because it's better than some other jobs you've had, that's for sure.

The guy puts the cigarette between his lips and takes hold of the doorhandle. He looks cold in his shirt, despite the shelter of the car and the heat rushing from the vents. He speaks around the cigarette, says, "He'd do it. He'd kill her. Christ, he'd just shot a cop, and anyway, the guy's a big enough prick." With that he opens the door and gets out. Then he ducks back. "Tell me if you find her."

"I don't even know your name."

"Zane—I'm here most mornings," and he swings the door shut.

## 17

AFTER PULLING OUT onto the main drag, the first thing Fisher does is crack the windows. Cold whistles in where his hat should be, across his scalp and his forehead, a freezing burn that he squints against. He's thinking: Brian shot a cop. The guy who's been step-dad to Bree, the guy Jan left him for, went nuts and shot a cop, and if he wasn't dead, he'd be out hunting for Bree and he'd shoot her too. Does it make him feel angry? Sure—but not as angry as thinking about why Brian was naked in her bathroom.

He thinks: Goddamn freak, he'd have killed her too.

He thinks: Always knew there was something wrong with him.

He thinks: Naked. In her bathroom. What the hell?

His ears are going numb. He tugs up his hood, never mind that it makes him feel like a deep-sea diver, his world shrunk to what's right in front of him.

The inside of his head's aching from Zane's smoke. The bottle of ibuprofen in the glove compartment's empty. He needs coffee. What happened to the coffee he bought at the convenience store? Must have left it behind, and now the nearest place is the coffee hut down at the intersection with Bartlett. He drives one-handed, the radio on high and his right hand punching through the pre-sets, but it's past the hour and there's no news on. The paper's behind him in its plastic bag. Part of him wants to reach back for it and pull over to the side of the road, right here, right now. C'mon Fisher, he tells himself, be better than that.

Although the fog's not so bad this morning, nothing's where it should be—the burger joint with its bright windows shining out into the murk when he thought he'd passed it, the gas station suddenly on his right, the turn-off to the coffee hut coming up so fast he has to swerve to make it.

A woman leans out the serving window in a pink knitted hat pulled down almost to her eyes. He tells her all he wants is a regular coffee. "Regular size?" she asks, and he tells her sure. "Medium roast?" and he says sure. "Cream and sugar?" and he says, "Go to town, why not."

The cup she passes him isn't what he'd call regular. At least, it's not what you'd call regular if you buy your coffee in convenience stores and diners. It's so big he has to stretch his fingers around it, so tall it towers out of his cup holder. He drives across the lumpy snow to the movie theater parking lot, which is empty except for two dead-looking cars. He pulls up far away, just in case, and spreads the newspaper over the steering wheel. Already his heart's jumping against his ribs. He turns on the dome light and there's his shadow across the paper, and it grows sharper as he leans forward to read.

This is what he finds out: last night local business woman Janice Armstrong returned early from a brief trip out of town and found a man's body on her deck. She didn't recognize him. The body was quickly identified as that of the missing trooper. He had a bullet wound to the chest. No statement about possible suspects has been issued. Mrs Armstrong was being questioned. Both her husband, Brian Armstrong, and fifteen-year-old daughter, Bree Fisher, are missing and the police are requesting information as to their whereabouts. No mention of the militia. No mention of missing guns and computer equipment.

Fisher thinks: he and Grisby had felt strangely safe in that house as they cleaned it and loaded up the car, as though no one was going to disturb them. Any earlier and they'd have run into the militia guys; any later and Jan would have walked in on them. For fuck's sake, he thinks, that house was like Grand Central Station.

And now another thing occurs to him. Somewhere—perhaps still at the hardware store, or driving back to the motel and mad as hell—is Ada. She'll complain to Fisher's dad about his useless son and then pour herself a cup of her watery coffee and prop herself against the reception desk with the paper in front of her. Fisher imagines the way her lips will tighten, how she'll lay a finger next to the paragraph at the very end that says the police are looking for Brian Armstrong and Bree Fisher. She'll smile to herself because she'll have caught a whiff of something not right, and there's nothing she likes better than ferreting out secrets.

He shouldn't have pissed her off, Fisher thinks. What was he thinking—dumping her like that in the hardware store? Because she won't forgive him for that, oh no, she'll find a way of paying him back. When Fisher was fifteen, she sent him to fix the toilet in one of the motel rooms at six in the morning. The police had been called during the night and the couple who'd occupied the room had fled leaving an unholy mess and a toilet that kept running. To Ada that was like letting money wash down the drain, so she woke Fisher and told him to fix it before he went to school. He remembers how the room smelled of sweat and cigarettes. From the bathroom came the slow rush of water. In the toilet bowl, cigarette butts swirled round and round. He lifted off the top of the tank and right then saw the problem: a plastic bag jammed in against the flapper and holding it open. He yanked it out and the flapper dropped shut. The bag dripped on his feet as he held it up. Inside, a stack of twenties held together with an elastic band.

He didn't say a word to Ada. He hid the money in one of his old running shoes under his bed then went to the office.

There he snatched up a donut from a box and gulped down some coffee while Ada watched him. At last she said, "Well? Gonna tell me?" He forced himself to look at her with as blank a look as he could come up with. He said, "About what?" but she wasn't having that. "Oh come on, you always get this look when you're hiding something. What's it this time, huhn? Find another bottle of bourbon? A box of condoms? Some porno mags? D'you hide them in your closet next to those photos of your ma?" and she let out a sour laugh. He wiped the sugar from his mouth and said, "I'm late," then shouldered his way past her.

When he got back that afternoon she was standing in the doorway with the spring sun harsh on her face and a cigarette trailing smoke behind her. She didn't say a word as he stalked past. Up in his room he put his hand in the shoe, but he knew already. The money was gone. Later that afternoon, Ada went out and insisted Fisher come along. She bought a brand-new TV, unfurling twenties from a roll she took from her handbag, and counting them out with her tongue smacking against the roof of her mouth. He said, "What's this all about?" but of course she just smiled, said, "Felt like treating myself. What's wrong? You don't like it?" She made him carry the box across the parking lot, and he remembers how badly he wanted to hurt her, and how she stood at the open trunk and watched him, leaned so close he could have shoved the box at her and she'd have fallen beneath it, and how she smiled like she was daring him to.

Fisher fills his mouth with coffee and its taste washes over his tongue. He tears open the bearclaw's plastic wrapper and takes a bite. Dry and over-sweet. He takes another sip of coffee and lifts the pastry like he's going to eat more. Only he's not hungry enough, not when his belly's all knotted up.

Nothing seems pinned down the way it should be, nothing feels safe. He thinks of Ada reading the paper, and Grisby with

Brian's stuff piled in boxes against his wall—even the gun used to kill him, for fuck's sake. What had he been thinking, letting Grisby take it? Because now it's not just a matter of Brian being dead, there's a dead cop too, and the militia guys all stirred up, and Bree lost somewhere out there in the darkness.

He was buying Grisby off to keep Bree safe. Isn't that why he let him take the gun, and all the rest of that stuff? Because Grisby's the kind of friend you can't necessarily count on otherwise, though what kind of a friend is that?

Fisher's fingers are sticky from the bearclaw. He licks them and they're still slick when he pulls his phone from his pocket and turns it on. Eight messages. From Ada, he'd bet. Christ, from Jan too, most likely, because mustn't she be out of her head with worry, her husband gone, her daughter too, and a dead cop on her deck when she got home?

But he doesn't check his messages. He calls Grisby's number, even though Grisby won't pick up unless he's on break. He leaves a message: "Call me, OK?" Nothing else. Nothing that could be incriminating. But he can't leave it at that. He dials the diner's number and the woman who picks up sounds real pissy, and she gets more pissy when he asks for Grisby because Grisby hasn't shown up for the breakfast shift.

## 18

I T'S CLOSE TO ten and the sky's brightened on its south-ern edge. When Fisher stops at an intersection and stares out toward the dawn, the sides of the buildings along the road are caught in a thin mid-winter light. It doesn't seem right that the sun should be close to rising when nothing else about the day is as it should be. Round and round in Fisher's head, like birds trying to land, come the possibilities of what's happened to Grisby: kidnapped by the militia; shot dead by them and dumped; wasted and still asleep in his own bed, dreaming of Hawaii; off to a pawnshop in his VW Rabbit, all pleased with himself because he has no idea what he might stir up.

The coffee was too much. A regular size that must have been a pint or close to it, and Fisher's head has turned brittle and light, his bladder's aching, and his heart's hammering in his throat. He drives up College Avenue with his foot too hard on the gas. Every now and then his tires slip on the icy road, and it doesn't matter because he's not quite here. There are two worlds sharing the same space, just like being at the movie theater: the bright dangerous world on the screen, and the world you're tugged back into when someone's phone rings, and there you are in your seat in the flickering dark with an empty popcorn box on your lap and your belly bloated and aching. Fisher doesn't see the road, or the school bus he overtakes, barely knows he's driving, because he's thinking of the dead cop on the deck, and Zane's creased face as he sucked on his cigarette and what the hell's up with Grisby that he's not even answering his phone.

Inside his gloves his hands are sweating. It doesn't help that when he pulls up at a stop sign and signals right the vehicle behind him does the same, nor that when he takes a left onto Beaumont, it follows close behind all the way into the parking lot. His hands are ready to wrench the steering wheel round and stamp on the gas, to flee back to the center of town, but the pickup swerves around him with a *blatttt!* of horn and pulls up at the far end of the lot.

Aurora Apartments is about as wretched a place as you could live in, even in this town: a U-shape of apartments staring back at each other so residents can't escape the sight of peeling paint and broken railings and snow sagging from the edge of the roof, not to mention fractured glass mended with duct tape or scorch marks above window frames. It's the place named in the paper when someone's been arrested for domestic violence or drug dealing, or found dead from an overdose. The sort of place where Fisher's had to chase down fares who bolted, where he's run as fast as his bulk would let him while his thoughts ground to slo-mo telling him, this is stupid, the little shit's high on meth and any moment now is going to pull out a knife, and I'll be dead over twenty bucks. But most little shits, it turns out, don't expect to be chased. They give in and find money they didn't know they had folded into the back pocket of their jeans.

Grisby's apartment is on the second floor and behind the curtains a dim light shows. The stairs haven't been shovelled and the snow groans under Fisher's boots and twists his ankles this way and that. You can't sneak up on Grisby, not when the snow and the shoddy wood beneath give you away. Before Fisher's even at the door a shadow has slipped across the curtains and the light has winked out. Stupid Grisby, he thinks. Like that's going to fool anyone. He knocks on the door, though the sound is muffled by his glove, then calls out, "Grisby? It's me. Open up."

He listens over the sound of his own breathing, thinks he

hears the creak of a floorboard just behind the door. He hisses, "Grisby, let me in!"

Even with his hood up, the cold numbs his ears and his head feels naked. He gives the door a kick and it shudders against its lock. "Don't fuck around. This is serious. Let me in."

Down below in the parking lot a car coughs and starts up. Its engine rumbles over the sound of traffic on the main road, a strange congealed sound in the frozen air.

"Grisby!" Fisher bellows, and his voice bounces back at him from the windows all around. When he closes his mouth his teeth are cold against his lips, and he tells himself he's got to shut up or someone'll call the cops, and then he'll really be in the shit.

He yanks off one glove and stuffs it in his pocket, then pulls out his wallet and feels for a card: anything, his driver's license, his bank card, what the hell. He works its edge into the gap between the door-frame and the door, wiggling against the cheap-as-shit lock while his fingers grow numb from the cold. He's not even sure it's worked, but he heaves against the door and it gives so suddenly he staggers into the darkness. A smell of cigarettes, of stale cooking oil. Then his skull splits apart and he falls.

# 19

THE DARKNESS IS as immense as the galaxy and pricked with far-off constellations. Here Fisher comes drifting through, huge and graceful and unwieldy all at once. This existence isn't unpleasant, not at all, and he wonders why he never found it before. It's not what you'd think—you don't need a spacesuit or a ship. Space is an element you move through like water in a gliding, comforting motion that takes little effort. He lets himself roll, then roll farther, but now everything swings drunkenly. It happens so fast his thoughts fall away and he reaches out to save himself, only his arms won't move. Or at least, they move together, awkwardly, somewhere behind him.

The blackness snaps to red. The red of blood coursing through eyelid skin. A light's been turned on. He tilts his head away. His mouth's dry and tastes of metal. There's something soft and sour-smelling beneath his cheek and cold's lapping across his face. He blinks his eyes open. Light shouldn't hurt, but this light sears across his retina and along his nerves to smash up against the inside of his skull. He winces and shuts his eyes again, but he's seen enough. A door—black scuffmarks from where Grisby's kicked it shut hundreds of times. A dull pink carpet. A sheet of paper bent like a chute where it's been folded.

A floorboard creaks. Fisher says, "Who's there? That's not you, Grisby, is it?"

But it can't be Grisby. Grisby wouldn't have tied him up. Grisby wouldn't have whacked him over the head. He'd have let

103

Fisher in as soon as he called out—unless he was scared shitless, and maybe he was. But by now he'd have seen it was Fisher he's hit and would be talk-talk-talking about being sorry and hey man, things have gotten crazy like you wouldn't believe, and better to be safe than sorry, right?

Not Grisby then. So who's in the room watching him? He opens one eye a little. All he can see is the stretch of carpet from here to the door. Everything's still. Everything held down by the iron-sided crush of pain in his skull. Better not to move, not yet. Instead he finds words, never mind that it hurts to push them out of his mouth: "I'm Grisby's friend. Grisby—you there? Tell them—I'm your friend."

A hand on his shoulder and he jumps. Another in his parka pocket, digging around, creeping under him to work its way into the back pockets of his jeans. He flings himself over, hits legs, hears a cry because whoever was emptying his pockets is falling, and Fisher tries to right himself before they do, but it's too late and all he can do is roll onto his back. Beneath him something hard. A plug. Attached to a cord.

Cords and papers everywhere, like a whirlwind's torn through here, and someone's scrambling, feet slipping on sheets of paper. A young woman. Her maroon sweatshirt's huge on her, her neck thin as a sprout, her hair light as cornsilk. Her ears are shot through with holes for earrings, but right now they're bare and all those holes give her a used-up look. For a moment Fisher thinks he must have made a mistake and that this is the next-door apartment—the same carpet, the same stained ceiling. But with a shift of his head he sees Grisby's lumpy black sofa and his TV on a plastic crate in the corner. As for the half-dozen boxes of Brian's stuff they'd stacked against the wall last night, some are gone and others are lying on their sides, their contents spilled across the carpet—a router, a portable printer, knots of electrical cords, white, gray and black. And everywhere a mass of papers: receipts, envelopes, bills, as though someone's flung it out in handfuls.

The woman watches him glance around. As soon as he looks back at her, her eyes meet his. He wonders: was Grisby lying about why he didn't want to go home last night? Was it woman trouble after all? "So," Fisher says, and his voice is all cramped up, "you're a friend of Grisby's? A girlfriend?"

She stares back at him with the wary look of an animal and he wonders if she's slow.

He says, "Where's Grisby, anyhow? I need to talk to him."

One eyebrow lifts. Fisher knows she's not going to answer, or not in the way he thought. That gesture's enough: she doesn't understand a word. She's not American.

Now that he's rolled onto his back, his weight's on his hands. He can't bear it. He tilts himself over onto his side. "My hands," he says. "Please. Untie me," and he wiggles them.

Instead she backs away. She snatches something up from the mess on the floor: his wallet. Then she retreats to the kitchen area without taking her eyes off of him. How small she looks, as though she hasn't quite outgrown childhood—her legs in tight jeans and—Fisher remarks with surprise—thick woolen bunched-up leg-warmers, the like of which he hasn't seen in years but that leave her bare feet looking flat and wide as fins.

Her hands reach behind her to a broom propped in the corner. It takes Fisher a second to understand: this is her weapon. This is what she used to knock him on the head, and the ridiculousness of it—that she could even find a broom in Grisby's apartment, for fuck's sake—makes him want to laugh. But he's tied up on his back with his soft belly exposed, and when she steps toward him with the handle angled like a spear, he realizes that she could kill him with that thing. Maybe she means to, because her face has turned hard. He lets out, "Whoa now, honey," and curls up as best he can to protect himself.

"No, no. I'm a friend! Grisby's friend, Mike Fisher. Look at my driver's license. Fuck," and he tries to sit up. She shifts the broom and he flinches.

"Christ," he says through his teeth and heaves himself into a ball, his thick legs hoisted toward his chest, and when she jabs he rolls to the side. The pain in his head's all stirred up by moving like that, but what the hell. He's close to her and he kicks, hard, and she folds up like a deckchair. As for the broom, it flails through the air then clatters against the wall, hits Grisby's TV, the wall, the TV again, and falls to the floor. Fisher lurches to his feet like a moose getting up. He pulls against whatever she's used to tie his hands: something flimsy and warm that bites into his wrists. When he twists them it gives, so he twists until it burns, because what does pain matter when she might kill him? At last it snaps, and a length of women's hose tumbles gently to the floor like the shed skin of a snake.

He reaches up to the side of his head. A pulsing swelling as fat and smooth as a chicken breast. The skin stings when he brushes his fingers against it, stings even when he just touches his hair, like the follicles have been damaged. Somehow this swelling has unbalanced him and he turns slowly, his head unsteady. He squints against the fluorescent light from the kitchen. There she is—tucked into herself on the floor against the kitchen cabinets. Around her lies a snowfall of sugar and cereal and ripped cartons, a cheese grater, a paring knife, a broken bowl. She's dropped Fisher's wallet and he comes close and snatches it up. He wipes off the sugar and shoves it back into his pocket without taking his eyes from her.

She's crying. He bends toward her and she sits up fast. In her hands, a barbecue fork. He grabs it and it comes free so easily it's like she wasn't even trying. He says, "No need for that. I'm a friend. Amigo. Freund. OK? I'm not going to hurt you. I'm looking for Grisby."

"Grisby." She says it oddly, buzzing the consonants and letting her voice dip on the first vowel. "Gone." She lifts both hands with their palms up, as though Grisby's ascended to heaven.

Fisher says, "Gone where?"

But all she says is, "Gone."

## 20

S HE SHOWS FISHER the bedroom with its drawers
pulled out and smashed, and the clothes dumped onto the
carpet, and the bed with its mattress pulled off its frame and
tipped up against the wall. "Two men," she says, and mimics
a gun with her hand. "Here," and she sweeps that same hand
toward the wreckage to indicate that they did this.

"What did they take?"

"Take? Take Grisby."

He runs a hand over his head. In the last few minutes he's
done this often enough to know exactly where the mound of
tender flesh starts. Despite the pain, he's let his fingertips rest
on it again and again, as though he can hold back the swelling.
"Yes," he tells her, "I know they took Grisby, but what else did
they take? Money? Pills?"

The delicate skin of her brow puckers like a disturbed pond.
"Pills?" she says, and the word's all stretched and strange.

Fisher steps toward the doorway and beckons for her to
follow. He gestures toward the wall, and the few boxes still
there. "Did they take the stuff that was in those boxes? Computer stuff? Guns?" He holds two fingers out like a gun barrel.

"Yes, gun," and she nods. "Two men, have gun."

"But they've ripped the place apart. What were they looking
for?"

Her lips look a little swollen and her eyes tired. On her
cheek, sugar sparkles in the light. Maybe she notices Fisher's
eyes going to it, because she rubs the sugar away. "I no understand."

Fisher bends and starts picking up the clothes scattered over the carpet, pretending to look under them. "The men were looking, like this, right?"

She stares back at him.

"Did Grisby know them? Did he say their names?"

She stoops too and picks up a flannel shirt of Grisby's, a lacy black thong, a blue sock, a pair of jeans, a leather skirt so short it must barely cover her crotch. Fisher stops her. "No," he says gently, "I wasn't telling you to clear up. The men—the men who took Grisby—they went through his things like this, didn't they?"

She strokes her fingers through her hair. Her bottom lip's pressed tight against her teeth and he knows she has no clue what he's saying.

"OK," and he heaves out a sigh. "What the fuck, hey? Never mind." He looks into her eyes and she looks back, her gaze flitting over his face. When he reaches out and gives her arm a squeeze, she flinches then lifts off the sweatshirt, and he sees that she's naked beneath it. Her breasts are surprisingly large against her thin chest and that chest's yellow and purple where bruises have bloomed over her ribs. "No, no." He waves his hand at her, even takes hold of the sweatshirt when she drops it and passes it back to her.

He walks out of the bedroom and has his hand on the cold knob of the front door before he thinks to say, "If Grisby comes back you have to call me, OK?" He mimics a phone with his little finger and thumb outstretched beside his head. "I'll write down my number." He pats his pockets. But what's he thinking? He knows he doesn't have a pen on him.

She's pulling on the sweatshirt, feeding her arms into the sleeves as she comes across the room.

"OK?" he says. "If you see Grisby, you call me, understand? Do you have a phone?" He makes a phone with his hand again and raises his eyebrows, never mind that it shifts the skin of his scalp and makes the swelling smart.

With one hand she's digging into the pocket of her jeans. A moment later, the black rectangle of Grisby's phone is sitting in her palm. She holds it out to Fisher. "This?" she says.

He reaches for it so fast she flinches.

## 21

T URNING THE KEY in the ignition makes Fisher's car bawl like a sick cow. How long was he out cold on Grisby's floor? Long enough to freeze the engine? No way, he thinks. Just after he'd come to, the light behind his eyelids changed—she'd hit him then turned on the light to see who he was. But maybe that wasn't what she'd done. Maybe she'd sat there with him in the dark with the broom handle at the ready until he'd moved. The clock on his dash says 10.55. He can't remember when he got here, can't think through the mossy throbbing in his head.

Stupid girl, he thinks. She panicked. Couldn't she hear in his voice that he hadn't come to hurt Grisby? That he was a friend?

But then, he'd broken into the apartment. What kind of friend does that?

He turns the key again. This time the engine catches, splutters, roars as he works the gas pedal. A cloud of exhaust rolls out behind the rear window, all devil-red from his taillights. He turns the heat up high and cups his gloved hands over his ears because they're prickling from the cold. A hat, he thinks—he needs to buy a new hat.

Two armed men, she said, and they searched the place. For the gun Grisby took from Jan and Brian's house? The gun that killed Brian? And that killed the dead cop? Or was there something else in Brian's stuff that they wanted? But then, why hadn't they taken it earlier in the evening? So much for the militia being a bunch of dumbshits. They've already tracked down Grisby. How long before they find him? Or Bree?

Maybe they've already found her.

His heart clenches with fear. No, he tells himself, it's not like that. Chances are, what happened to Grisby has nothing to do with Brian and his wacko buddies. Grisby's one of those people who treads on the rotten edge of things: dealing Percocet and Vicodin, getting himself just a little high, just a little low, doing favors here and there with money changing hands. Now he wonders: did that guy Grisby was scared of come back for him? Or was it a robbery plain and simple, because someone who deals Percocet is going to have money around the place? But then, why take Grisby with them? Did he owe someone more money than he had in his apartment? And as for the girl, who the hell is she? Some East European working girl? Some poor kid brought to the States, who had no idea what kind of work would make someone fly her all this way? Did Grisby pick her up last night? No, he thinks. Working girls don't hang around until morning like that. She knows Grisby and she's scared, but she's got nowhere else to go, or nowhere else she wants to go.

And if Tessa calls around and finds her there? Grisby didn't say a word about breaking up with Tessa, not that that means much of anything. Hell, maybe she's already found that girl and is mad as hell. But Christ, not mad enough to get her brothers to bust into the place and take Grisby away.

The sky's brightened enough for the lights stuck on the outdoor walkways of the building to look small and mean. Fisher nurses the cold engine and huffs through his gloves to warm his hands. He has the radio on loud above the hiss of the vents, but there's no news, not now. But here comes a pickup heaving across the snow, and it parks a couple of spaces away. It's nothing, Fisher tells himself, just someone going about their business. The trouble is, the pickup just sits there with its engine churning and no one getting out and no one getting in. Panic flutters in his chest. Maybe he's got it all wrong. Did the girl call someone? Could it be that she's working for the guys who came for Grisby? Hell, just because he found her in Grisby's apartment doesn't mean she knows him. She could have been told to wait there in case some friend of Grisby's showed up, and Fisher did, like the dumbass he is.

Wouldn't she have opened the door in that case? Wouldn't they have left her with a gun? And she gave him Grisby's phone—why the hell would she have done that?

Unless it's a trap of some kind.

Don't be fucking paranoid, he tells himself, it's not going to help. Still, the pickup rumbling away disturbs him. He glances over the roof of the car between them, thinks he can make out a guy at the wheel. He slips his car into reverse and backs out fast, yanks the wheel around and speeds out of the parking lot with his eyes on the rearview mirror. Sure enough, the pickup's reversing too. Could be chance, he tells himself, but he's too scared to believe it and sends his car swinging out across the road so fast that it slides and slides, nearly into the oncoming traffic, and he straightens it up only just in time.

※

When eventually Fisher pulls up it's on a residential street between two parked cars. From his mirror comes a dazzle of lights. A bus, huge and bloated on this narrow street. It doesn't stop. He waits. Nothing else moves.

Soon his eyes are staring at nothing: how easy it is to not pay attention. The houses behind their chain-link fences, the western edge of the sky the blue of a tropical sea, the upturned cups of streetlights spilling out light for nothing, because the sun's here at last. A coil of exhaust. Lights. A car pulls out of a driveway and its headlights flash off the snow, passing Fisher, turning off at the next block. In his heart he knows he lost the pickup at the first intersection, but he can't help checking his mirror. He wonders if it was following him at all.

He turns up the radio. An old Tom Petty number: he can't bear it and snaps the music off. In the quiet there's only his car engine murmuring away and the rush of air through the vents. He pushes back the hood of his parka. Even the slight pressure of the fabric against the swelling is too much. It sends fingers of pain across his skull. That's the last thing he needed: a pain on the outside of his head to match the raw ache inside.

But at least it's not a concussion, or not much of one. He can drive, he can function. He can still find Bree, can't he?

He pulls out his phone. If bad news comes, it'll have the same bleating ring as any other call, the same bland numbers on the screen. Should he call Jan? If he doesn't, won't it seem strange? Hell, their daughter's gone and a dead cop's been found at her house. If he hadn't dumped Brian's body, what would he do? He'd talk to her. For sure.

He takes off his glove so he can make the call. The battery's so low he's surprised the screen doesn't go blank. His heart's beating a little faster. He tells himself, *I was home last night. Grisby came over. We had a few beers and hung out. That's all we did. And this morning Ada woke me and I drove into town, and things have gone crazy since I saw the paper, and where the hell's Bree? The paper said she's taken off.*

On the other end, a flat buzz then another, then his call's sent to voicemail. He hears Jan's voice bright-edged and cheery, because she's Jan Armstrong of Armstrong Realty and values your business, so she'll return your call as soon as she can. He lets his head tip back against the headrest, turns it slightly so that the edge of the swelling just touches it and the pain reminds him, *Watch yourself now, Fisher.* After the tone he says, "Hey Jan, it's me, Mike. I just saw the paper. Christ, a dead cop? What in hell's going on at your place? The paper says Bree's taken off. Why didn't you let me know right away? Call me back and let me know what's up, because I'm real worried, OK?"

He ends the call with a jab of his finger and takes a deep breath. But almost straight away the phone rings and he lifts it. Nothing. Dead air. Like holding a rock to his ear. Has the battery just died? But then, that's not his ring tone. It's not his phone ringing, but the one in his pocket. Grisby's phone. He pulls it out and lays it on his knee. In its case it's the size and shape of a bar of soap, but black and slick, as if worn smooth by Grisby's hands. After the fourth ring it cuts off.

Grisby has six voicemail messages. The first is from a guy called Jed saying he'll make a purchase and will meet him out back at ten. The second's from Desiree, who wants to stop by because she's running low, and where the hell was he last night when he'd said he'd be there? The third's from Tessa and she calls Grisby a scumbag motherfucker, then hangs up. The fourth's from a kid saying he's got Vicodin to sell but he wants fifty a pill and he's got a whole bottle, then he laughs and leaves his number.

The fifth message makes Fisher lean forward onto his elbows and plug his free ear with his finger. A guy called Manny who says simply, *Yeah, I'm interested. Stop by and show me, OK? I'll be in by eight.*

One more message. It takes him a moment to recognize the voice: his own, curiously flat, saying, *Call me, OK?* How odd to be outside yourself for a few moments. He remembers sitting in his car outside the movie theater. Calling the diner. Calling Grisby. As though Grisby had gone in to work, or was at home, when he'd been taken away by two armed men.

He plays Manny's message over again, and a third time. He thinks, that's why Grisby didn't go into work. He was going to try to sell Brian's stuff. The question is, did he meet Manny and offload anything? Or did those two guys get to him first?

There's only one way to find out. Manny's number is right there on the screen. He calls it and a guy picks up and says in one well-worn rush, "Arctic Gun and Supply, can I help you?"

## 22

FISHER CAN'T HELP himself. Crossing the bridge he slows to forty and his eyes search the ice turned yellow by the low sun, the ribbon of black water, the turn-out where emergency vehicles would have pulled up if a body had been found. But there's nothing except the ice and the water, the scrawny undergrowth on the slope he slipped down last night, the blur of fog beyond, and then the river's gone and he's turning off the highway onto a back road.

Arctic Gun and Supply is a ramshackle cabin down by the power plant, a God-forsaken part of town where the wash of the new laps up against the old. The store sits by itself on a patch of ground, bare except for a couple of black spruce leaning toward each other that do nothing to block the view of the blank-walled power plant across the road, with its chimneys and glaring lights. Despite the daylight, a single bulb lights the store's sign: a grizzly holding a rifle. Of all the stupid things. As bad as Bear Cabs, for fuck's sake. And as he thinks it, he realizes he's had that thought before. He's seen that logo, and recently too. He tries to catch the memory, but it slides away.

He intended to park some distance off, just in case, though in case of what, he isn't sure. In the end there's nowhere to park without giving himself away, so he pulls up close to the door, beside an old pickup sitting low on its tires that has a couple of crates in its bed.

He hurries toward the steps and up onto the porch. Already a dog's barking from behind the door, deep chesty barks that mean Fisher knocks instead of going in. He waits, then knocks again. When the door swings open a fat guy in his sixties is standing there in a flannel shirt and overalls. Manny. He says, "It's a store, for God's sake, just come on in."

The dog's chained up over by the counter, a German shepherd that's sniffing the air for his scent. It's fallen silent now but watches Fisher without moving, and Fisher stares back. It lets out a growl.

"Just ignore her," Manny says and swats at the dog. "Cut it out—you know better than that." He leans onto the counter with his hands gently curled into fists. Their skin's loose and mottled, and the counter's glass top is all scratched up. Beneath it, ranged on two shelves, sit rows of handguns all pointing the same way. One of them is so small Fisher could close his hand around it and it would vanish. Guns give him an odd feeling: they're just lumps of metal, but look at what they can do. A bullet from one killed his mother, the bullet from another blew a hole in Brian's head. Fisher used to keep one tucked next to his seat when he drove nightshift and sometimes he wishes he still does. He's only been robbed twice. The first time was by a guy in a suit who held a knife to his neck. The second was at five in the morning by a woman with a crooked nose and a tooth missing right in the front. She shoved her hand in next to the seat like she knew the gun was there and took off with it and all his earnings for the night.

The old guy sniffs long and hard. "You just looking?"

Fisher glances up. "It's like this—" he starts, but Manny's already got his hands up, a strange gesture in this place, and is saying, "Whoa now, just tell me what you need, son, I don't need the whole story behind it."

"My friend called you about some guns he had to sell."

Manny's staring back at him, his eyelashes so pale that his eyes look strangely naked.

Fisher says, "Did he show up? See, I'm worried about him. He hasn't been answering his phone, and—"

"You playing babysitter to your friend? Is that it? Seems to me what he does is his own business."

Fisher runs one hand over his head, rests it on the sore lump and looks back at the guy. "Thing is, he's gotten himself into trouble. They weren't his guns, see."

Manny's lower lip is wet and shines as he says, "And now you want them back. Is that it?" Behind him his dog's claws scratch the floor. It lets out a sound that's half yelp, half growl.

"I'll pay you what you paid for them."

"What makes you think I'd buy anything from a guy who just comes in off the street? Huhn? D'ya think this is the only gunstore in town?"

"You're the only one he called."

"Your guns, are they, son?"

"He's in trouble."

"And you want to help. You're just a Good Samaritan, aren't you, because we don't have enough of them around here." He smiles and his dentures show, an unearthly white against bubble-gum pink gums. "But that's not what I asked you."

"You wouldn't want to sell stolen property, would you?"

Manny laughs and a delicate thread of spittle hangs across his open mouth. "You want to watch yourself or someone might take that as a threat." He leans on the counter again. "See, you could get yourself in a whole mess of trouble, and there'd be no way out of it. Wouldn't want that now, would ya?"

Fisher's gut turns cold. "OK, OK, we can forget about it," and now he lifts his own hands.

Which is funny, because only then does Manny pull out a shotgun from beneath the counter and train it on Fisher's chest. He says, "You can forget all you want, son, but I'm not the forgetting kind."

The black eye of the barrel stares at Fisher, and his bladder feels too small, and all he can think about is not pissing himself. He fills his lungs as best he can, has to force out his voice to say, "You shoot me, and you're gonna lose this place and spend the rest of your life behind bars. You want that?"

"It's not so hard to make people disappear."

"I wasn't dumb enough to come here on my own."

"Oh, right," Manny says, "I can see your buddy standing there right next to you. Sure thing."

"Outside," he says. "Told him to go get help if there was any trouble." Even to Fisher, this sounds lame beyond belief.

But Manny's head tilts slightly to one side, like he's listening to something beyond the log walls of the cabin. "Open the door," he says, "go on now."

Fisher backs toward the entrance. He feels behind him with one hand until he finds the doorhandle.

"Easy," Manny hisses. "Now get those hands back in the air and kick the door open."

Only as the door swings wide and the cold hits his face does Fisher understand—he's on display for whoever's supposed to be waiting for him in his car. Except, there isn't anyone, and the old guy's going to figure that out any second now because the car's just sitting there churning away, and there's no face staring out from behind the window. This is it, Fisher thinks, and before he can tell himself not to, he's thrown himself across the porch and down the steps, and a helluva blast shatters the air. He's barely at the car, is swinging the door open, when the dog's on him. Its teeth sink into his sleeve. He shoves the dog hard against the side of the car and tips himself in across the seat. The dog's on him again and he kicks it, kicks it in the face then wrenches the door shut.

The second shot hits the edge of the hood. Fisher jams the car into reverse, and there's the dog, its teeth snapping uselessly against the glass, and Fisher floors it as a third shot crashes through the air.

## 23

OFF FISHER GOES, off up Airport Road. His head's still singing from the blast of the gun. He can't loosen his hands and they grip the wheel so hard they hurt. Plus he's cold. Beneath his armpits his T-shirt's not just damp but wet, and in his crotch his boxers stick uncomfortably. Christ, he thinks, did he piss himself after all? But that can't be right because he still feels like he needs to take a piss. In fact, he needs to take a piss real bad.

He's hearing himself think over and over, *That fucker tried to kill me.* His eyes are everywhere: in the rearview mirror, in the wing-mirror, up ahead where, over the rucked-up bare metal where Manny's bullet went through the corner of the hood, he can see vehicles waiting to pull out onto the main drag. Only when he spots a trooper's car easing along behind him does he flip on the turn signal and switch into the right-hand lane behind some small white import barely doing thirty-five, and follow it as though every muscle in his body weren't taut with the urge to race ahead.

One thing's for sure: Grisby made it to the gunstore that morning. Manny must have bought Brian's guns from him, and Grisby was as happy as a fucking clam and took off home with a wad of cash in his pocket. How long was it before those two guys showed up? Long enough for Manny to have called someone and set them after Grisby. That would have been easy enough—*Son, I need to see your ID before I can buy these here guns from you* and Grisby would have been just dumb enough, and just greedy enough, to fall for it. By the time he got home, Brian's militia buddies were onto him. He didn't stand a chance.

But how would Manny have known to call them? Fisher brakes late, comes close to rear-ending the small white import. Brian loved those guns. He collected them. He wasn't the kind of guy to buy his guns at the supermarket and load them into his cart with his groceries. No, he'd have gone to a gun dealer. One whose store sign was a grizzly holding a rifle. Same as on the magnet on the filing cabinet in his office.

Shit. Manny must have sold Brian the guns. No wonder he knew who they belonged to. Maybe he sold guns to Brian's militia buddies too, the sort of weapons a straight-up dealer wouldn't touch with a ten-foot pole, and when Grisby showed up with Brian's guns, Manny'd have known exactly who to call to find out what the hell was going on.

The trooper hasn't pulled ahead. He's gliding along beside Fisher, cool as can be, even gives him a glance now. Fisher's tongue has turned dry, his throat raw when he swallows. "Go on, get out of here," he mutters thickly. Then the dazzle of red and blue lights starts up, and a siren whips through the air, and Fisher would have floored it but for the small white import a few yards ahead of him. Then, like a miracle, the trooper hurtles up the road, through an orange light, and on toward the airport.

Fisher sinks back in his seat, saying, "For fuck's sake, Christ Almighty."

꧁

Fisher stops. For one thing, he needs to take a piss. For another, all of a sudden his legs are shaking so hard he can't keep his foot on the gas. He pulls over onto the forecourt of a tuxedo rental store and parks any old how. His legs are twitching like he's just climbed all the way to the top of Henderson Dome and back. His neck's so taut it hurts. As for the lump on his head, he'd swear it's the size of a whole other head now, for all that when he runs his fingers over it, it doesn't seem much bigger than before.

Where should he go? He doesn't know.

What should he do? He doesn't know.

All he knows is that he needs to take a piss, but for now he just rests his forehead against the steering wheel and keeps his eyes closed. Bree, he thinks, where the hell are you? He can find her, can't he? But how can he think? His head's hurting inside and out: those smarting sinuses, the lump where the girl hit him, the blast of the shotgun still rattling inside his skull. Christ. He walked into Arctic Gun and Supply like a real dumbass, like nothing was going to happen if he started asking questions. How come he's so stupid?

Arctic Gun and Supply: so much for the cute grizzly on the logo. But the thought of that logo triggers something else. Jan and Brian's office. The filing cabinet with its magnets. A metallic one in the shape of a key. And he remembers. A small gadget attached to Jan's keyring. A chunky thing for letting a realtor into properties for showings. Brian must have had one too. So where is it now?

Fisher lifts his head. He says, "You're a clever girl, Bree, oh yes you are." He tugs his phone from his pocket and yanks off his glove with his teeth. The battery's low, but a quick search, that's all it'll take, surely. Problem is, even with the heat spinning out from the vents, it's cold in here, and his fingers are stiff, and the goddamn screen's so small, and he needs to piss real bad, so bad he can hardly think.

He lifts his head. There, just up the road, salvation. He puts the car into gear and sends it careening over the snow.

## 24

I T'S YEARS SINCE Fisher's been in the public library and the smell catches him off guard—the reek of old paper, of unwashed bodies and barely dispersed farts. It's a place where the discarded and unloved end up, or at least the hopeful among them who don't understand that life's left them behind. Maybe he fits right in. His clothes are dank from sweat, and a flap of material's hanging loose from his parka sleeve where the dog ripped it. When he gets to the bathrooms he even pisses a little on his longjohns, he's been holding it for so long. Here, he's just another loser.

He has to reserve a computer to use it; for all that, out of the eight ranged along the wall, only a couple are occupied: at one, a saggy-faced woman in a green sweater whose thighs spill over the sides of her chair; at the other, a skinny guy in a baseball cap with a ravaged face who sits with his nose a few inches from the screen. Fisher tries to lower the seat of his chair, but the lever's stuck and he's perched ridiculously high, can't even get his legs under the desk. The fat woman wheels herself over on her chair. She whispers loudly, "Give the lever a good tug, that one sticks."

Instead he gets to his feet and swaps the chair for the one at the next computer, and the fat woman glares at him. The librarian looks up from behind the counter and opens her mouth as if she means to say something, but Fisher looks away.

He sits hunched, the bulk of him squeezed around the rectangle of the keyboard and his head hung low to stare at the screen. From close by comes a stifled belch. The fat woman.

Into the small window of a search engine he starts typing

"Armstrong Realty Alaska" but the keyboard's grimy and the A sticks so that he has to pull it up with his fingertips each time he's pressed it. Fuck that, he thinks, and glances over his shoulder. In a moment he's rolled his chair to the next computer. He's barely had time to open up the search engine when the fat woman's hissing at him, "Number five. You reserved number five," and the librarian's head jerks up. Next thing he knows she's coming at him. She leans in close and her silver bear-foot earrings catch the light. She whispers, "Do you wish to reserve a different computer?"

Fisher explains the keyboard problem. She insists that he come to the desk to change his reservation, and fusses with the sign-up sheet, and whiteout, and her pen, until he can scarcely bear it. Then he's back at the computer, his fingers awkward because this keyboard's big, not like his laptop, and the system's slow, each new web page he pulls up appearing from the bottom like a glass being filled. He's just thinking, fuck this, fucking fuck it, his arms tensed to push himself away, to rush back outside, when there it is, huge and bright, just a foot from his face: a list of Armstrong Realty properties. He scrolls through them and clicks on the photos of their interiors. Each time he sees one that's empty, he thinks, bingo! Five of them, two in town and three in the wilderburbs around town, not far away but just far enough. Bree's a smart kid: if she's going to hide, she's going to do it right.

He sits back and lets out a sigh. Hell, he feels pleased with himself. This was easier than he imagined. He's created a list like he's some sort of prospective homeowner out to buy a place, and now he hits the print button and gets an error message.

The fat woman at the end of the row belches again, then tries to cover the sound with a cough. When she moves her chair squeaks beneath her weight, and she moves often, turning to look at Fisher and he feels it each time, those eyes on him.

He slumps back in his chair and rubs his face. Someone hisses at him. The fat woman. Her face is red above the flat green of her sweater, and she says, "You know what? You're sighing. Over and over. How can a person concentrate?"

He doesn't say a word, just turns back to the screen. He hears, "That's just plain rude."

He digs in a small basket where scrap paper's been cut into squares and jots down the addresses. He doesn't notice the librarian until she's at his side again. "Sir?" she says. "If you disturb our other patrons I must ask you to leave." Her face is pinched in annoyance.

"Sighing is a disturbance? How about her belching?" and he nods toward the fat woman.

The fat woman blinks a couple of times, then sits with her hands settled in her lap. "I can't focus when one of the other patrons acts in a hostile manner." She says it as though she's learned it by rote.

The librarian leans toward Fisher. Her teeth are a little gray, and a strand of hair catches on the corner of her glasses. "We have a zero-tolerance policy—" she starts, but he's on his feet.

"Zero-tolerance for sighing, I get it. Belching, that's OK. Well, I guess that's why you're so busy in here." He tucks the piece of paper into his pocket and heads for the exit.

# 25

H E STARTS ALL hyped-up at the idea of his own clev-
erness. First he tries the houses in the hills: one not far
from home for Bree, perhaps too close, because he peers in the
windows, even goes to the length of smashing a small window
by the garage and letting himself in, but the place has the grim
look of having been empty for months.

The second place is farther out. He leaves his car at the
bottom of the driveway, just in case, and runs in a crouch up
to the door. No fresh tire tracks in the snow, no footprints. He
circles around the place. Three doors: at the front, on the side,
on the deck. He tries the deck door last, and to his surprise
it gives. Inside, the house is cold and the air stale. He creeps
through the deserted rooms. No signs of cooking, no signs
of anyone having slept there. He checks the fridge, checks the
closets, stands in the empty garage with his hands on his hips.

The next couple of places are the same: their windows as
soulless as the eyes of dead fish, their rooms big and empty,
their driveways rutted with tire tracks even he can see are old.

At the last house a window round the back's already been
smashed and left open. Inside, wrappers from burgers and a
couple of plastic cups from fastfood joints lying on their sides,
the small pools of drink inside them frozen solid, what with all
that cold air coming in. Fisher feels hope bloom as he wanders
through the place. Someone's been here, not so long ago: dark
hair in the washbasin, a mug left by the sink. He kicks at the
wrappers and plastic cups on the carpet in the living room, but
he's smiling because Bree's been here, he's sure of it.

When he pulls the door shut behind him, he glances up to see a neighbor at a house a good stone's throw away watching from his deck. The guy's brought his coffee outside, steam rising off it thick as smoke, and he makes a point of watching Fisher as he takes a sip, and takes another, as though it's the most natural thing in the world to stand outside drinking coffee at fifty below.

Fisher gives him the finger, though probably the guy's too far away to notice. Fuck it. Bree's not here now, he missed her because he was too slow working out where she could be. For a moment he thinks: she'll be back. But no, she's not that stupid. This is the sort of place where the neighbors keep watch.

His car door yawns as he yanks it open, then he folds himself in behind the wheel. He left the engine running but the car doesn't feel warm, more like he's carried the brutal cold in with him. He reaches out to crank up the heat, only it's already on high. For a few moments he leans close to a vent, letting its warmth lick across his face, then he shoves the car into gear and takes off, the frozen tires jolting across the snow.

# 26

FISHER DOESN'T NOTICE the needle for gas has tipped over to empty until he's already close to town. Empty. Like his soul, like his heart, like his life. He came so close to finding Bree. Hell, maybe she'd only just left. And now she's either on the road south, or driving around town in Brian's brown Highlander. He needs to spot her before the cops do. Or the militia. He tells himself it wasn't them who hauled Grisby away. Christ, couldn't it have been the guy Grisby was hiding from and a buddy? Trouble is, Fisher can't make himself believe it. Who goes to that much trouble? And if it was the militia who took him—well, Grisby doesn't have it in him to resist a little pressure. By now he could have told them everything. Brian dead in Bree's bathroom, Bree's frantic messages. Fuck it, if they weren't looking for her already, they will be now.

He needs to do something, some damn thing, anything for crap's sake. Except he doesn't know what.

As soon as he gets back to town he pulls in for gas at a supermarket. The sun's as high as it's going to get, a thumb's width above the horizon, and it's turned the world gold and pink and lavender, like this is a gentle place when the time-and-temp display at the bank across the road says fifty-two below.

He zips his parka up above his mouth and undoes his seatbelt. It's no easy matter to pump gas in this kind of cold. The buttons on the payment pad are so small he ends up taking off his glove and stabbing at the frozen plastic through all its YES and NO questions, can hardly slide his card through the reader, his hand's so numb. Who the hell comes up with these machines? Some fucker in California? Not some guy who's ever had to stand outside in this kind of balls-numbing cold, that's for sure.

It doesn't help that the nozzle won't stay on and he can't retreat inside his car. No, on this morning, this cursed morning, he has to stand holding the fucking nozzle at the fucking gas tank while the cold of the metal seeps through his glove and into his hand, chilling his blood and that chill swimming up his arm and flooding his body so that soon he's shivering so hard it's almost more than he can bear to stand here. Of course, it doesn't help that he's lost his hat, because a hood's just not the same. Air leaks in around your neck, it touches your ears, it slips over your scalp. And it doesn't help either that his belly's squirming and hollow. All he's had this morning is a coffee and a bite of bearclaw. As for last night's dinner, he threw that up in Bree's bathroom. No wonder he feels emptied out.

The nozzle clicks off. He has to wrestle it back into its holder because the hose has gone stiff from the cold, and it takes three tries to screw the gas cap back on. He revs the engine a few times and watches the needle creep up to full. He checks his phone. No messages. And damn it, he needs to charge it. It sits on his palm like an egg about to hatch. He wills it to ring, and for Bree to be on the other end saying, *Dad? Come get me, I'm over at Walmart* or *Dad? Can you pick me up? I need to crash at your place.* Instead it just sits there, the screen gleaming in the delicate light of this sub-arctic morning. Who can tell him where Bree is now? Jan, maybe. A big maybe. He calls her number, listens to it go to voicemail, says, "Hey Jan, call me if you hear from Bree. I'm worried sick here," and hangs up quickly. He's relieved, he realizes. He didn't have to talk to her. Didn't have to make out like he didn't know her husband's dead, shot by their daughter, and that their daughter broke into one of the properties they're trying to sell because she's shit-scared—

He stops. Something about that's not right. He pictures himself at that last house, climbing out of his car and walking round to the back through the snow. Just like he did with the other places. Except the back window was already smashed and left open. Why the hell was it smashed when Bree could have just let herself in?

He tells himself maybe she didn't take the realtor key after all. So she smashed the window instead. Only, he doesn't believe it.

Was it someone else? Some other kid who needed a place to stay? For Chrissake, it wouldn't have been hard to work out that the place was empty. But his mind won't settle on that thought. Those footprints leading around the house. More than one set. Maybe one person going back and forth, or maybe more than one person poking around. Looking for someone. Breaking a window because whoever was inside was too scared to answer the door.

How hard would it have been for someone else to work out where Bree was hiding? A realtors' kid: for sure she'd hole up in an empty property. Any dumbass could work that out.

An SUV edges in close behind him to use the pump, but Fisher doesn't move. He feels the earth's gravity dragging at him so hard his head's an unbearable weight and his hands want to slump into his lap. Fuck, he thinks, have the militia got Bree?

A blare of horn behind him but he doesn't move. He needs to think but he can't. He can't hold his thoughts together.

He tells himself, I'll call the cops. But what would he say? That his daughter killed her militia-gonzo step-dad, and he dumped the guy's body in the river to hide it, but could they please go rescue her from a bunch of second amendment nut-jobs?

He thinks, I'll buy me a gun and go after them. Oh yeah, that's what someone in a movie would do. But he's just a sad-ass, overweight, useless-fuck of a cabbie. He doesn't even know who these guys are, or where they are.

Then it comes to him. He's got it the wrong way around. If the militia nuts've got Grisby and Bree, they'll be looking for him too. And if he's not home, how would someone find him? By calling his cell and asking for a ride. Or by calling Bear Cabs and asking for a non-smoking cab. Just like Grisby does. And it wouldn't take much to get Grisby to talk. He's a candy-ass, and besides, loyalty isn't his thing.

It's been months since Fisher's gun was stolen and he hasn't bought another. But there's the supermarket entrance, just a few dozen yards away, and while he's in there, he can pick up some ibuprofen too.

## 27

T HE DAY NOW has a curious splintered feel to it. Every
time a call comes through, Fisher starts to sweat and a
tense ache runs through his butt, and his hand goes to the
gun tucked between his legs. But so far all he's had has been a
fare from the supermarket to the apartment complex down by
the hospital—a young woman who tried to chat, like maybe he
needed conversation—and another out to the airport, a smooth-
faced older guy in a pricy wool coat who didn't say a word
the whole way, and a few shorter rides from a box store to a
nearby housing development and another from the university
to a Thai restaurant just down the hill. Through the window
he glimpses people chatting and smiling and lifting forkfuls of
steaming food to their mouths. His own lunch is fries already
gone cold and a soggy burger. Down the front of his parka cling
limp strands of lettuce and drips of sauce he wipes at with the
wrapper. His belly doesn't feel full, just less empty than before.

He turns up the radio for the hourly news, but there's
nothing about a body being pulled from the river, or a teenager
being kidnapped; nothing except a repeat of the news about
the dead cop, and a car wreck out on the highway, then the
weather forecast that says the cold's not going to let up for
another couple days.

No wonder Fisher feels out of sorts. It's not just what's
happened, or that sense of waiting when nothing out of the
ordinary's going on, but the fact that Reggie didn't let him
take the Ford he usually drives, said the brake drums need
replacing. He's mad at Fisher for calling in sick, and madder

at him for showing up hours late, so he's given him the rest of Gabe's shift, because Gabe didn't show up either. Reggie's a big enough jerk that he insisted Fisher take the Plymouth Villager because, Christ, it's no-smoking isn't it? And it's just come out of the shop with a new transmission.

So this afternoon Fisher's driving the Barf Mobile. It's no one's favorite. A minivan means kids yelling or crying or throwing things, or a carload of drunks in suits staggering after lunch at some fancy restaurant who want you to drop them all over downtown, who fight over paying or try to stiff you because hey, didn't Bob or Pete or whoever the hell else pay the fare before they got out? As for a tip, forget it.

The reek of vanilla air-freshener's almost too much. Fisher tries not to breathe it in, but why resist? He's going to have to put up with it until he gets off shift at six. But better that sweet stink than what it's hiding.

At least the fog's mostly gone, just a few pockets here and there like wind-blown snow caught in corners. He drives up Airport Road and turns onto Fifth. The air has a crystalline quality to it and everything's bronzed by the setting sun. How about that, he thinks, sundown already, and the sun's so far away there's no warmth to it. Instead it casts a syrupy glow over the snow along the road, and the exhaust lingering in the air, and the frost bearding road signs and fences and heating vents.

A little after two thirty and Fisher's given up any hope of finding Bree today. She vanished and all he could think of to do was go to work and hope she found him, or the militia found him, or someone who knows what the hell's going on found him. So here he is driving round and thinking up excuses for when she asks him what the fuck he was thinking: is he really so useless, so lacking in imagination?

To which the answer is yes, he decides. He's that useless, and he's that lacking in imagination. Words her mother used against him. Funny that, how he's putting them in their daughter's mouth. As for Jan, he wonders where she is. At the police station? After all, she hasn't called him back. He pictures her distraught, the way her mouth goes slack and her eyes empty, and he feels a twinge of pity. Except she doesn't know the worst yet. That their daughter's shot her husband dead and he's lying in the river and might not be found for months.

Poor Jan, he hears himself think. Her world's coming apart. Then a meaner part of him decides she deserves to know what it's like, because isn't that pretty much what she did to him when she left and took Bree with her? No warning, no explanation. He'd been driving a truck route to Prudhoe Bay and got home to find her stuff gone and Bree's too. It took him three days to find where she'd moved to. He stood on the doorstep of her apartment and asked, what did I do? She'd kept the door half-closed so Bree couldn't run out to him and said, if you don't know, there's no point explaining it, is there?

He's wearied by it all, by what happened long ago and his own still sore resentment. Be better than that, he tells himself, but he knows he can't be, and that's been the trouble all along.

He glances at the clock on the dash. Still just after two thirty. Three more hours to go, unless he quits early. Fuck Reggie if he doesn't like it and goes on about Bear Cabs' reputation, and needing to have cabs at the ready and all that crap, when he should wake up and see that Bear Cabs is on the way out.

He's got a pick up at Fifth and Dunkel. On the corner sits a low square building housing a bar on the ground floor and a pool hall upstairs. He pulls up just past the entrance and checks his mirrors: some guy leaving the doorway with his shoulders hunched against the cold. A black down jacket. A black knitted hat. Fisher snaps on the radio while he waits, finds his hands rubbing the steering wheel and his breath whistling through his teeth with the music.

He lets his eyes close and thinks about how Bree was when she was small. How she'd sit on his knee and plant kiss after kiss on his jaw, very intently, and hold his head if he tried to turn away. The first few times after he and Jan split up, when he went to fetch her for a day out together, she'd throw herself at him in joy. That joy had quickly evaporated. Soon he had to go into the apartment to carry her out and she'd cry and hit him, even if he told her his plans for the day, made up on the spot: ice cream and a train ride at the park, wouldn't that be fun? No, no it wouldn't, she hated him, she hated train rides at the park. It was like she'd soaked up every drop of her mom's bitterness at having once loved him when he'd turned out to be a loser, a nothing. And what's he done since except try to prove that wrong, and failing over and over?

The side door slides open, and he looks around. The guy's not wearing a hat. He's wearing a black ski mask. That's not so unusual when it's this cold, right? The guy has to duck to get into the minivan, and he only comes half in. It's then that Fisher notices two things: the guy doesn't shut the door, and when he straightens up there's a gun in his hand.

## 28

I**T'S A DIFFICULT** business kidnapping someone, never mind that when Fisher's hauled out of the cab his brand-new gun tumbles into the snow, or that he doesn't go for the pocketknife in his parka. There are two men, both with ski masks pulled down over their faces, and both wearing black down jackets like it's some kind of uniform. The first guy wants to tie Fisher's hands behind his back, but the other guy says, "So anyone looking out the bar's gonna see him with his hands tied? Getting into my truck? Screw that."

The first guy's voice has a tightness to it like air escaping an overfilled balloon. "You want him getting away? Huhn?"

"Just hold the gun on him and make him drive. I'll follow."

"Oh sure. And he's not gonna see where we're taking him. Is your brain up your ass?"

"Just until we get out of town, fuckwit."

The first guy waves the gun at Fisher. "Gas station on the Lewis Highway. Got it? And no funny business."

The second guy lets out a huff of exasperation. "Not the gas station. Christ. The pipeline-viewing spot. There won't be anyone there."

"There's always someone there."

"At fifty-fucking-below? Get real. Let's go, I'm freezing my balls off out here."

They shove Fisher back behind the wheel of his cab. Where his gun fell there's empty snow—which of them grabbed it? He doesn't know. It's gone now, a dumb idea anyway.

The first guy gets into the passenger seat. He keeps the

138

gun on Fisher, and when Fisher reaches for the gearshift—an awkward damn thing, up by the steering wheel—the guy's eyes follow. He must notice the same moment Fisher does, and the same thought occurs to him: the cab's radio. The guy's hand whips out and snatches the handset, wrenches it so hard the coiled wire stretches straight. Then he gives a jerk and the cord snaps back and swings emptily against the dash, and the handset's just a lump of plastic in his hand. He looks at it, then lowers the window and tosses it out into the street.

When he looks back at Fisher, his eyes peering through the holes of the ski mask have a meaner look. He holds the gun right up against Fisher's head, cold metal against Fisher's scalp, and the lump where the woman hit him sings with pain. Fisher doesn't flinch, though, he doesn't move. He lets the guy dig around in the pockets of his parka and pull out his phone, his wallet, his pocketknife, his bottle of ibuprofen, and the guy gives a snort of laughter. "Now drive," he says, "and don't try nothing stupid or you'll be sorry."

So Fisher drives. And he doesn't do anything stupid. He indicates each lane change, he stays under the speed limit, but not so far under that a cop would stop him, and though this is what he wanted, to be on his way at last to the men who might have Bree, a terrible fear's clawing at his insides.

## 29

SOMETHING SO SIMPLE as tying someone up is no easy matter at fifty below. Fisher could have warned them about that. The duct tape's been lying in the back of the second guy's pickup and the glue's frozen, and when he does manage to pull off a length he can't get it to stick around Fisher's wrists. They've got him facing the pipeline—a steel tube thicker than the trunk of any tree in the Interior, coming crooked as a bendy straw down the hill into the valley then vanishing up over the next rise on steel legs like saw horses. A viewpoint for tourists. Busloads of them are brought here in the summer. Christ, thinks Fisher, might as well go and view the power plant. At least it has lights.

There's a warning sign on the pipeline, bristly with frost. Don't climb onto the pipeline. Don't fire your gun at the pipeline. What to do in case of flames coming out of the pipeline. It takes his mind off the cold, at least, because his kidnappers have taken off his gloves, and they've been fucking around for so long with the duct tape that his hands have gone numb from the fingertips down to where his fingers meet his palms. A throbbing starts up in his left thumb then slowly fades, erased by the cold. The first guy's smoking now and his cigarette looks obscene sticking from his mouth in the middle of that ski mask. As for the second guy, he's still struggling with the tape. "Hundred and one freaking uses," he mutters, "except to tie a guy up. Should write and fucking complain."

The first guy's passing his gun from hand to hand. He huffs between his teeth and his breath spills out in great wobbling clouds toward whichever hand he has free. His gloves aren't thick enough, and you just try holding a piece of metal while it's burning your hand with cold. He draws hard on his cigarette as though that's going to warm him, and the smoke billows around Fisher. He turns his head—not so you'd notice really, he thinks—but the guy steps closer and breathes the smoke straight into his face, those cut-out eyes staring right at him.

The second guy says, "That'll have to fucking do. I'm not gonna spend all day on this shit," and he tosses the roll of tape back into the truck.

"How about his eyes, man?"

"Give him your mask."

"Fuck no! Use the goddamn tape."

"It's shit in this cold. Give him your mask and pull it down."

"It has freaking eyeholes."

"Backwards, you moron."

The first guy snaps at Fisher in his tight voice, "Shut your eyes," and he does. The guy's rough. He wrenches the mask down, but with his gloves on he can't get a proper hold and it bunches up over Fisher's eyes. The guy paws at Fisher's head, knocking the soft lump where the woman hit him a lifetime ago, trying to pull the mask all the way down without taking off his gloves. He puffs under his breath as he tries again, jerking Fisher's head to the side, and a second time, and that's when Fisher lets his eyes open for an instant. By a miracle the guy doesn't see, he's so intent on the mask. Then it comes down over Fisher's face, and his chest tightens as though he's been hit. Not because of the second-hand warmth, or the stink of greasy skin and tobacco. No, because of what he's just seen, a strange face, blank as an egg. No hair, no eyebrows, the skull rounded and gleaming and bare as a knee, the eye-sockets scarcely more than a slight dent in the flesh. The sight of that egg face leaves him with a sick feeling of fear.

Behind the mask he opens his eyes. Blackness patterned with tiny lozenges of light, everything blurred. He tilts his head to where he thinks that monstrous face was, tries to make it out through the weave of the mask, but the guys are moving about, their boots squeaking over the snow, and besides, it's all just dizzying speckles of brightness against the dark. He shuts his eyes again. Is this what it's like to be a worm, he wonders, living in darkness as though that's all there is? A tube of blind flesh exposed to all kinds of dangers it can't see?

A roaring from the highway, a car storming down the hill toward them, the noise of its engine fractured in the cold air. Fisher leans forward as though the sound's reeling him in, but an arm falls across his chest like a bar. The second guy says, "Don't get any ideas." Then he calls out, "Open the truck door so we can get him in."

Mr Egg Face, the guy with the tight voice, must be standing a few yards away now. He shouts back, "Fuck no—put him in the backseat of the cab."

"We're ditching it."

A crunch and squeak of snow. The second guy's voice is louder now. "How big a fuckwit are you? Weren't you listening? We keep a low profile."

"You're the one wanted him to drive it out here."

"And you're gonna drive it up to—fuck it, the rest of the way. OK? Then we can ditch it."

"Your fucking idea, you drive it."

"If you don't like it, you should have brought your own goddamn truck." There's the crunch of boots on snow, the groan of a door being opened. "Get on with it, we're already late and the Commander's not gonna like it. Just don't go and fucking wreck it." A door slams. The tone of the truck's engine swoops upward and suddenly the air stinks of exhaust.

Mr Egg Face isn't pleased. He grabs Fisher by the back of

his parka and yanks him nearly off his feet. Off they stumble, off to where the cab waits, then Fisher's shoved inside. His face slides against the seat. Even through the ski mask it feels cold. He shifts his head so that the sore lump is cooled by it. Lying like this, he opens his eyes and makes out a square of bright sky that flickers as the cab lurches off along the road. He remembers a Hitchcock film where some guy tries to remember the sounds he heard as he was driven around blindfolded, but there's nothing to hear except the engine. He thinks he should try to work out the route by the turns the cab takes—isn't that what a clever man would do?—but although he knows this road, each curve and climb and dip, all the way out to the small settlement of Beecher, he's lost within minutes.

It doesn't help that the guy's driving the cab so hard the engine whines and the turns are too tight. Every once in a while he shouts out, "Any trouble and you're a dead man—get it?" and, "Stay down or you'll get one between the eyes." So Fisher stays down and twists at the tape binding his hands. He forces his hands apart until the tape stretches a little and its glue pulls at the hair on his wrists. Fuck, he thinks, tied up twice in one day—what are the chances of that? Only the duct tape's tougher to escape from. He tugs and tugs, feels the bite of it into his flesh, the way it sticks as he tries to pull one hand free, works at it so hard it rubs his skin until it smarts. But he keeps trying. He imagines himself wrenching open the door and jumping for it. He pictures how he'd fall, and the crush of his bones against the road. He thinks how, if he's a goddamn lucky sunuvabitch, someone will see him and pull over, and Mr Egg Face will just have to let him be saved. He can almost taste it: the sweetness of relief, of safety.

And Bree? The thought of her makes him breathe too fast, makes his face sweat beneath the mask. He's so damn scared he's going to save himself, when the whole idea was to find her and get her away from these guys? Isn't getting caught what he wanted? Isn't this a lead to where she might be? He forces himself to lie still, letting the cab rock him, tilting him forward a little as it brakes, pushing him back against the seat as it turns off the highway and onto a lumpy side road.

One thing's clear: they're out in the wilderburbs where houses and cabins are half-hidden in the trees, and where you can fire off a gun as many times as you want and no one's going to pay it any mind.

## 30

THE CAB COMES to rest badly parked, its nose up against what must be a snow bank and the whole thing canted at a careless angle. The door slides open and Fisher's hauled out. He stumbles and falls face down in the snow. "Fucker," spits Mr Egg Face, then something hard and narrow sends a new pain bursting through Fisher's cheek. He hears, "Don't worry, sir, I've got him" in that tight voice, then he's dragged to his feet and across the snow, and the whole way he can taste blood.

Already his hands are stinging, bare in that splintering cold and the tape sticky against his skin. The snow beneath his boots is firm from being trodden down. Through the mask the light dims slightly. The snow sounds hollow. He stumbles on a step and pitches forward because he can't catch himself, staggers against a doorframe. Warm air. On it, the smells of bacon grease and cheap coffee. Despite himself, saliva pools in his mouth. A hand yanks him forward and he's on a wooden floor, boots thudding across it with other boots, and he's shoved this way, then forward, then to the right where the light through the mask brightens again. The air's too hot, he's gasping like the damn mask is suffocating him, and maybe it is because more than anything right now he needs the coolness of fresh air filling his lungs. He manages, "Can you—"

A blow to his belly. He bends over and gags. The acid stench of the contents of his own stomach fills the mask but he hasn't thrown up, not quite, and he swallows, swallows. Hands drag him up and push him onto a hard chair with his arms angled around its back. Now's he tied well and good with rope this time, so tight his skin prickles. He's sitting tipped to one side, he knows that, but he can't right himself, not now when his guts are burning and his breath's shredded, and his whole self is clenched against another blow.

Footsteps, the creaking of floorboards, then muted voices. People in another room. One voice lifts above the others and Fisher catches, " . . . stupid bastards! . . . around town—huhn? Can't you think for yourselves? It isn't just your own asses you've . . ." Other voices wash in, then that same insistent voice is back: ". . . fuck it up with this one. Get it? I handle it. You fucking blew it with the last before we . . ." Then the sounds are muted, like someone's pushed a door shut, and there are only the closed-in noises of Fisher's own body. He wonders, am I alone? He lifts his head then forces himself to straighten up against the pull of the bruised muscles in his belly. All he can make out through the pinholes of light coming through the mask is the white rectangle of a window.

It's so still in here that when he coughs the sound of it hangs on the air. He shifts his feet, too, coughs again and listens. How odd it is to hear a room instead of seeing it, but he's sure: this is a bigger room than he thought. Sounds shimmer away rather than being eaten up by the air. He moves his hands, testing the knots, but there's no getting loose this time.

A woman's voice close to his ear hisses, "Try that again and you'll be sorry." The inside of his stomach falls away. She must have leaned in right beside him because her breath brushes his cheek. "Thought you were on your own, didn't ya? Well, you ain't." She stretches that *ain't* all about: a Southern accent, but the voice itself is raw and it's no surprise when he catches the smell of her now, the stale cigarettes and the warm stink of sweat.

"I don't know what this is all about," he says, and he feels like he's betrayed Bree already.

Her hand catches him on the side of the head where the broom-handle landed just a few hours ago and the pain of it splits across his scalp again. He can't help it; he cries out and she comes around in front of him, blocking what little light he could see. "Big mistake to get mixed up in all this, huhn? You're not so tough. No, you're not tough at *all*," and she gives him a shove, except he's large enough that it only jerks his head back.

From the other room comes the tail end of a voice, then the hollow clattering of boots on floorboards, so many of them his heart seizes. The woman's still beside him and she calls out, "This one shouldn't give us much of a problem, Commander, he's scared shitless already, even of little ol' me," and she laughs.

A man tells her, "Shut it."

They've arranged themselves around him. From his left, a whisper of cloth on cloth, from somewhere off to his right, a sniff then a stifled cough.

The blow to Fisher's jaw comes out of nowhere. It snaps his head and sends him flying backward, the chair coming down on his arms tied behind its back, all his weight on them, then his head thudding against the floor. Lights flash across the darkness inside his skull and his breath comes out all wrong. All he can think about is his weight pressing the chair onto his upper arms so hard he wants to cry out. Someone's standing over him and he moans. Without thinking he pulls up his legs to protect his soft belly, but he's not quick enough. A boot presses down on his middle, not quite painfully, not yet at least, but he can't breathe, the air's been knocked out of him, and he's like a fresh-caught fish left gasping on the floor.

"Now," says a man—the Commander, Fisher thinks, the guy who told the woman to shut up, "you cooperate, you go back to your sorry-ass life. You don't cooperate, you can kiss that life good-bye and go into the Great Beyond crying for your mama. We're gonna make it easy, just two choices, see?" The boot pushes harder against his gut. The toe touches his ribs and the heel scrapes his hip bone. "See?" the man says again, and only now does Fisher understand he's supposed to answer.

He tries to nod, he gulps at the air, and finally he manages a soft, "Yeah, I see. I'll help you. Just let my daughter—"

The heel rams into his gut and Fisher yelps. Then the boot lifts away and the voice turns almost gentle. "Tell us where Brian Armstrong's hiding out. Just that, and you can go."

"Brian . . ." and his voice snags as his thoughts catch up. They want Brian. They think he's alive, then, and they're pissed as hell at him. What's Bree told them? Did she make up some story about Brian taking off because that's what they wanted to hear? He tries to breathe against the pain in his belly, says, "Canada."

That boot presses down harder, half on his belly, half on his chest, and he tenses himself against it too late. The Commander must be leaning his weight on it, because the pressure grows horribly. "Don't . . . fuck . . . around . . . with . . . us."

"True," and Fisher almost sobs. "Let—let my daughter go. I—I'll tell you everything."

There's one beat of silence before the Commander answers, and Fisher understands: this guy's been caught off guard. Maybe Bree's not here. Maybe they're not even looking for her. Fuck, what if Grisby didn't mention Bree? And now he has himself, like the fucking dope he is? If they don't have her, this is all for nothing. They might kill him and it won't help her one bit. The thought of it lodges in his throat.

The Commander says, "Ah yes, your daughter," but his voice has slowed. "She's been asking for Daddy, poor thing, she wants to go home. We don't want to hurt her. But we will—understand? You'll hear her screaming when we set that pretty hair of hers on fire, or break the bones in her hands. Is that what you want?"

It's all fake: the menace curled into his voice, the idea that they've got Bree. The Commander's making it up. Bree's hair's not pretty, not since she had it cut short.

"Tell us where he is, or she's going to hurt real bad."

"Canada."

"Bullshit. Brian hates fucking Canada."

The mask pulled down over Fisher's face is stifling, his belly and chest half-crushed by the Commander's boot, and that boot presses down harder now and the pain of it sears through his ribs, his guts. He bellows until it lightens up, then he cries out, "Fuck, he's dead. Shot dead."

"Dead? Are you saying you killed him?"

"No," and it comes out as a sob.

"Think of your daughter, you fucker. You want us to hurt her like we're hurting you?"

"She called. My daughter. She was scared. Brian was going crazy."

"When?"

"Evening."

"You're full of shit." The boot presses harder against his ribs.

Fisher half sobs, says, "It's true."

"What she say?"

"To come get her. Brian was going ape-shit. That's all."

"And you went over there?"

"Too late. Wasn't there. Brian . . . he was dead."

"Been thinking of what to tell us, have you? Bedtime stories to put us to sleep?" His heel jabs down and Fisher cries out. The Commander's yelling, his voice wound up in a fury. "This is a load of shit! Just shit!"

"It's true," and Fisher's words stretch into a moan.

The Commander stamps down against his ribs, and again, and he yells, "What did she tell you? Huhn? What she say?"

Like he's forgotten that she's supposed to be here, like that doesn't matter any more.

Fisher can't roll over, can't protect himself. The wool of the mask clings to his face. He shakes his head as though he can free himself of it, because he can't help thinking, if only he could breathe cool fresh air and see these guys, the pain wouldn't be so bad, he could bear it. He opens his mouth but the damp wool sticks to his chin. Another kick, this one so hard he retches, and the woman cries out, "Oh c'mon, not in here. Not on my new rug."

The Commander hollers, "Shut the fuck up, Darlene."

"Christ Almighty," she says. Footsteps, then she's leaning over Fisher. "Know what I got here?" Something sharp pushes against his upper thigh. "Oh you felt that, huhn? Well, listen up: this knife's gonna cut off your balls if you don't tell me the truth. Got that? Not fast and less painful like, but slow. Can you imagine how it's gonna feel? It'll sting first, going through the skin, then it'll start slicing into all those nerves in there, and blood's gonna be oozing down your legs, all sticky. Feel that point?" She pushes it into the soft skin of his thigh. "That hurt?"

He nods.

"Good." She must have a cigarette in her hand because there's the crackle of burning paper and tobacco, then the air's full of smoke. "Now tell me where that fucker Armstrong's hiding out."

"Dumped him. In the river. Down from the power plant."

"You still telling me he's dead?" The point of the knife presses hard against his jeans and longjohns.

"Shot through the head."

"How much he pay you to say that, huhn? Because, we know it ain't true. Now," and the knife slices into his skin in one fierce burst. There's a rush of warmth as blood seeps out around the blade. "Why don't you tell us what really happened? And what that little girl of yours saw?"

It's not the pain that makes him go cold. It's the futility of what he's done: setting himself out like bait when these nut-jobs haven't got Bree. Was she trying to run away from what had happened with Brian? Or was she so scared of these militia buddies of his that she ran from them, not knowing they weren't looking for her?

Militia buddies. Ex-buddies, he thinks. Whatever Brian did, he pissed them off big-time.

Fisher's shivering and his teeth are juddering against each other. He swallows, feels Darlene's breath on his face. The blade shifts in his flesh and pain gapes through his thigh. He says, "I—I went over. Searched the house. Brian . . . was dead. Wrapped him up. Dumped him in . . . the river."

"Oh hon, you weren't on your own. C'mon now. You need to stick to the truth or you're gonna be real sorry." She lets her accent stretch that *real* so long that Fisher flinches. "Oh yeah," she says, "being afraid's good, because you've got every reason to be afraid. See, we talked to your friend. He said Brian took off in a hurry to Denver. And then you tell us he's in Canada. And now here you are saying he's dead."

From somewhere close by comes the shuffling of feet. A cough. Darlene says, "If you don't wanna watch, you can make yourselves useful and put on more coffee." The knife wobbles a little in the wound, and through the wool of the mask Fisher gulps in a lungful of air. Darlene leans close, one hand on his hip. "Where did he want a ride to?"

Fisher shakes his head. Fucking Grisby, he thinks. What exactly did he tell them? That Brian called for a ride? For fuck's sake. But then, maybe he was trying to leave Bree out of it. Doing what he thought Fisher would do too, and keep her safe.

Only, he's fucked that up well and good.

"Need a little something to jog your memory, hon?"

The knife's a cruel pressure in his flesh. Then it shifts a little, slicing through nerves and he's almost choking. He calls out, "I told you—he's dead! Go look. Just south of the Larsson Bridge. I wrapped him in a tarp," and his voice breaks, "I did—I dumped him. Please."

The knife turns and his whole self becomes lost in that pain. He hears, "Tell me again. What did your little girl say when she called?"

He wants to keep the words down. He doesn't want to let what he suspects about what Bree did come loose, not here. The knife grinds farther into his flesh and his own mouth betrays him, it shouts, "He was going ape-shit. That's what she said. She was scared!" He sucks in a breath. "Your guys took my phone. Listen to the fucking messages."

In an instant the knife's gone and in its place there's the angry warmth of damaged flesh. Cigarette smoke hangs on the air and someone's stepping around him. He gets the feeling that there's some discussion going on above his head, carried out entirely in looks and gestures. Footsteps cross the floor: two or three people, by the sound of it, and then there's the oomph of a door nearly closing.

This time Fisher doesn't make the mistake of believing he's alone. He lies perfectly still with his whole self held in around the raw throbbing of his thigh, and the bone-aching pressure of his weight on the chair bearing down on his upper arms. He waits, and he listens. From somewhere not far away come voices blurred by walls. If he were to guess how long he lay there and waited, he couldn't say. Five minutes. Fifteen. An eternity.

When the footsteps clatter back into the room, someone's saying, "Don't be an asshole. Keep it on, maybe he'll call."

The light breaks up. These guys must be blocking a window. The Commander says, "OK, you two, take him out."

152

A lazy voice asks, "Want me to help?" Fisher knows that voice, he's sure of it.

"No, go find the girl."

Fisher's skin fizzles in fear. He calls out, "She's just a kid."

A laugh. The lazy voice again, saying, "Want to tell me where Brian's headed?"

"He's dead. I told you." There's desperation curled into his voice.

"Then she's dead too."

Now the Commander butts in. He must have turned away because his voice's muted. He says, "You two go take care of him. Do it properly this time."

## 31

E VEN WITH THE ski mask over his face Fisher can tell the sky has ripened to a sunset orange. The air's harsh against his skin, and beneath his boots the hardpack of snow groans and creaks like the surface of an alien planet. The wound in his thigh smarts like a live thing, like a promise of what's to come. He thinks, I'm gonna die, out here, today. He thinks, I know they haven't got Bree, I know they haven't, but part of him won't believe it. That voice saying, *Then she's dead too.* Only she's not. She's not. The Commander said, *Go find the girl* because they don't have her, they never had her. They think she's still got that pretty hair that came halfway down her back. But last night she took off and today, like an idiot, he drove around in his cab, hoping these guys would find him, thinking he was saving her.

He doesn't care that he stumbles along. Soon he's going to be dead. Fear unbalances him. Any moment now they're going to tell him to stop—by a tree perhaps—and shoot him in the head. Like Brian. His head with an extra hole in it and his brains and blood leaking out the back. But these guys didn't shoot Brian. They're looking for him.

The light dims. The ground's more uneven here and he lurches. He wants to cry. How sad to die like this when he had so much life ahead of him. When Bree will never know he tried to help her. He thinks, is Grisby out here somewhere? A hole in his head?

One of the guys grabs Fisher's arm and forces him to a halt. Close by, a squeak of hinges, the flapping of a door hefted open too fast against its frame. He's pushed forward. From beneath his boots comes the hollow thud of a wooden floor, and all about him hangs a closed-in stillness. This is it, he thinks, and his whole self tenses, his neck, his spine, the bulge of his belly, his thick thighs. Just don't piss yourself, he thinks, not that, not in front of these guys. Mr Egg Face's tight voice says, "Take off his parka."

The second guy—Fisher's sure it's the other kidnapper, the guy who drove the truck—says, "No way. Did you bring the tape to tie him up again? Huhn? Besides, it don't stick well in this cold."

"This's gonna take forever. I gotta get back to town."

"Won't fucking take forever, not in this cold." Something tugs at his parka. There's the buzz of the zip being undone, then a swell of cold against his body.

"Let's just get it over with, Marty."

"Put his fucking wallet in his pocket. He had an accident, no traces. Get that into your fucked-up head, will ya?"

Something's shoved into his parka pocket, then the door slaps closed. Hands fumble against the door, then something scrapes over the wood, securing it Fisher realizes. The first guy bangs hard against the door, like you would with a truck that's ready to go, shouts, "Don't go catching cold in there, you fucker," and laughs. Boots crunch away over the snow, and before long a distant door thuds shut.

Fisher waits. He stands perfectly still, as though someone might be watching. His ribs hurt, and his belly, his head, his jaw, but worst of all is the cut on his thigh. Already the blood on his longjohns has frozen and it pulls at the wound like it's drawing in the cold and letting it course through him. He's supposed to freeze to death out here, and for it to look like some dumb-ass accident. He concentrates and lets his hearing slink out of him like feelers, exploring the air, checking it for the slightest sound, because he's not going to get caught out twice. But it's cold. Already his hands are losing feeling.

Fuck freezing to death, he thinks, fuck standing here like a fucking cow waiting for the fucking bolt through its brain. He bends forward and works his numb hands apart, using his butt as leverage, biting his teeth together against the sting of the tape over his wrists, and pulling and pulling until that tape is slipping over his skin, up over the mound where his left thumb starts, pulling so hard he's caught in a cocoon of his own heat inside the mask.

Then the tape comes loose and he lets out a laugh because his stiff arms, tied for so long, are rising up of their own accord like he's thanking the good Lord for saving him, and what a heady feeling that is. He lets them float up, up, then catches himself and swings them down, swinging them over and over until the blood's forced toward the lumps of flesh that are his hands, and even if it doesn't help much, at least his arms feel like part of him again.

He hears voices. Not close, not yet, and his poor hands scrabble at the ski mask, his fingers as cold and useless as a dead man's. Not frostbitten, not that bad, but he claws at the mask, bunching it up as best he can when he can't feel what he's doing until the raw air slides up over his face and he blinks in the sudden light.

They've shut him into an outhouse, for fuck's sake. At least it's too cold to stink. He tucks his hands inside his sleeves and breathes down the twin tubes of the cuffs to warm them, then he fumbles for the zip-pull on his parka. Four tries before he manages to zip it up to his chin.

He puts his eye to the crack between the frame and the door. Those voices are clearer, closer, and a car door slams shut. He shifts his head, but all he can see is a house, three pickups parked in front of it, and the minivan with its ridiculous smiling

156

bear logo and someone walking toward it. A guy in khaki who pauses to press his fingers against his nose and blow it clean onto the snow. That slanted way of standing, that way of resettling his hat. With a start, Fisher recognizes him: Lyle. Ada's nephew. That lazy voice saying *Want me to help?* when they were going to take Fisher outside. Lyle's voice. No wonder he couldn't help Ada at the hardware store this morning. He was too busy with these guys.

Lyle climbs into the minivan and a moment later its brake lights flash on, then its white reversing lights. It whines backward across the snow and out of sight, and Fisher shoves his face against the cold wood, breathing hard. Shit. Is he off to find Bree in the cab? No wonder they picked Lyle to look for her; he met her once or twice when he first moved to town. Maybe he'd recognize her if he found her. Christ, that was Lyle saying Bree was as good as dead. Fisher tells himself Lyle was just screwing with him, he's that kind of shit-for-brains. But that's not all there is to it. There's always been something off-balance about Lyle, not just that he's done time, but the way he has with Ada of smiling and being Mr Charming when any fool can see something crouched in his eyes, something calculating and dangerous.

Fisher's so tense his shoulders ache, but the cab doesn't come rolling back past him and down the driveway. No, across the thin air rumbles the sound of its engine, then the creak and slap of vehicle doors. When finally he catches the cab's engine being put into gear again his heart seizes and his mouth goes slack. He crams his eye against the crack and watches it lumber back into view, then pull up beside the pickups once more.

The cab's engine's still running and from it exhaust balloons onto the air. There's Lyle, half in the cab and half out, like he's trying to make up his mind about something. Fisher wills him to get the fuck out, not to go after Bree, not yet. And, like a miracle, Lyle hunches his shoulders and heads into the house. Soon after another couple of guys follow, one of them with his voice spitting and curling, complaining about something by the sound of it, though Fisher can't make out what.

Soon all's still again. Fisher swings his head about and huffs on his hands. He needs to get out of here, but he's never seen an outhouse like this: built out of two-by-fours and fully framed, for crap's sake. Who the hell wastes good lumber on a hut to shit in? He backs up, never mind that there's no room in here and the bench of the toilet seat digs in against his shins, then he launches himself at the door. It rattles but doesn't give. Did he expect it to? No, he'd hoped, that's all.

His shoulder aches where bone mashed against wood. He brings his eye back to the bright crack between the door and its frame. There's the house, a dark log thing with two windows facing his way, and smoke from its chimney twisting into the dying light. There's the shit-brown Barf Mobile parked between a couple of silvery pickups, like a manatee between sharks. Lyle's left it running, letting it warm up, or going to fetch something before he takes off. But that means the keys are in the ignition. All Fisher needs is to get to it. He lets his eye track down the crack to where it darkens. A latch of some kind to hold the door shut in the wind. He remembers the scrape of something against wood; something propped against it too, then. A shovel maybe, or an ax.

He looks about him, as though there's something he's missed that would help him get out of here. The baby blue expanded polystyrene of the toilet seat. Two rolls of toilet paper stacked on top of each other. An air-freshener with its white plastic bars over a frozen yellow gel, which of course smells of nothing at all in this cold. And that's it.

If this were a movie, he'd come up with some way of using this stuff to escape. He'd be cleverer, he'd be faster, he'd be better than this Mike Fisher trapped in an outhouse. And he wouldn't be freezing to death. But as he breathes on his hands and looks about him, he doesn't get any smart ideas. I'm gonna die, he thinks, like the stupid fuck I am. Maybe I can wait for someone to take a crap, but what then? Stab them with the air-freshener? Gag them with toilet paper? Besides, that house doesn't look like the sort of place that doesn't have plumbing. So what the hell is this outhouse for? Then he remembers: those voices. Those other doors shutting. There's more to this place than he's seen. Cabins, most likely, and not far away, because who wants to walk far to take a dump? He gets up on the bench and tries to find a hole to peer through in the wall. But there's nothing more than tiny cracks and a crescent-shaped vent in the side wall, too high up to be of any use.

He lets himself down onto the bench and rests his head on his arms. The wound in his thigh is pulsing horribly, his guts and ribs and head, all radiating pain like it's a contamination he'll never rid himself of. What is he but a broken man? He would cry, but he doesn't even have that left in him.

A trill of sound. A phone ringing in his pocket. Grisby's. The guys didn't find it.

His hands are so cold he fumbles, nearly drops it, claws at the cover to open it then holds the freezing plastic to his ear. Too late. It cuts off in mid-ring. Fisher sags for a moment, but hell, that doesn't matter, does it? He has a phone. He breathes on his fingers. He thinks: who to call? Not Grisby. Not Jan. Ada, he thinks. Because when she hears that Lyle's out here, messing around with these militia guys and that he just blew her off this morning, she's going to be mad as hell. Madder than she is at him for ditching her in the hardware store.

He's so cold his fingers miss the numbers on the screen. He has to try four times, then there's Ada's harsh voice saying, "Alaska Travel-Inn, how can we help you?"

"Ada," and he's half-whispering, as though someone's going to hear him, "it's me. Mike."

"You think you can do that to me? I waited half an hour, even had them page you."

"Ada, look, I've—"

"I don't know what you're up to, but it's going to bite you in the butt. You get that? Because I'm going to make sure it does."

"Ada, I've been kidnapped. Some guys are trying to kill me."

"If they don't kill you, I will."

"This is for real. Lyle's part of—"

"Nothing with you's for real. You get yourself down here by six to help me unload or I'm gonna be wondering why you've got Brian's bag in your closet when he's taken off and a dead cop's been found at his place. You get that? Because I *am* for real." And she hangs up.

He cradles the phone in his hand. If he wants to live, he should call the cops. Who else is going to come get him? He could call Reggie: hell, Reggie must be wondering what's happened to him, he took off to pick up a fare and didn't call in again. If things are busy Reggie'll be mad at him too, but not as mad as Ada.

He's about to call when he realizes: he doesn't know where he is. No GPS on Grisby's phone. It's a cheap piece of crap. What's he going to say? That he's locked into an outhouse at a place not far off the Lewis Highway? Who could find him in time?

Then it has to be Jan, he decides. Wouldn't she have some clue who these guys are, and where they're holding him? He calls her number. It goes straight to voicemail, and he says, "Jan! Christ, I don't know how to explain this. Brian's militia-nut friends are looking for Bree. OK? This isn't a joke, they're deadly fucking serious. You've got to do something: find her before they do. Call the cops. OK? And while you're at it, they've shut me into an outhouse at a place off the Lewis Highway, three or four miles out of town, I guess. They've left me to freeze to death. I could use some help too," and stupidly he laughs. "Sorry, Jan. They're serious and I'm starting to lose it. And Jan? Watch your back. These guys don't mess around. They're pissed as hell about something."

The cut in his leg's seeping. A trickle runs down his thigh, a warm slide that's soon cold. He should stay still or it won't close up. Fuck that, he tells himself, if he stays still, he'll freeze to death. He tucks his hands behind his neck in the warmth of his hood and jumps up and down, just a little at first with his boots barely clearing the ground, getting his blood moving, never mind that the cut burns and his head's soupy from being hit, and his ribs are so bruised each impact makes him grunt. He thinks. He has to think. The crack between the door and the frame's bright with the last of the daylight and he keeps his eyes on it as he jumps.

Then something falls. A light thud like snow frozen onto a branch coming loose. A roll of toilet paper toppled by his jumping. He's about to kick it to one side when he realizes: this could be his salvation.

It's no easy matter to push the cardboard tube out when he can scarcely feel his hands. He wraps the toilet paper around them for warmth then lays the roll down and stamps it flat with his boots.

His breath billows out as he picks up the crushed tube and forces it into the gap between door and frame. The corner slips in, bends, sticks. The tube's still too thick. He catches a strange half-swallowed sigh, the sound of his own disappointment, like he's already leaving himself behind. He stares at the tube, then brings it to his mouth and bites down along the edges, a couple of inches on each side. He pushes it up against the crack again and shoves the end through.

The fit's so tight it's hard to move the tube up the crack, and harder still because his fingers are wrapped like a mummy's in toilet paper. The cardboard scrapes along toward the latch, then the end pushes through the crack tips down. It's caught. The latch: it's too heavy. He leans his head against the wood. Gonna die, he thinks, and he isn't afraid, just disappointed. He yanks out the cardboard tube and sits down again. Somewhere out there Bree is lonely and frightened, and now he can't help her. Fucking Grisby, he thinks. He stirred this up. First thing this morning he took off to sell Brian's guns when only a fool could be so stupid.

Outside a raven calls, tock-tock, like one piece of hollow wood hitting another. Fisher says, "Yeah yeah."

Soon he'll see Lyle leave to hunt for Bree, and when Lyle's gone he'll have nothing to do but freeze to death. In a few hours those other guys'll be back. They'll turn the wooden latch that held him in here and drag what's left of him out across the snow. Between them, they'll heave him into the bed of one of those pickups, and cover him with a tarp, and take him away to dump him. He'll just be one of the stupid fucks who tried to walk somewhere in this killing cold, and Lyle will find Bree, because really, what chance is there that Jan will do anything, even if she believes his message?

The raven again. Tock-tock. Soon it'll fly away. It'll take off from its perch high in a tree and spread its dark wings, circling over the house and this small wooden hut, then it'll tilt itself and flap off across the hillside, away from the wood smoke coming from the chimney, away from the car engine left grumbling into the quiet, away from the outhouse where Fisher will be freezing to death beneath a slanted roof of corrugated plastic. He looks up. The roof. So low over the bench seat that he could stand and easily reach it. Not much wind in these parts, he thinks. Not much need to nail down a roof too hard, and besides, those nails will have shrunk a little in the cold. He heaves himself up on the seat, never mind that the wound in his leg rips with pain. He lifts his arms high then shoves at the roof with all his might.

32

IT'S JUST TOO damn easy, that's what Fisher thinks as he
eases the cab out across the snow, steering it clumsily with
his frozen hands, down the driveway so fast it bounces and
the wheel jerks, nearly out of his hands. He forces himself to
brake. The whole time his eyes are tugged back to the mirror
because someone—surely—is going to come after him. The
road's narrow and turns sharp left. Snow sprays into the air
as the right fender cuts into the bank and he can't think, can't
tell where he is.

He drives downhill, always downhill, and too fast. He sends
the cab lurching around a beaten-up car climbing the road
toward him, sees the panic on the face of the old guy driving.
Then just past a stand of birches there's the scarlet eye of a stop
sign, and beyond it, like a miracle, the highway back to town.

❧

Here are the things Fisher discovers about suddenly being free
from death: that his thoughts are scattered like a bomb's gone off
in their midst, that he's more afraid now than he was before, and
that—where's the thrill of having survived?—his hands throb
horribly where the cold's scorched them. In fact, where doesn't
he hurt? There's his thigh, his ribs, his jaw, plus his head, inside
and out.

As he belts along the highway, he runs a hand over his scalp
and touches the swollen mass where the broom hit him, as
though he can soothe away the pain. An old pain really, con-

sidering what else he's just been through, and he's surprised by how it still hurts. Of course he can't think: everywhere he aches is a reminder of what just happened and nearly happened, and what will happen if Lyle and his militia buddies catch up with him again.

Three times he reaches out for the cab's radio, sees as his hand gropes empty air those wires hanging loose like the roots of an upended plant. He thinks: I've got to hide. He thinks: I've got to find Bree. He thinks: how the fuck am I going to do that?

He's gone miles before the minivan's warm enough for his hands to really thaw. Eventually the feeling that his blood's boiling through his skin gives way to a more insistent ache deep in his bones. He holds on tight to the steering wheel and doesn't slow down. He can't. He's so scared that he's sitting hunched low, and every vehicle that overtakes him makes him jerk his head for a look at the driver. A blonde in a sleek red coupe smoking a cigarette. An old guy with a hat pulled down to his eyes. Not Lyle, then. Not that guy with the strange egg face either.

Soon he's so close to town the route's marked by the glare of streetlights, and the late afternoon traffic surges toward him with lights ablaze. The sun's fallen away below the hills and is dragging in darkness behind it. At least the night will hide him, but hell, he's driving a minivan with a bear painted on it. How inconspicuous is that?

He needs to get across town and pick up his car. He switches lanes, brakes, is about to rush an orange light when the phone in his pocket rings. Grisby's phone.

He holds it to his ear. "Yes?"

"You come—yes? Right now." A woman's voice, hushed as though she's afraid. The foreign woman from Grisby's apartment.

"What's happened? Christ! Is it Grisby? Did he make it

back?"

"You come . . . please."

Fisher shifts his fingers on the phone. "Not now. I can't. I have to find my daughter."

"Daughter?"

"My daughter."

Her words barely make it through the phone. They're little more than disturbances on the air, but he's sure he hears, "Bree-yan, yes? You come," and she hangs up.

## 33

I T'S NIGHT BY the time Fisher pulls into the parking
lot outside Grisby's apartment, never mind that the clock
on the cab's dash reads only 4.35. The day feels over, a leaden
exhaustion weighing him down, and it's all he can do to guide
the cab between two cars and put it into park. The woman said
*Breehan*, that accent of hers tugging at the sounds. Somehow
Breehan's here, or has been found. A wash of relief slips over
him. It's all over, isn't it? The worst of it, at least.

The cold wraps around him as he swings the cab door shut.
No gloves: he should stop by the store and buy some, though
maybe Breehan won't want to, maybe she'll want to go home.
No, not home, not to her home, at any rate. So he'll have to tell
her: Brian's gone. No trace of him left. He'll explain all that
before she tells him anything. Won't that be easier?

The snow on the stairs creaks under his feet. Of course
the woman hears him before he knocks. The door opens just
enough for her to see out, to let him slip inside. She's wearing
a short purple dress and so much makeup he wouldn't have
recognized her. It makes her look not just older, but old: the
lipstick too dark, the skin around her eyes almost bruised. She
says, "Grisby? You find?"

"Grisby? No," and he shakes his head. "No, no sign of
Grisby. But Breehan—is she here?"

The woman's face tightens. "Bree-yan? I tell you, you drive,
I tell you. OK?"

"Why don't you tell me now? Is Breehan here?"

Her eyes are already on the door. "Please," she says. "We go."

His heart slips inside his chest. "Where's Bree? Tell me that, at least. Is she OK?"

She walks past him and pushes her feet into her snowboots, pulls on a parka. When she lifts her hood she says again, "We go."

Outside the world feels abandoned, the darkness thick except where lights push back at it: the yellow glow of a bulb at the end of the stairs, the twin stare of the cab's headlights. Fisher and the young woman don't say a word, but hurry through the cold with their breath leaving trails of frost behind them.

She sits in the passenger seat and presses down the door lock. She's got a quick, nervous look about her, peering around, her hands twitchy as they hold her bag on her lap. She's afraid, Fisher realizes, and now he's looking about too, staring over his shoulder, watching a car turn in from the road, bumping over the snow, and he reverses out too fast, and pulls away, too fast, and the woman grips the edge of her seat. Headlights glare in his mirror: a pickup looming so close that Fisher shields his eyes and can barely see down the road. A jolt—the pickup's hit them, and Fisher panics and stamps on the gas. He says, "Fuck it, fuck it, fuck it," like that's all there's left to say, because they've found him already. How could he have been stupid enough to come back to Grisby's place?

Beside him the woman's curled into herself on the seat. He's driving too fast. Up ahead a light turns red and he bites his teeth together and keeps his foot hard on the gas. A car's coming toward them and swerves, but the pickup's still on their tail, comes closer and closer, and Fisher accelerates, up toward the railway tracks and the small strip of stores beyond, but there's another jolt and the cab's tires shriek, another, even harder, and his head bumps against the headrest and this time he can't keep the cab straight. It swings around on itself and he brakes, but it tilts, tilts, rights itself and comes to rest just beyond the tracks. There's no escaping now because the pickup's pulled up right beside them.

You'd think someone would call the cops. You'd think someone would stop at least. But cars buzz past leaving only their exhaust muddying the air, and when Fisher turns to look out the window, a guy's standing on the passenger side with a crowbar in his hand. He brings it down hard on the hood with a dull clang then steps closer with it raised again and Fisher holds up both hands in surrender.

The woman lowers the window and cold air rushes in. The guy wipes his nose on the back of his glove, says to Fisher, "Sorry about your cab, mister, this isn't about you," and he leans toward the girl. "Where's that freak Grisby? Huhn?"

She shakes her head quickly.

"C'mon," he says, "I ain't got time for this." His face has bunched up, his mouth small and angry.

"Hey," and Fisher spreads his hands, "she doesn't know where he is."

"She's fucking with me," and he swings the crowbar. It hits the wing mirror and it dangles like a dead thing, wires exposed, glass shattered. He glances at Fisher. "Sorry, mister. The insurance'll cover it, right?" Then he holds the crowbar at the open window. "You ain't gonna be worth much to Grisby with your face all smashed in. You tell me where he is, or no one down at the Mirage is gonna pay to fuck you again."

She shies away from the window. She says, "Gone. Men, this morning. Took him."

"Then you pay me back. Five hundred bucks. Got it?"

She shakes her head. "No have."

"Sure you do. How many tricks you turn last night? I saw you down at the Mirage. You weren't home washing your hair."

"You ask Grisby. He have five hundred bucks."

The guy sucks in his breath. "Nice little arrangement Grisby's got himself. He clears out for the evening, you turn your tricks, and he comes home to a warmed-up girlfriend and cash for his Hawaii fund. Oh yeah, I know all about that. Thing is," and he presses the end of the crowbar under the woman's chin, "he's not gonna get to Hawaii by ripping people off. Not in a town this small. You pay me back and I'll forget about it. OK?"

Her head's tilted up away from the crowbar, but her hands are at her bag, tugging at the zip.

"Nice and slow," the guys tells her. "You try anything, you're gonna lose some teeth."

In her hand, a roll of bills. With the crowbar under her chin she can't look down, can't do more than pass the money to him, and he plucks it out of her grip. "That'll do nicely," and he stuffs the whole roll into his pocket and the woman, her face all stiff, her mouth jerking, raises the window then folds over on herself. "Go," she tells Fisher at last, "we go now."

## 34

F ISHER'S HANDS ARE shaking. He pulls over at the strip mall because he doesn't trust himself to drive, not until the fear thrashing inside him subsides. He turns to the woman. "You could've told me."

Her face swings toward him. Under their makeup, her eyes and mouth are dark and sinister.

He says, "You knew he was waiting, didn't you? That's why you were afraid—that's why you called. And now look," and he nods at the dented hood, the wing mirror dangling from its mount.

She turns away. "Who help me? No one. Grisby—where he gone? Not come back, and man shouts at door. Angry, very angry. Not go away."

His hands are still on the wheel and he leans his head against them. "But someone else came over too. Breehan."

Her eyes are glassy and wide. "Breehan gone. Colorado," and her tongue trips on those four syllables.

"What?"

"Gone. Colorado."

"So she came by the apartment? Fuck," and he closes his eyes for a moment. He let himself be taken by the militia, had been so pleased with himself because he thought he was going to find Bree and rescue her, and all the time she'd been in town planning her own escape. Maybe she came by his house, and of course he was out. So what did she do? She came by Grisby's place.

The woman must be watching him. She leans close now and says softly, "You drive. Mirage Club. OK?"

Down at the parking lot beside Bear Cabs Co., some fucker's unplugged his car. Reggie, Fisher thinks. It's just the sort of small-minded crap he'd get up to.

Everything's stiff: the door, the steering wheel, and when he tries to crank the engine, nothing happens. The seat's like a block of ice beneath him. Bree's taken off to Colorado. Brian's dead. Grisby . . . well, who the hell knows for sure.

He locks up the car, plugs the cord back into the socket by the wall and takes off in the cab, the broken wing mirror banging against the door. Fuck Reggie, he thinks, fuck them all.

## 35

WHEN FISHER GETS to the supermarket checkout, the cashier gives him a look that runs from his head to his boots and back again, then won't look at him any more, as though the sight of him bothers her. He watches her ring up his purchases and stuff them into bags, is ready with a couple of bills to shove at her, then snatches up his shopping and heads for the washroom. In the mirror he stares at himself: his parka's torn, his jeans stained with blood, his eyes watery as undercooked eggs, and on the top of his head sits the ski mask, all bunched up. A thug's hat. He has to admit he looks like a man who's been up to no good.

He shuts himself into a stall and unzips his jeans. His fingers are raw from being frozen, and his longjohns peel painfully off the wound on his thigh. The cut's smaller than he imagined, but still oozing. Blood's run all the way down to his socks and crusted in his leg hair. He wipes what he can with toilet paper, then fumbles with the ointment he's bought. He tries to close the wound with butterfly stitches, only they stick to his fingers, and the plastic bag hanging from his wrist, and by the time he gets them on there isn't much stick left to them.

The effort's left him sweating. He lets himself out of the cubicle and yanks off the ski mask. One short toss and it's in the trash. He holds onto the washbasin as though he might be sick. The wound's stinging deep down into his muscle, and it's riling up all the other pains he's suffered. At least he bought some ibuprofen, and he pops open the bottle and shakes four into his hand. To tide him over, he thinks. Until he's driven home and can take some of the Vicodin Grisby left him. The thought of those little white pills hangs golden and warm in his mind.

The faucet's low, but he holds his head under it and rubs in soap from the dispenser. The swelling on his skull feels overripe, like it's about to burst. An old guy with a pinched face pushes open the door. He gives Fisher a quick glance and looks away, says, "We've all been there," and shuts himself into a stall.

Fisher dries his hair as best he can on a paper towel, and his face too, then he digs into the plastic bag. He pulls the tag off the hat he's just bought, a green woolen thing with *The Last Frontier* embroidered across the front. He's bought gloves too, and he slips them on as he walks out into the lobby where the ceiling heaters shed their red glow, and the air's hot and cold like milk heated too quickly.

The afternoon's barely over and already it feels like it's been night forever. His hair's still damp. Even with the hat on, it chills his head the moment he steps outside. But that's better than the ski mask with its stink of greasy skin and cigarette smoke and besides, the cold makes him hurry, the plastic bag swinging against his hip.

Already his hands are aching, despite his new gloves. They haven't forgotten the awful cold of the outhouse, won't forget it for months, for years, perhaps. He thinks about calling Jan and telling her Bree's OK, that she's gone down to the States, to Colorado, of all places. Soon, he thinks. First he's going to drive home and let Pax out, he's going to put the pizza he's just bought in the oven, then he's going to take a Vicodin and watch an old movie, John Wayne maybe, then he's going to sleep. Tomorrow? Well, Reggie's not going to swallow a story about being kidnapped, and another guy taking a crowbar to the cab. He'll have to come up with something else: a fare who went nuts and knocked him out—he has the lump on his head to prove it—but hell, how's he going to explain not calling the cops? Fuck Reggie, then. He'll buy some new clothes and get a haircut and apply to City Cabs, and if they don't want him, hell, he'll try Northstar Cabs, or Eagle Cabs. And this time things won't get fucked up.

He's bought duct tape and he tries to tape up the smashed mirror. It's too cold for the glue to stick—he should've known that—and besides, he hasn't got the patience, not now. He tosses the duct tape onto the floor and steers the cab out onto Airport Road with the mirror still banging against the door. It's the end of the workday and traffic's heavy, or as heavy as it ever gets in a town this small. In places ice fog hangs like cotton wadding, in others the air's so clear that the lights of the town seem polished and hopeful. Fisher follows along behind a red Subaru, watches the warm gleam of its taillights all the way through town and out along the highway to his turn-off where he slows, gently, drives across the earth bridge that bends across the old dredge pit, then he guns the cab up the hill. Here the trees close in like a tunnel leading him home. The cab lurches over ruts, squeals in the hollow at the corner and there, behind the trees, is his porch light, reeling him in.

He pulls up and turns off the engine. Silence washes over him. He sits there for long enough to take a few breaths and let them out slowly. This time yesterday he pulled up here and Grisby was beside him. Everything looked the same. The porch light shining out, the snow banked up along the path to the trailer, the timbers of his unfinished house behind like a broken box. Grisby. Have the militia guys killed him, he wonders? Did they lock him up to freeze to death too? Or did he get away? But if he got away, where's he now? An urge tugs at him: go find Grisby. But he's too worn out, too beaten down, to even think of doing anything.

It takes an effort to open the door, to pick up his bag of

groceries through his thick new gloves, to root through the snow for the end of the electrical cord and plug in the cab. It's stiff and he has to force the metal prongs into the plastic. Then he walks the few yards to his trailer and up the steps with his key in his hand.

He doesn't have a chance to use it, though. The door opens and there, with a gun held casually like this is all a joke, stands Mr Egg Face.

## 36

MR EGG FACE isn't alone. Behind him, in Fisher's re-cliner with a can of beer in his hand, sits Lyle. "You are so *freaking* stupid," he says. "You go to all that effort to escape, then you come *home?*" He rubs his chin with the back of his hand. "I mean, for fuck's sake, Mikey. I didn't think you were *that* dumb."

Mr Egg Face has a knitted hat pulled down to where his eyebrows should be and it lends him a sullen babyish look. He gives Fisher a shove and the groceries knock against his leg. "I was supposed to have a date tonight—now look how I'm spending it, you asshole."

Lyle gets to his feet and the recliner squeaks. "Christ, shut the fuck up, Al."

Pax is huddled by the wall in the kitchen. He looks up at Fisher, doesn't lift his head or wag his tail, just glances up then away, as though in warning. Then Fisher sees it: a pile of clothes on the floor. Brian's. Shirts, pants, underwear. Beside it, gaping open, Brian's bag with its silky lining ripped and its mesh pockets torn loose. One of these guys has taken a knife to it and a shiver of fear runs through Fisher.

Lyle tilts back his head to take a gulp of beer. His adam's apple sticks out like a knot on a branch. The underside of his chin is so pale it's like it's never seen the sun. He wipes his lips on the back of his hand and belches. "You even buy shitty beer, Mikey. You're a total fucking loser and always have been." He empties the can onto the carpet in a twist-ing yellow stream, then drops it and stomps it flat. "Now, why don't you tell me what that bag was doing in your closet?"

The label's gone—how the hell did they know it's Brian's? He thinks, Ada. Lyle called her, or she called him. Christ—does she know he's in the militia? Has she always known?

Fisher's tongue has turned heavy in his mouth. He can barely make it say, "It's just a bag, Lyle."

Lyle smiles. His two front teeth are crooked and he has a habit of holding up his hand to cover them, so Fisher's not ready when that hand belts him across the face and sends him staggering against his sofa. For a moment his arms wheel, the plastic bag looping through the air, then he falls against the cushions.

Lyle's mouth is pulled into a thin smile. "You fucking liar."

Behind him Al stoops and snatches up the bag of chips fallen from Fisher's groceries. He rips it open and cradles it against his chest, the gun in his right hand pointed at Fisher and the left feeding chips into his mouth. He says, "Want me to shoot him?"

Lyle doesn't look away from Fisher. "No, fuckhead, because then he won't be able to tell us where Brian is."

Al looks around him, licking crumbs from his lips. "How about I shoot the dog? He stinks anyway."

Lyle holds up one finger. "First let's see if he can remember where Brian's hiding." He bends from the waist toward where Fisher's lying on the sofa and says gently. "Is it coming back to you, Mikey?"

Fisher's too hot. His hands, his head, his face, they're pulsing with the warmth of his blood and a tremble's started up in his gut. "Brian's dead. How many times do I have to tell you guys? I dumped him in the river."

Al walks over to the kitchen. He takes a chip from the bag and holds it out to Pax who barely sniffs it before letting his head sink back onto his paws. Al balances the chip on Pax's nose, and another, and the dog shuts his eyes.

Lyle sighs. "But somehow Brian's bag ended up here. Isn't that weird? I mean, it's like you're looking after it for him. You know, in case he decided to go someplace, like, say, Colorado."

So Ada did read the label. *Colorado.* Fisher hears it again in his head with the syllables off kilter. That's how the foreign woman said it. *Breehan gone. Colorado.* And he understands now. She found the luggage label. She took it from his pocket after she hit him with the broom. He'd ripped it off the bag while Ada was here and stuffed it into his jeans. The label that he wrote. That he'd meant to make it look like Brian had left town. Brian. Or, if you were foreign, *Bree-yan.*

Breehan isn't safe. She hasn't gone to Colorado. She's still hiding, all alone because Fisher gave up looking for her.

He hears a sigh and braces himself, imagines Lyle's hand smacking into his face again, or a boot catching him in the groin, but instead Lyle, stupid, lazy, rat-faced Lyle, saunters to the kitchen. He takes the bag of chips from Al and tries one. "Do you only buy cheap crap?" he says and tips them out over Pax like a fall of petals, then drops the bag on him too. From the pocket of his flannel shirt he takes a pack of cigarettes, lights one, and pulls his lips tight against his teeth as he sucks in the smoke. Next he snaps his fingers at Al, who swings his round bland face toward him.

Al says, "What?"

"Your gun, fuckhead," and Lyle holds out his hand.

"Use your own. I mean, what the hell?"

But Lyle snatches it from him and Al shoves his empty hands into his jeans pockets.

Lyle turns the gun over like he's never seen one before. He says, "Thing is, Mikey, we're busy men. We've got better things to do than ask you nicely a dozen fucking times where Brian fucking Armstrong's hiding out." He plucks the cigarette from his lips and forms his mouth in an odd O-shape. Out of it floats an off-center smoke ring. He tilts his head to watch it wobble and fade. "Last chance, Mikey."

Fisher gets to his feet. "C'mon Lyle," he says, but his voice sounds lost. "I've told you, he's dead."

Lyle lifts the gun and shoots. The sound's curiously flat. The dog's body jerks and the legs splay out. One's missing a paw. It ends in a bloody stump, and a soul-curdling whine fills the trailer.

Lyle looks at the end of the gun, then lets it hang loose from his hand. "Feel like telling us now, do you? 'Cos I'm just getting started."

Pax is trying to get to his feet. His claws are scraping against the floor and blood's everywhere, like he's scratched it up out of the linoleum. He slides in it, his eyes on Fisher, and when at last he heaves himself up, Lyle kicks him under the chin. Pax flies against the wall, a ghost of a dog with a flaring red stump where a paw should be.

Fisher's barreling across the room. Fuck them, he thinks, fuck anyone who'd shoot a goddamn dog, then the gun's pointed at him and he keeps going until Al kicks his legs out from beneath him. From the floor he yells, "Christ, he's just an old dog. What's wrong with you?"

Lyle's turns the gun back to Pax. "Five . . . four . . ."

"He's hiding out someplace. Wouldn't tell me where. OK? OK?"

Pax is on his feet again but he's shaking hard.

"Three . . ."

Fisher's on his knees. He crawls toward his dog and lays a hand on his head. "Fuck—of course he didn't tell me where! He wanted me to keep the bag in case—in case he decided to fly down to the States. Wasn't going to go home again and pack, was he?"

Lyle's thin face has twisted. Deep under his brow, his eyes

are nothing but dark specks. "Down to the States—listen to you. You sound like a good ol' sourdough, don't you? Except for the fact everything you said's a pile of crap." He lifts the gun again, cocks an eyebrow. "Where is he?"

"I don't know. He's a shit—I'd tell you if I knew, if—"

That flat sound again and Pax's old body judders. The white fur of his chest is a slick red, then he's still. All Fisher can hear is his own breath. When he looks up the gun's aimed at his crotch. Lyle spits, "Talk, you fucker."

Fisher's filling his mouth with words, any old words, anything to fend off Lyle and the bullet about to come at him, when a phone rings. He recognizes the bland bleating. His phone. The skin around Lyle's eyes tightens. He gestures at Al, and Al pulls Fisher's phone out of his coat pocket and slaps it into Lyle's hand. Lyle says, "Y'allo?" Then his eyes widen in delight. "No, but this is his phone... Well, he's kinda busy. What's this about?" He bends his head to listen. "No, this is a friend of his ... Oh sure ... Yup ... Really? ... Just a second." He stares at the phone for a moment, then presses a button and Fisher hears Jan's voice all tinny through the speaker saying, "Mike? You there? You've got to help me—you saw the paper, didn't you? And Brian's taken off with Bree. Christ, I could kill him. You there?"

"Yeah," he calls back. "But I thought you were supposed to take her to Anchorage."

A sigh. "She was being a little bitch. So I come home and ..." She stops, like she can't find the words.

"You want me to find her?" His voice is knotted up.

"You sound weird, Mike."

"I'm OK."

"Can you go after them? Out to the cabin?"

Fisher says, "The cabin?"

"Your mom's old cabin. Brian sold it for you like he said,

Mike, only he bought it for himself. Christ, even I didn't know," and she laughs, "not until Marcie asked what he was doing out at Moose Lake all those weekends. I thought he was off camping in the White Mountains. That's what he told me." She laughs again and the sound of it makes Fisher wince. "Now I'm worried. Real worried. He's got himself mixed up in some dangerous stuff." He can hear her breathing, too fast like she's been running. "He's gone too far, way too far. But why'd he have to take Bree?" and her voice catches.

"I don't know, Jan. It's not like they ever got on."

She's crying now, her voiced stretched and loose. "It's been so hard. The last few years. I was . . . well, we all make plans, don't we? But for now, we have to find Bree. They're watching me, the cops are, and you know how Brian can be. He might do something crazy."

Fisher cranes his head closer to the phone. "It's all right, Jan. I'll find her. I'll head out there tonight, OK? And the moment I find her, I'll let you know."

"Want me to take care of Pax?"

Fisher can't bear to look where what's left of his dog is lying at the foot of the wall. "No," he says quietly, too quietly probably, then more loudly, "Pax's dead. But—look, if you don't hear from me, call Ada. Tell her Lyle's coming with me. He's Brian's friend, after all."

"Who's Lyle?"

"Her neph—"

But Lyle jerks the phone away. "Talk to you later, Jan," then he turns it off. He rounds on Fisher. "You smartass fucker," he says. He balls his fist and goes to hit Fisher, but Fisher ducks. When he straightens up Lyle's aiming the gun at his crotch again. "I don't forget crap like that, you hear me? You'll pay for it, well and good." He steps closer. "Now, where's this place?"

"On Moose Lake."

"Christ, which fucking Moose Lake?"

"The one out by Tomlin."

He calls out to Al, "Make some coffee, for fuck's sake, and find a thermos."

Al runs a hand over his head. "You're fucking joking. I'm not driving all the way out there in this kinda cold."

"Think about it, Al—how else we gonna find him? And if we don't . . ."

They give each other a grim look, then Al starts opening cupboard doors and slamming drawers, and the whole time he's muttering under his breath, "Fucking Moose Lake, fuck."

## 37

T HE WHOLE WAY out of town, Fisher wonders about
something: when Lyle slammed the door of the trailer
shut and saw the cab parked in the driveway, he let out a roar
of laughter and said, "The cab? You're kidding me. This is too
fucking perfect."

Only it isn't, is it? The cab's too conspicuous to be perfect.
That's what bothers Fisher as he takes the highway east with
Lyle in the passenger seat and Al following in his truck, too
close for comfort, the headlights glazing the inside of the cab
and glinting off the rearview mirror so that he curses, quietly,
as he drives. It doesn't help that Lyle lights up and won't crack
his window. He sits with his seatbelt strapped across his chest
and a gun in his lap, and every now and then he says something
like, "You don't even drive good. Isn't there anything you can do
right?" or "Don't try anything clever, Mikey, you're not up to it."

It's hard for Fisher to keep his mind on what he's doing.
Instead of the minivan's headlights spilling out ahead of the
hood, he sees Pax juddering as he died, and his leg with its
paw blown away. In a few weeks Pax'd have been dead anyway,
but to die like that—into the darkness Fisher says to himself
over and over, I'm sorry, Pax, I should've saved you. The fact
that he didn't, or couldn't, stirs up an anger that sticks in his
throat, and makes him drive too fast, taking the curves sloppily,
making Lyle sway and hold onto his seat until he lifts the gun
and pushes it into the soft skin beneath Fisher's ear. "Cut it out."

"Or what? How d'you plan on finding the cabin without
me?"

Lyle shoves the barrel harder into Fisher's neck. He cries out and the van swerves. "There's always your ex. I can have one of our men go pick her up. You want that? Huhn?"

Fisher doesn't say a word, but slows the van and hunches over the wheel looking as defeated as he can until the cold barrel of the gun lifts away. But he's thinking, why haven't the militia picked her up already? What's to stop them? Then he realizes: Jan said she thought the cops were watching her. A dead cop found on her porch. Hell, yeah, they'd watch her. They're waiting for Brian to show up, or for her to try and contact him. A cop-killer: they're going to go all out to find him. But so's the militia. To turn him in? To get the heat off them? Something about it doesn't make sense. Gun nuts like Brian's buddies don't help the cops, not ever. Besides, why would Brian leave the dead cop on his own deck? Was he planning to dump him after he'd taken care of Bree? But hell, you don't end up naked in your step-daughter's bathroom if you're trying to shut her up for good. Not unless someone is trying to set you up.

Now Fisher wonders: what if Brian didn't kill the cop? What if one of the other guys did? He remembers Zane sitting beside him in the car—hell, just this morning—the hoops of his earrings catching the light, sucking hard on his cigarette between telling Fisher what he thought had gone down before Bree fled: the militia guys holding a meeting, the cop snooping around. But why leave him on the deck? A warning to the rest of the cops? A warning to Brian? But the Commander, Fisher thinks, sounded pissed, like everything had got fucked up. That voice full of menace. That foot kicking hard into his belly. Anything to get Fisher to spit out what he knew about Brian.

The Commander's the guy who's been telling the IRS to go fuck themselves, Fisher realizes, the guy Zane was talking about, the guy that's been in the news. Getting hauled into court, saying he was a sovereign citizen, pulling all that crap to get out of paying Uncle Sam, and rounding up a bunch of shit-for-brains guys with guns as back-up.

He must have expected things to turn out differently. Only, Brian's vanished and now the militia are the ones running scared.

Before long there are no headlights coming toward them and no taillights up ahead. The few lit-up signs for bars or small stores have fallen away. The world's nothing but icy blacktop, an occasional row of mailboxes where a side road branches off, and Al's headlights shining into the cab.

Lyle's so close Fisher hears the bright rustle of paper burning whenever he takes a drag on his cigarette. Already his head's clogged from the smoke, his thoughts slow and awkward. Fucking Lyle, he thinks, fucking little shit that he is. That laugh when he stepped outside and saw the minivan, as though Fisher had obliged him without knowing it. But that doesn't make sense. Neither does the fact that they didn't bring sleeping bags or blankets, didn't stop for supplies at the grocery store, are driving a hundred and fifty miles in the darkness with nothing more than a thermos of coffee.

It's years since he's been out to the old place. Fuck Brian, he thinks, buying the place on the sly, like there had to be something dirty about it. He went out there every summer with his dad until his dad ballooned up from sitting around so much at the motel, and eating donuts and candy and chips like he just couldn't stop himself. Even carrying their supplies the couple of dozen yards from the truck up the path to the cabin got to be too much for his dad and he made excuses for not going out there, and soon Fisher stopped asking.

Ada must have thought the cabin was his dad's. Maybe his dad let her believe that because, after Fisher got married, after Bree was born and things had started going wrong between him and Jan, somehow it had slipped out that the place was Fisher's and always had been. Ada worked on Fisher until he sold it. A fresh start for him, she said, a nest egg it was time to hatch out. He thought about going to the community college and getting a diploma—as a mechanic, maybe, because he was handy at fixing things—but that didn't work out. Besides, Ada had other ideas. A new roof for the motel, and a paint job inside and out, new furniture too, and he spent the whole summer fixing up the place without getting paid a dime. She said it made him a business partner, that he'd get a share of the profits. But when has Ada ever given him any of the profits? The one time he brought it up, she rounded on him with her cigarette held high, asked if he didn't think she'd done enough for him, buying him books for school, making sure he had clothes and shoes and snowboots, feeding him, and what had she asked for in return? He should have told her: hours of cleaning motel rooms, and picking gum off carpets, and scraping dried puke off bathroom walls. But he didn't. He knew he'd lost.

And of all things, Brian bought the place and never told him. A sick feeling wells up in Fisher's gut. Was it Jan who suggested he use Armstrong Realty to sell it? Was she already sleeping with Brian back then? Or did that damned place somehow throw her into Brian's path?

He wonders, is he cursed? Is he weak? Does he bring bad luck to everyone? To Pax, who should have slipped quietly from this world when his old heart gave out? To Jan, who was easy prey for someone like Brian? To Bree? To Grisby, because what the hell's become of him? Did they let him go when he told them how to find Fisher? Or has he been dumped like garbage out in the woods and won't be found until spring?

No wonder this trip feels doomed. It is doomed. Even if they make it out to the cabin, what are Al and Lyle going to do when they find out Brian's not there? And if Bree's hiding in the cabin, she'll be scared out of her mind when she sees two vehicles drive up. But is she there? She doesn't have her license, she's never driven anywhere. Why would she drive Brian's car a hundred and fifty miles through the crushing cold of January just to hide out when she could have taken a plane to Anchorage and vanished?

He hopes she's there, and dreads it too. One thing's for sure: he needs a plan, and he drives with his face bunched up, trying to think, as though somehow one will come to him.

# 38

WHEN LYLE'S HEAD starts to roll and drop and jerk up, Fisher pretends not to notice. He stares out the windshield at the snow along the road, doesn't shift his grip on the wheel, doesn't sniff though he's dying to, doesn't cough despite the pressure building in his chest. Out of the corner of his eye he watches the bounce of Lyle's head, and only when it comes to rest against the back of the seat, and a hollow snoring starts up, does he drag off his glove with his teeth. First he reaches for his own seatbelt. He pulls it over his chest and jams the tongue into the buckle. Next he lets his bare hand reach toward Lyle's buckle. He doesn't even glance at what he's doing. He feels for the release: a click then the belt sighs as it slips up across Lyle's chest. The ripple of his snore doesn't change.

Good enough, Fisher thinks. He glances at Lyle's lap. He's still cradling the gun but there's no helping that now and he accelerates until the road's reeling dizzyingly under the hood. Then he takes a breath. He braces his arms against the wheel and stamps on the brake.

The force of it throws him forward and the seatbelt cuts into his neck. Beside him Lyle's flung against the windshield like a doll. There's a crack as his skull hits the glass, and his face bursts open in shock. The gun tumbles into the darkness at his feet.

The cab's spinning, tipping, and Fisher can't help it, he wants to save himself, and he steers into the slide. A flash of snow, of gaunt black trunks, of headlights bearing down on him, then the cab's going slower, straighter. Fisher glances beside him. Lyle's slumped between the dash and the seat. He moans and Fisher's reaching out, that damned seatbelt that just saved him pinning him down now. He releases it, steering wildly with one hand, grabs for the shiny metal finger of the passenger doorhandle. Impossible to open it like this. He brakes again and the cab swoops. It's almost at a stop and he throws himself across the seat and shoves the door wide.

The dome light blinks on and cold air rushes in. Lyle's got both hands over his head but he understands, he's ready when Fisher leans back and kicks with both legs. He shields his chest with his arms then fumbles for a grip. One hand hooks itself over the edge of the seat, the other on the doorframe. His face is a mass of blood. One eye's shut, the other glares at Fisher as he kicks again. Fisher's boot glances off Lyle's chest, and again. Fisher heaves himself across the cab and lets his weight fall against Lyle's shoulders. One of Lyle's hands comes free but the other's still clinging to the doorframe. Their faces are only a few inches apart. The stink of blood's everywhere and the cold's closing in, drowning them like seawater. Lyle butts his head forward. Fisher's not fast enough. The blow grazes the side of his head, then Lyle's face is buried in Fisher's coat. Fisher understands: Lyle's reaching for the floor, his hand's searching, lifting, holding the gun up, black and shining in the meager glow of the dome light.

Fisher flails against him. His hands claw at that bloodied face, and as the gun swings its eye toward him, he lashes out. His knuckles hit something knobbly and resistant. Lyle's gasping. He's hit him in the throat. Fisher heaves himself forward, never mind Lyle's weight or the gun that threshes the air beside his ear. Lyle's hand snatches at his parka. The fingers grip, slip off. Fisher punches out then Lyle's weight's gone, and the light changes because there's Lyle's falling onto the gleaming snow with his arms splayed and his mouth wide.

No wonder the snow's gleaming. Al's pickup. The head-lights are dazzling around Al as he runs toward the cab. Fisher scrambles. His knee hits the steering wheel, his elbow bumps the window. He jerks the steering wheel to send the cab back out into the road and his foot's searching for the gas pedal because there's Al with his pale egg of a face, and he's holding onto the doorframe, and Fisher's not even looking where he's going. He's staring at Al, sees his mouth widen as Fisher's foot hits the gas and the cab jolts off along the road. The dark chips of Al's eyes soften, his face strains, then he's gone. Fisher guns the engine and sends the cab screaming down the road with the door open and the dome light on, everything the light touches looking small and shabby.

❧

He drives like the devil himself is chasing him. Off along the straight stretch of road where the snow folds away on both sides, staring past the web of cracks where Lyle's head smashed into the glass and there, twitching green across the sky in electric waves, is the aurora, magnificent tonight when nothing deserves to be.

Fisher lets himself laugh and the sound of it sets him on edge because there's something crazy about it. It's miles before he stops and shuts the door. By then the cab's bone-achingly cold.

## 39

FISHER GETS GAS in Sumner. A wind has picked up and scours his face as he watches the numbers on the pump change. Every few seconds he turns his whole upper body so that he can peer out the funnel of his hood. Along the highway comes a pair of headlights, and another, but they slide on by.

Fisher wonders: just how badly hurt was Lyle? Bad enough for Al to drive back to town? Or is Lyle just bruised and furious, and right at this moment he and Al are scanning the few bright lights of Sumner, looking for him? And here he is, under the glaring lamps of the gas station, beside his ridiculous cab with its ridiculous bear logo. Thinking about it gives him the shivers worse than the cold. The pump clicks off and he fumbles the cap, has to try three times before it catches on the thread. By then he's all twitchy with fear. He wants to take off into the darkness but he knows better than that; what chance will he stand if he leaves without supplies? What good will he be to Bree if he arrives with no food, no nothing?

If she's even there, he reminds himself. This is just his best bet, that's all.

He parks around the back of Sumner's small supermarket where the mouths of the dumpsters gape with half-flattened boxes. Inside there's a deli and a bakery, and Fisher's so hungry saliva wells up in his mouth in painful spurts before he's even decided he has to eat, because what good will he be to Bree half sick from hunger?

The woman behind the counter has her black ballcap pushed way back as though to tell the world she doesn't care about the acne scars that pock her forehead and cheeks. She holds out an order form and a stub of pencil. "Closing up in a few minutes—all we got's what's in the cooler." She turns away.

"Just give me a pastrami on rye."

She's wiping down a plastic chopping board. She doesn't turn around until she's leaned it against the wall. "All we got's what's in the cooler." Her voices presses a little harder on the words this time, like he must be stupid.

But it's hard to look in the cooler when his eyes are tugged toward the doors. Every time a customer leaves those doors whoosh open, and he's so afraid that his chest turns hollow and the air seems too thin to support him. He's barely looking at the dishes of cut meats and salads laid out in front of him. Instead he sees Lyle falling backward out of the cab with his arms stretched like a diver's and his face taut with shock, sees the door hang open for a moment, and Al's face like a demon's. He remembers the surge of relief that made him shove his boot hard on the gas, and how the door had swung and flapped for miles until he stopped to close it. But it wasn't just relief. There'd been a measure of raw joy in it too: Lyle's hands grabbing at his parka, his fingers slipping, the weight of him suddenly and deliciously gone. Lyle, lazy fuckhead Lyle, Lyle who's so psycho, so sick in his head, that he shot Pax.

The supermarket doors slide open and Fisher's eyes jerk up. A man. His breath catches. An old guy with a face sharp as an ax. Not Lyle. Not Al.

Behind the counter the woman has given up on him. She's rinsing out containers in a hiss of water. He looks at the order pad: a mass of choices his head's too clogged to make sense of. He calls out, "Just give me a cold cut on whatever bread. OK?"

"Choose your cold cut from the cooler, and mark it down on your order form."

He makes himself stare at the steel dishes. Most of them

are empty. Some have a spoonful or two of what looks like egg salad or tuna mayonnaise. On others slices of ham lie greasy and limp. But what the hell. "A ham sandwich. OK? Just give me a ham goddamn salad sandwich." He slaps the order form onto the cooler. "And a rootbeer."

Her lips vanish and two creases appear on her brow, thin and deep as claw marks. She doesn't look up.

"Be back for it in a minute," he says, but she keeps her head down over the bread she's buttering for him.

A line of yellow bearpaw prints leads toward the back of the store and out through a pair of swinging doors to the bathrooms. There's something bleak about the backrooms of stores, something that makes the lights and packages and shining fruit laid out up front seem as luring and ill-intentioned as a trap. You push through the doors with their scuff marks and blurred plastic windows, and in an instant the light's thin, the walls stacked with pallets of plastic-wrapped boxes, and the air's slippery with the smells of cleaning fluid and old coffee, because this is what life really is.

On one wall hangs a clock for employees to punch in, a handwritten notice in lazy capitals above it saying, YOU MUST CLOCK OUT ON BREAK OR BE DOCKED AN HOUR'S PAY! THIS MEANS YOU! Here the pawprints are grimy and their yellow paint flaking away. In the corner, propped up like a drunk, a mop stands upended in a metal bucket, and Fisher catches the piney stink of disinfectant, a smell that reminds him of throwing up at school in the corner of the classroom and being given the mop to clean up, because didn't he know better?

The men's bathroom reeks of smoke and a cigarette butt's floating in the toilet bowl. Fisher's hands are cold against his dick, and his dick's soft and damp in his hands. As he pisses the butt bobs like a lost ship and tiredness drags at him, like part of him's escaping. The warmth of his soul maybe. It's just leaking away and there's no stopping it. With a shiver he tucks his dick back into his boxers. For a moment he thinks about checking the cut on his thigh. It's stinging, of course it is. But what can he do about it? Instead he zips up his fly and turns away.

The washroom sink's gray with dirt and the faucet so loose it wobbles then gushes when he barely touches it. He rubs soap and water over his face, then stares at himself in the mirror over the paper towel he dries himself with. Twenty-four hours and he's a changed man. Before he had the forlorn look of the abandoned. Now he could be a long-time drunk, or a guy living homeless, his face bruised and pale, his stubble uneven, his eyes with a desperate look. Who's he to save Breehan? he thinks. Who's he trying to kid?

The small supermarket feels like a place out of the past, before stores grew so big that you couldn't call out to someone from one end to the other. Its ceiling's low and the shelves reach just below head-height. He pays for his sandwich and steers a small cart across the worn linoleum. It's light as a toy, at least until he piles in cans of chilli, baked beans, spaghetti and meatballs, ravioli, condensed milk, then bottles and jars of everything from water to powdered coffee to apple sauce, plus sugar, and chocolate, toilet paper, even a couple of cheap dusty sleeping bags stuffed into a bottom shelf because hell, there's nothing more dumb than heading off to a cabin that's miles from nowhere with no supplies. At least, back in the days when he was driving a truck up to Prudhoe Bay, through hundreds of miles of nothing, he always took off with a shitload of supplies, never mind that he had God's own luck and never broke down, or not for long enough to need them.

He eats his sandwich as he goes, leaving wisps of shredded lettuce on the floor, wiping his lips on the back of his hand. At the end of one aisle, in a dim corner where the light doesn't quite reach, he runs his hands over pocketknives hanging from a display. Cheap crap, he thinks, not knives that'll become a familiar weight in your pocket, that you'd use every day, several times a day. Like the knife Al took from him, a good goddamn knife, for all it was one he'd taken from a fare who wouldn't pay or couldn't pay. And now, when he needs a knife most, he doesn't have one and is looking at these pieces of junk. One of them has a can opener and a decent blade, a screwdriver, a small fork even. Better than nothing, if not by much.

It's a serious business, this venturing out into the heart of winter: one slip and you're a goner. You forget to bring matches. The small gas bottle doesn't fit your camp stove. You lock your keys in your car. You let the cabin door snap shut behind you when you're in nothing more than a sweatshirt and underwear, because you were just stepping outside for a piss. Then the cold swamps you. Even now, in the warmth of this supermarket, Fisher remembers the crush of the cold when he was locked in the outhouse. Dear God, he thinks, and Bree's out there somewhere. She's not prepared. She's the sort of dumb kid who wears sneakers in January to look cool. The few times he took her camping—at Blair Lake and down in the state park—she sat in the car until he'd set up the tent, then sat in the tent with her knees folded up to her chest and said, "What now?"

Ahead of him at the checkout is a sinewy old woman in work jeans and huge white bunny boots. Beneath her hat her hair shows as rough and gray as iron. She stares shamelessly into Fisher's cart then sucks in her lips like she's seen it all before, that there's something he's doing wrong, poor fuck.

Fisher's purchases fill six plastic bags to bursting. They hang from his hands and bang against his legs. In the small foyer he sets them down and digs around for the pocketknife. It's a job and a half to get it out of its plastic, then there it is, a bright red lozenge in his palm. He stares at it for long enough that it looks like something he'd own, then slips it into his pocket.

Outside the cold makes the wound in his thigh smart but he walks slowly, slowly enough to let his eyes search the glow condensed beneath the parking lot's few lights. He keeps to the shadows as he makes his way around the building. There's the cab, the eyes of the cartoon bear eerily distinct in the darkness. Already it's cold inside and the steering wheel stiff as he does a u-turn and heads back to the road. Headlights behind him. A small silver car. He eases the cab onto the highway heading east. He's so pleased with himself he doesn't notice the pickup that slides out onto the road behind him and no wonder: its headlights are off. By the time Fisher does notice it—when the driver flicks on the lights just where the streetlights of Sumner give out—it's too late. The town, such as it is, is gone.

※

You'd think there'd be something Fisher could do to escape his pursuers. And there is, he tells himself, there surely is. He just hasn't put his finger on it. He could lead Al and Lyle away from Bree—but then, how will he find her? Besides, there aren't many roads to turn off on, not out here, and everything's telescoped in by the darkness. You want to turn off? You peer down the beams of your headlights for the pea-green of a road sign, and in an instant, there it is, just a few yards away, half hidden under a layer of frost. Too late. You've passed it.

The lights of the pickup distract him, as does the uneven thunk-thunk of the broken wing mirror banging against the cab door. He needs to think. He reaches into one of the plastic bags and yanks out a bottle, unscrews the cap and pours the iced coffee into his mouth. It's as sweet and thick as melted ice cream. He drinks it anyway, then stretches his neck this way and that. Only now does the cab feel comfortably warm. Over the coffee on his breath he detects another smell, muddy and unpleasant, so slight at first that it's barely there.

He has to lose Lyle and Al, he thinks. He can do that, can't he? Doesn't he drive for a living, for fuck's sake?

He drains the last of the coffee and tosses the bottle behind him. A moment later his foot's hard on the gas pedal and the engine's roaring. He sends the cab slicing across a bend, then the next, for all that his heart's frantic against his ribs. For whole seconds at a time the pickup's lights vanish. All he needs is enough time to pull off and kill the lights, to let Al and Lyle pass without spotting him, but here comes the pickup once more, tearing up the road behind him. A crack splits the air. A shot. For fuck's sake, and he pushes harder on the gas, but it's no good. The minivan's not built for speed. He takes a curve too fast and the tires slip enough to scare him. He's shifting his foot to the brake when the rear window fractures into a cobweb with a dark hole at its center.

In seconds he's shivering from the cold being sucked in. Funny how you can forget about the temperature outside when the heat's blasting. But now—now he hunches into himself for warmth, and the pickup settles in behind him once more. On he leads them, eating up the miles between Sumner and the cabin because, for the life of him, he can't think what else to do.

## 40

IT'S THE STILL heart of the night, a time when darkness takes on the depth of permanency and your soul clenches at the sight of it. The cab's headlights catch a flash of green: Moose Lake 5 miles. Only five miles. A panic trips inside Fisher. All he's doing is leading Lyle and Al straight to Bree, and they're not going to take it well that Brian's not there. Will Bree know enough to be scared of them? Or will she get mad if they won't believe Brian's dead, and things'll get out of hand?

He has to think. He tells himself there must be something he can do, only he's thinking so hard he's not concentrating, doesn't realize how much he's let the cab slow until the pickup's so close its lights dazzle off the mirror. He hits the gas hard enough for the cab to shimmy and slip, sees the scabby trunks of spruce, a snowbank all yellow in his lights, all of it sliding past him, then he's wrestling the steering wheel until there, there's the blacktop again.

He recognizes where he is: the small bridge over Deadman's Creek that rattles when you pass over it. At the end of a track there's a short row of mailboxes nailed to one end of a railroad tie, like a few tenacious teeth in a moose jaw; then there's the gas station that hasn't been open in years, the building collapsing in on itself. Jensen's, that's what it was called.

Then it comes to him, like a match struck in the darkness: he doesn't have to lead Lyle and Al to Bree. All they know is that the cabin's on the lake. He can take the third turn-off instead of the fourth and they won't even pass the old cabin. Instead he'll lead them up past Pa Jensen's place with its mounds of busted-up cars, and buckets from the dredge that's been gone for sixty years, all of it just bumps under the snow in his vast yard, and down to Jim Jensen's cabin, right on the lake. With any luck, Jim'll have been out there recently enough for the place not to look deserted.

And then? Fisher can't imagine. But hasn't he thought it far enough through for now? And he drives on like a man possessed.

⁂

When Fisher pulls up close to Jim Jensen's cabin, the pickup pulls in right behind him. In the glare of the headlights, the cabin's more ramshackle than he remembers, the plywood more stained, the cheap glass of the windows gleaming thin as soap bubbles. The place looks like it's sagging into itself, but then, it looked that way fifteen years ago when he banged on the door in a panic the night Jan went into labor early with Bree.

When Fisher gets out he smells woodsmoke on the air. No vehicle parked here, though. Could be the smoke's drifting in from across the lake, held down by the cold air. He steps up onto the narrow porch. It's stacked with boxes and garbage bags three deep.

A shudder and a grunt behind him: the pickup's engine shutting off, then its headlights. The cabin's bare windows, the bags of garbage heaped on its porch, the raw teeth of a saw hanging from a nail by the door, all lose their gleam as the night sweeps in.

Beyond the dark shape of the cabin lies the frozen lake. Under the crooked peel of moon hanging in the sky, Fisher can make out its flat expanse, a curiously luminous blue. Close to the horizon, just above the trees, a few stars glitter, but the air's too choked with ice crystals for much else to show.

200

He tugs at his hat. The soft, bruised flesh where the woman hit him throbs, fluids dammed up where they shouldn't be, and the cut on his thigh prickles horribly as the cold slices into his flesh. How old he feels, his chest sore, his ribs aching, his whole self broken apart and weary. Dear God, he thinks, how did that happen so quickly? He remembers his younger self, bulky as a bear, standing outside this cabin with a suffocating tightness in his chest at the thought of his wife bunched up and moaning on their bed, and his child being born out here where there was no help to be had. Now here he is again, fifteen years later, still trying to save Bree.

Boots grunt across the packed snow and Fisher turns, catches a flash of shadow in the darkness, then he's reeling and Lyle's on top of him, his fist sharp against his chest. He's yelling, "You fucker! You goddamn fucker!" Fisher's face down in the snow. He can't breathe. The cold's everywhere. He shoves hard and Lyle rolls off him, far too easily. When he's struggled to his feet he understands: there's Lyle, lopsided, one arm hanging strangely. Broken, perhaps, or the shoulder dislocated, and Lyle's stoked up a crazy anger, is coming at him again, crouched forward and his injured arm swinging like an ape's.

Snow's stuck to Fisher's face, his neck. It's got into his boots and squeaks as he shifts his weight to step back. Someone's behind him. Al. He hears, "Stop right there, fucker, or I'll shoot you in the head." Then Al lifts his voice, calls out to Lyle, "C'mon now, you can finish him off later. Brian's here someplace."

Lyle turns and his face catches the moonlight. One eye's swollen, the other furious. "Don't be a fuckhead, Al, he's gone. Fucking gone!"

Al steps forward with a cigarette between his lips, then he leans into the flame of his lighter. "What the fuck?"

"How'd he get here? Fly?"

Al lets smoke drift from his mouth and looks about him, slowly, like he's taking stock: there's the cab Fisher drove, there's his own pickup, there's an old car with a thick crust of snow over it.

Already Lyle's climbing the couple of steps to the porch, and the door's squealing open, and it's dark inside like a space where a tooth used to be. "Get it now, fuckhead?" he yells. "Mikey here must've warned him!"

Fisher barely has time to taste his fear before Al shoves him hard up the steps, holds the bitingly cold end of the gun against his neck. As soon as he walks inside the cabin, Fisher catches the smell of grilled meat, the pissy stink of old beer, feels the warmth of the place swamp him. Al's right behind him. Together they stumble through the darkness, knocking against a table, a chair, Al cussing under his breath. A rasp, then a wavering light falls across the cabin: Al has his lighter held high. From the beam hangs a lamp and Lyle unhooks it, shoves it at Al, who sucks hard on his cigarette then fiddles and cusses some more over it, pumping it hard, then holding a flame to the mantle.

The room bursts into light. The cabin's barely twenty feet by fifteen, dishes and pots on a shelf in a corner by a plastic bowl tilted up to dry, a barrel of a woodstove against the far wall where longjohns and socks and felt boot liners hang from nails, a narrow bed with a pillow and blankets on it.

"Frisk him," Lyle snaps at Al. Al shoves Fisher against the wall. He bats at the legs of his pants, squeezes the bulky pockets of his parka then plunges his hand in. He pulls out the new pocketknife. For a moment he looks at it, then he drops it to the floor and stamps on it with his heel. The plastic casing splinters and the short blade and tiny fork, the nail file, all its miniature tools splay out. With another stamp they come apart, and Al kicks the pieces to one side. "Piece of shit."

Lyle turns toward Fisher. His skin looks thin, like a dying creature's. "You better know where Brian's at or you're a dead man. Freezing to death'd be too easy this time. You understand?"

"You took my phone—how could I call anyone?"

With his left hand Lyle reaches for something on the windowsill and holds it up. A hunting knife. The end of the blade's curved like a claw, meant for severing joints and sinews, for slicing apart muscle, and it shines wetly as Lyle comes close, his head tilted against his eye that's swollen shut, his lips tight, his arm dangling all wrong.

But Lyle's good eye slides off to the side and no wonder. The churning of an engine rough from the cold, and the three of them stand perfectly still in the hissing light of the lamp. Then Lyle says softly, "Gotcha."

What must Jim Jensen make of two strange vehicles pulled up in his driveway, one of them a cab, of all the freaky things, with its back window shot out and its wing mirror hanging loose? No wonder the engine churns away outside. There's no sound of a door slamming, no hollow crunch of boots across the porch, because Jim Jensen must be staring out his windshield and considering what to do.

Lyle snaps, "Kill the lamp, Al."

"What?"

"Lamp."

Al lays the gun on the table and reaches up. He turns the knob and shrinks the flame to nothing just as Lyle's left hand snatches up the gun. Lyle hisses, "Take the fucking knife. Slice his throat if you have to."

"That's my gun."

"Shut the fuck up."

"Fuck you." But Al takes the knife from the table and twists it in the glare of the headlights coming through the thin curtains. He walks softly toward Fisher and holds the blade against his cheek. It's icy from lying on the windowsill.

Lyle's nothing more than a shadow pulling back the edge of the curtain with the gun and peering out. His holds the gun awkwardly and uses the same hand to wipe the frost from the glass. Then comes the sound of his breath, a little fast, and a creak of the floor as he shifts his weight. But just as he dips his head toward the gun, as though it's a rifle and he needs to aim carefully, the door bursts open. There's no one there, just the dazzle of headlights. Lyle wheels around. His face is all knotted up. From a few yards away a shaky voice calls out, "Who's there? What's going on?"

A tension inside Fisher comes loose because here she is, safe after all, and he's found her, but the relief won't fit into his chest. Al's breath's in his face, his arm hooks around Fisher's neck so that the blade's biting into the soft skin beneath his chin. Lyle's lurching toward them, Lyle with a fierce look in his good eye made all the fiercer by a wicked joy. He spits, "Tell our friends to come in, Mikey."

Dread pools in Fisher's belly. No, he thinks, no fucking way. He sucks in a breath, the air already cold, colder than the blade against his neck, and he yells, "Jim! Get out of here!" His words come out ragged. He wrenches himself to one side, feels the blade slip over his skin and he swings his arm. The knife flashes through the air and he kicks, hard as he can, into Al's groin. A shot—from Lyle, he thinks—and another, then a click, but he's falling and hits the floor so hard his bones bend, he'd swear, and his organs flatten themselves, and it's all he can do to open his eyes and stare between the table legs toward the doorway. Ice fog's boiling into the cabin but there, sharp against the brilliance of the headlights, is the unmistakable outline of a shotgun barrel. A man barks out, "Quit f-fighting or I'm gonna shoot you all stone dead."

## 41

J IM JENSEN'S NOT the man Fisher remembers. That Jim Jensen was a slack-shouldered, paunchy bird of a man with chicken-bone fingers and a flushed look to his face, a man whose tan Carhartt's were so covered with stains from where he'd wiped his hands on his thighs that they looked like maps of unknown continents, and whose beard was so thin it barely covered the livid marks on his face, either acne or sores or something worse. That Jim Jensen had stood with his door open only a couple of inches while Fisher told him over and over that his wife was in labor, that he'd trained as a goddamn EMT, hadn't he, and he had to come help. That Jim had tried to shut the door in Fisher's face but he'd jammed his shoulder into the gap and yelled, "You come or I'll fucking kill you, you bastard." He must have sounded wild because Jim Jensen came out and let Fisher hurry him along the dirt track through the trees to the cabin. He'd done nothing much but tell Fisher to help ease out the baby, to wait for the afterbirth, to cut the umbilical cord, and the whole time he'd looked anywhere but at Jan with her tuft of brown pubic hair dark against her skin and blood smeared over her thighs, and as soon as Bree'd been wrapped in a blanket he'd taken off without a word.

And now, here's Jim Jensen bellowing into the hollow space of his own cabin, a broad man whose weight looks carelessly slung onto him, hanging from his shoulders and his ribs and the bones of his face, as though he could shrug it all off if he wanted. But it's Jim Jensen all right: that same slight stutter when he yelled, "Quit f-fighting," that slouching way about him as he steps across the threshold with the shotgun sweeping the room. He says, "Light the lamp," and it's Bree who comes to the table, who pulls a box of matches out of the table drawer and lights it like she's done it before. The glow unfolds across the cabin, and Jim kicks the door shut.

His beard's long and matted now, his parka patched with duct tape. His red hat has earflaps that give him a dumb-dog look, but his eyes are everywhere—on Al curled up on the floor by the wall, on Fisher standing by the kitchen counter—but they settle on Lyle, and Lyle gives him a sly grin because he's got the handgun aimed at Jim's chest. Lyle says, "Drop the gun, motherfucker, or I'll shoot you."

Jim hefts the shotgun higher. "I'll take my chances."

From the table Bree's watching. Fisher's shocked how fragile she looks, her cheekbones curved and delicate like pieces of broken shell, her lips pale, her eyes distant beneath the ragged line of her bangs. This is the first time in months he's seen her without makeup, he realizes. His little girl. He doesn't recognize the hat she's wearing, a black ugly thing too big for her, nor the dull blue coat. She must have left in one helluva hurry. Horrified at what she'd done to Brian. But that jerk deserved it, Fisher tells himself: for fuck's sake, he was naked in her bathroom.

Bree's holding onto the back of the chair so tightly that Fisher could swear it's trembling. She doesn't take her eyes off Lyle. He's stepping forward with that handgun raised. "Brian Armstrong. Tell me where he is, or I'll blow your fucking head off."

Jim blinks. "Brian? What the hell?" Now he glances at Fisher. "What's this all about?"

Lyle's got a swagger to his walk as he comes closer, never mind that one arm's hanging useless and his shoulder's sloped at an unnatural angle. He leans against the table, so close to Bree that she recoils into the corner between the woodstove and the bed. She half-stumbles, half-sits on a stack of cut logs. On the wall above her hangs Jim's long underwear.

Lyle swings the gun after her. "Then maybe you know, ugly girl. Why don't you tell me so I don't put a bullet in your brain?"

Jim's lips part like he's about to say something. Instead he lets out a laugh and cradles the butt of the shotgun against his shoulder. "You dumbass, coming in here like you've got a right to, when you don't know shit." He licks his lips. "Go on—shoot."

In that instant Fisher's in motion. He's coming at Lyle without thinking, feet paddling against the floor, hands outstretched, his head jutting forward like a man struggling against the pull of a river. The air's so dense it won't let him through fast enough, and he's too late, surely he's too late. There's Lyle's twisting the gun toward him, and the dark hole the bullet's going to come bursting through is pointing at his face. He throws himself at Lyle with his eyes shut against the thought of what that bullet will do to him.

Only, the shot doesn't come. Instead one hand glances off Lyle's chest, and the edge of the table catches him on the thigh, just above the cut, and the wound smarts ferociously. As for Lyle, he staggers back against the plyboard counter. A bowl rattles, a glass tumbles over and falls to the floor but doesn't break. The gun's still in his hand, and he pushes himself straight again.

Jim says, "Might as well drop it, seeing's as it's empty, you stupid f-fuck."

Fisher's got one hand clamped over his thigh. Through the denim comes the warm seep of blood. He looks over at Bree. She's covered her face with her hands but she's not crying. Fisher says softly, "You OK?" She stares out over the dark mounds of her gloves. Her head jerks with each breath, and she doesn't say a word.

Jim rocks a little from one foot to the other, tilts his head back. "One of you'd better tell me what's going on." He glances from where Lyle's got his back against the counter, to Al still tucked into himself on the floor.

Lyle weighs the gun in his hand, smirking. "You're a friend of Brian Armstrong, right?"

Jim's face closes up. "I'm asking the goddamn questions. Tell me what the hell's going on."

Lyle licks his lips with a tongue as pointed and quick as a lizard's. "See, Brian's managed to piss some people off."

"You?"

Lyle gives a shrug. "Yeah, me and a few thousand other people."

"Say what?"

"Heard of the Alaska Citizens Guard?"

A flicker crosses Jim's face. "Those guys who dress up in uniform and play at being soldiers? Oh yeah, I've heard of them. What the hell did Armstrong do? Sell them some land at the bottom of a lake?" He snorts.

Lyle's got one hand lifted and he presses down on the air, a strange gesture. "Oh no," he says softly, "nothing like that."

Fisher thinks how odd it is that Lyle comes toward Jim, keeps coming even when Jim barks at him, "You stop right there or I'll shoot your goddamn balls off."

"You wouldn't want to do that. See, there are thousands of us and we've pledged to stand together."

"Thousands? You people make me laugh. How many really? A dozen? Half dozen?"

"Numbers like you wouldn't believe. When the time comes, no one's going to stand in our way."

Now Jim's grinning. " When the time comes? F-for what?

We talking world domination, or you just gonna hole up some-place with your buddy who doesn't wanna pay his taxes, and wait f-for the f-feds to come blast you out?"

Lyle's mouth's gone hard. He reaches up to the lamp that's gently hissing and sends it swinging. Its light gapes and yaws across the cabin. "You don't want to talk that way, not if you want a long and quiet life."

"You threatening me, you dumb f-fuck? Who the hell's holding the gun?" He lets out a snort of a laugh.

Lyle juts his chin forward a little. "Tell me where Brian is, and we'll forget about all this."

"How the hell would I know where he's at?"

"See, here you are in his cabin and all . . ."

Jim's cheeks flush a deeper red and his eyes turn wet and small. "You're dumber than you look. This is my cabin. His is down the next turn-off."

Lyle's jaw pulls tight. He looks around him, at the table, at the door, his good eye swimming a little, his mind calculating, adjusting. "Well now," he says at last. He hasn't looked at Fisher and Fisher can't help feeling that Lyle's saving up his fury, that to look at him now would be to put a flame to the fuse too early. "That doesn't matter, not in the long run," and he wipes the back of his hand over his mouth. "You can still be of use. Take us to his cabin and we'll leave you and your daughter in peace."

Jim's face twitches in surprise. Lyle catches that flicker of muscle and skin and stops dead still. "Oh my, wrong again? Here I am in the wrong cabin. And that girl—not your daugh-ter?" He licks his lips and moves his hand up his useless right arm. He's thinking, his brow pulled down a little. "So if you're not *Dad*, then . . ." and now he turns to Fisher, "you must be. How about that? Your pretty little girl went and grew up into this ugly bitch. Honey, I just didn't recognize you." He smiles and the furrows beside his nose deepen.

Something in Fisher retreats, scrambling, as though he can hide inside himself. He takes a breath and the sound of it trembles. He wants to say something. He has to say something, to fend off Lyle. But what? Out of the corner of his eye he sees Bree turn away to the wall. Lyle says softly, "Well, how about that, you ashamed of him, is that it?"

The lamp's swinging only slightly now, like it's caught in a draft. Jim settles the butt of the shotgun higher against his shoulder. "You're starting to piss me off real bad. Get outta here. Go on, right now."

Lyle turns and he's smiling. He lifts one hand, fluttering the fingers ridiculously, like some old-time dancer hamming it up. Jim stares at him and it's like he's trying to decide whether to shoot when Lyle jerks his head.

It's odd, that jerk. It's like it's yanked on some invisible mechanism that lets fly a blade of light, and that light knocks Jim Jensen back on his heels. His shotgun tips up and a crash of sound knocks a small hole right through the cabin roof. The gun slips out of his hands. It clatters to the floor and Jim stands unsteadily. It takes him a few seconds to notice the horn handle sticking out through his parka close to his heart. He touches it with his fingertips, trying to understand what it is, and what an effort it takes, because his breath saws in and out, loud enough for Fisher to hear above the ringing left by the blast.

Lyle steps in front of Jim. His grin's tight, his left hand up and his fingers dancing through the air again. "Oh yeah," he says, "that's right, watch the hand, watch the hand." He snorts. "Not so bright, are you, asshole?"

Jim coughs. Blood trickles out over his bottom lip and through his beard. His eyes are still on Lyle's hand, and that hand shoves him full in the face. He tilts back against the wall like a felled tree then slumps to the ground.

From behind the table, Al hauls himself to his feet. "Stupid fucker was pissing *me* off."

"Silent but deadly, that's you, Al."

Al comes around the table and puts his foot on Jim's chest. He's bracing himself to pull out the knife when Lyle says, "Leave it."

"Hell no, that's a good knife."

"Under the radar. Remember?"

"Hey—for fuck's sake. It's gotta be worth a hundred bucks." He wrenches it out and wipes the blade on Jim's Carhartt's. It leaves a glistening smear. Fisher's looking at it when he catches Al staring over at him. "And he's pissing me off too. Wasting our fucking time. The girl can take us to the cabin. We don't need him."

Lyle doesn't move. When at last he looks up, he touches his swollen eye and says almost lazily, "Slow down. We've got to think it through. Remember?" From his pocket he pulls a box of ammo and lays it on the table. He starts loading his gun, awkwardly, one-handedly, sliding in one bullet at a time like he's got all the time in the world.

Al's cheeks quiver slightly. His mouth's oddly small and pulled in. "All you chicken-shits just talk talk talk—*I'm a sovereign citizen, we're gonna secede from the Union, we've got ourselves a people's army*—well fuck. None of you does anything but talk. Except me."

Lyle pushes another bullet home. "I'm trying to cover your ass, Al."

Al blinks. His eyelids are thick and slow-moving, and his eyes dark beneath them. "Hey—what the hell?"

"Covering it. Again. So stop fucking around and give me the knife." He lifts the gun and tucks it under his arm. The other hand he holds out to Al.

Al holds the knife up close to his chest. He holds it so tight his skin's stretched over his knuckles. "We were fucking sitting ducks."

"Well you got him good. Now give me the goddamn knife."

"Not him. Not fucking him," and he kicks Jim in the belly.

Lyle's still got his hand out. He says quietly, "I'm not blaming you for that, OK? What happened, happened."

"The fuck you aren't."

Lyle bends his head close to Al's and Fisher has to concentrate to hear him above the hiss of the lamp. "We used it to our advantage, didn't we? So what's it matter?"

Maybe Al doesn't notice Fisher there listening in. Maybe he doesn't care. His voice comes punching out. "Except Brian took off. So much for your fucking plan."

There's such fury in him that Fisher edges along the wall, and farther along, up toward where Bree's huddled on the small stack of wood. What's he planning? He doesn't know. To throw himself over her if Al looks her way with that knife raised? To hold her in his arms and feel her breath against his neck, the way he used to in another life?

Lyle's eyes flit toward Fisher but Fisher keeps moving toward Bree. Lyle says softly to Al, "Doesn't matter. The cops are still after him and that suits us fine. By the time we're done, he won't be telling them anything. We just need to be careful."

Al's hands lift to his head and spread like a cage over his hat. "Fuck it! Fuck it!"

"I've got it all worked out. Just give me the knife."

Al's face looks like a ball of clay smoothed over, his closed eyes just slight hollows, his nose a half-formed thing. When he opens his mouth again it's wide and dark, and from it he bellows, "This needs to be over."

"It will be. Go on out there and bring in the other guy." He pushes his face close to Al's again, but Al's not looking. His eyes are still shut and his mouth's wet and gaping.

Fisher can't bear the sight of him. He stares at his boots on the floorboards and makes them move one more step. Then he's there and he crouches and rests a hand on Bree's shoulder. She flinches and hunches into herself. She won't even look at him, as though this is all his fault. And she's right, isn't she? Didn't he lead these guys to her when she'd run away? When no one should have found her out here?

His head drops. He needs to think. Surely if he tries hard enough he'll find a way to save them both, but the stink of blood's filling his head and all he can think about is Jim lying dead a few feet away.

## 42

THE OTHER GUY Lyle wants brought in. Grisby. No wonder when Lyle saw Fisher was driving the cab he said, *This is too fucking perfect.* Fisher had brought Grisby out here in the back of the minivan. That slight smell: Grisby, dead, hidden in the cab's narrow trunk.

Now it's almost more than he can bear to see Grisby curled on the cabin's narrow bed with his knees up to his chest. His face is stiff and grizzled with frost as though this isn't Grisby but some nearly-finished model of him: the awful whiteness of his skin, its blue marbling, the flat eyes, a small hole in the middle of his forehead like a dead third eye. But it's him all right. Al dragged him through the doorway while Lyle held the handgun on Fisher and Bree, as though they might rush him and run off. Where could they run to when the sub-arctic night's as inhospitable as an alien planet? Fisher had exactly that thought as Al dragged the body across the floor. It hit him at the same time: that it was like Grisby's thoughts leaking into his head, that it was Grisby being hauled toward the bed. His green parka. His dirty white bunny boots. His face frozen into a grimace when he was hoisted up, legs bent at wrong angles and arms crossed over his belly.

Inside his head an unearthly whistling has started up, the sound of the world pressing in with all its menace. A person— someone like Grisby, like him, like Bree—is nothing but meat and bone that a bullet could rip through. Each lungful of air feels like a miracle, the grace of a fragile system that could easily falter. How has he managed to live this long? And Bree: she's barely begun her life and any minute now it could be crushed out. He reaches a hand to her shoulder and squeezes. She shakes it off and looks at him over the sleeve of her coat with eyes full of reproach. He opens his mouth but she's quicker, hisses, "Don't fucking touch me."

His hand's still outstretched. He folds his fingers toward his palm and settles his hand on his knee. "I love you, sweet pea," he says softly.

Her bottom lip's loose. It pulls to one side like it's been snagged by a hook, then she says. "You're as big an asshole as the rest of them."

He stings with the shock of it. He opens his mouth but she buries her face against the sleeve of her coat, and there's Lyle almost upon them with the gun in his hand and the skin around his swollen eye turning an odd shade of blue. "Don't move, fuckhead, not even your lips."

He tips his head toward Al, and Al nods. He has Jim's shotgun open and slides in two cartridges from a box on the counter. Then he steps over Jim's body and hoists the gun to his shoulder.

The air's suddenly too thin. Fisher's body is as awkward as a balloon, his head dizzyingly high above the floor. He grabs Bree and tries to hold her to him only she shoves him off, and when he looks back the shotgun's not aimed at them but at Grisby. Lyle snorts. He says, "Aim for the head, Al."

The force of the shot jolts what's left of Grisby. The front of his parka's like a corn kernel popped open, all white and fluffy except for the darkness in the middle. Fisher's belly seizes. He can't help himself. He bends forward and vomits between his boots, hears Lyle moan, "Oh for fuck's sake, you missed his freaking head."

A second shot and Fisher can't look except at the puddle of vomit at his feet. It's mostly water with shreds of ham and lettuce. The sandwich from the supermarket in Sumner. When he looks up, Grisby's slid to one side like a doll. "You didn't have to do that," he says. "You didn't have to kill him in the first place."

Lyle rubs the barrel of the handgun along his jaw like a razor. "Two guys dead in a cabin. A fight—over what? Who the fucks knows? Who the fuck cares? It's winter, that's enough."

The cabin's starting to grow cold. No one's fed the woodstove and a draft's leaking in through the hole in the roof. A hole the size of a fist already downy with frost, and beyond it, the night sky. Fisher hunches his shoulders. "You killed him for nothing."

Lyle shows his teeth. "So loyal. But you know what? Your friend here was so scared he sang like a fucking bird. Christ, he'd have sold out his own mother. Must've thought we were pissed at him for taking Brian's stuff, like Brian had changed his mind and sent us after him. He didn't get it." He sniffs. "As for you, he said it was all your idea and hey, if we wanted you, all we had to do was call Bear Cabs and ask for non-smoking. Worked like a fucking charm. Pity he got out of his blindfold, because he could have been useful, but there you go. Life's a bitch."

"You killed him because he saw you?"

Lyle purses his lips. "Al gets worked up about things like that. But who wouldn't? You can't feel secure if you know some little shit might rat on you. Any friend of Brian's, oh yeah, a rat for sure."

Fisher wants to say, *He wasn't Brian's friend* and *He couldn't have recognized you. Some days he didn't even recognize me,* but he doesn't. He doesn't say a thing because he feels his loyalty deflate. Grisby giving in so easily. Giving him up to these guys, and look what's happened because of it. But there's this too: Grisby didn't tell them about Bree. Maybe he was too scared to tell them what had really happened, but

216

either way, he didn't make things worse for her, and that's something.

Al's bent over Jim. He swats at his face, at those eyes staring up at nothing, then pulls out the kitchen chair and sits down spread-legged. Lyle waves him off.

"Find a cloth or something and wipe down anything we've touched. Just in case." Then he reaches up and dims the lamp so far the mantle's a dying sun and the room's swimming with shadows.

Behind him, Al puts his gloves back on and rubs the door handle, the gas bottle hanging from the lamp, then he looks around, looks at Fisher as though it's just occurred to him that, if they're being so careful, why the hell's he still alive?

Fisher glances down. Beside him Bree's still perched on the stacked wood. She must be uncomfortable, but she doesn't move. She's staring at Al, her eyes glassy and big like a night animal's. Even in the half-dark she must know Fisher's watching her, but she won't look at him, and he feels it like a pain in his chest. He's done something to make her hate him, to distrust him. Not showing up when she called? Coming too late? She's no idea that he and Grisby cleaned the house and dumped Brian's body, that what she did isn't going to hang over her because, by the time Brian's found, the trail will be too cold for the cops to follow it back to her. And even if they did, well, he's the one who dumped Brian, isn't he? He's the one they'll come after, and she'll stay free.

Lyle's face must be hurting because he winces. He doesn't let go of the gun, but touches the skin around his closed-up eye with the back of his knuckles. His other eye glares out at Fisher. "You try anything, I'll shoot you dead. Get it?" Over his shoulder he calls to Al, "You about finished?"

"Fuck yeah."

"Then it's time."

217

Al picks up Jim's gun. He must think he's taking it with him until Lyle scowls and beckons him over. "No way," he says, "that thing won't be much good to you with her in tow."

"What the fuck? I'm not taking her."

"Sure you are. Insurance. And reload that thing."

"Why the fuck, if I'm not taking it with me?"

"For me, dumbass. Mikey here had a major disagreement with the dead guys—what a shame. Shot dead."

Al slides a couple of cartridges into the shotgun and passes it to Lyle. Lyle slaps the handgun into Al's palm, and Al holds it loosely, only it's pointed at Bree. "How far?"

Bree's head comes up. "Quarter mile." The words have sharp edges, like she hates every one of these men in this cabin.

"What's he got with him?"

"A forty-five. Couple of semi-automatics. An assault rifle. Whole bunch of ammo, some grenades and pipe bombs."

"Night vision scope?"

She shrugs. "Dunno."

Al lets his breath hiss out between his teeth. "Fucking great."

"Smoke him out," says Lyle.

"He'll be expecting something like that."

"So what's he going to do? Hide outside and wait for someone to burn his place down? Not in this kinda cold. Not even he's that hardcore." Lyle leans back in the chair, looks at Bree. "How long you supposed to be gone?"

Bree's twisting her fingers together. "'Til morning."

"Fucking sick," and Al smirks. "But I guess we knew that."

Lyle tips himself forward a little. "So what the hell—why he send you here?"

For a few moments the silence pulls in tight around them. Then Bree turns to face him straight on. "He's expecting trouble."

"Someone warn him?"

218

"Yeah." Her eyes slide toward Fisher and they're bright with hatred. "Him."

※

When you take a knife to a fish just pulled from the water, it'll jerk in your hands and keep jerking even when you've sliced it from its throat to its tail, even when its guts are spilling out cool and slippery on your hands. It'll stare out at the world with a flat look that can't show panic. But it feels panic all right. It feels betrayed, because the world's never done this to it before. So why now? It can't make sense of it and never will because it's already too late.

That's what Fisher thinks when he bends his face away from his daughter. It's the end. It's over. The world's never done this to him before, not this way, not so painfully, and it's all he can do to keep breathing. He doesn't reach out when she gets to her feet, doesn't even look at her when she pushes past him to the door where Al's waiting.

Lyle calls out to him, "Use her as bait. And be careful."

"Of course I'll be fucking careful."

"Of her." He sniffs. "And Al? Only shoot her if you have to. She could be useful. OK?"

"You want to do this? Huhn? Then get off my fucking back." He zips his jacket right up to his chin and takes a flashlight from a hook by the door. He turns it on and shines its thin beam on the floor by his boots.

"Four knocks."

"What?"

"When you get back. So I don't shoot you by mistake." Lyle gives a smile that shows his teeth. "Wouldn't want to do that now, would I?"

# 43

W HEN AL OPENS the door to take Bree outside, the last of the cabin's real heat seeps away. What's left is faint, the used-up breath of a dying fire.

Fisher presses his arms against his sides. He could have reached out to Bree as she passed him. Could have squeezed her hand, or at least looked up at her, but he wouldn't let himself. That look. That *Him*, like he was something to toss away so she could slip free herself.

He shouldn't mind. He came here to save her, didn't he?

But he does mind. That look. The ill-will behind it. What did he do to deserve it?

He tells himself he's being stupid. It's all over for him but not for her, and she knows that. Besides, she's a clever girl and gutsy with it. She'll have a plan. Is she going to make a run for the cabin and barricade herself in? Or take off in Brian's SUV, because she's sure to have parked it nose out as Brian always did? But the silence outside's getting longer, and she's out there in the dark, trudging across the snow with Al toward the empty cabin, and if she doesn't do something soon Al's going to swing open the door and see the place is empty, and then what's to stop him from killing her?

Fisher stares down at the slit in his jeans where Darlene shoved the knife into his thigh, at the weave dark and shiny with dried blood. The pain's sunk into him as though the blade's still stuck in his flesh.

A scrape of wood against wood, and Fisher looks up. With the lamp turned down the cabin's dim as an old photograph.

What a scene it is: Jim sprawled by the door, Grisby on the bed with his jaw askew and half his skull blown away, Lyle beside him with the shotgun barrel propped across the table. Of course. He only has one hand to hold it because the other's useless and lying in his lap. Now he swivels it to point at Fisher's chest and heaves a sigh.

"There's more to you than I thought, Mikey. Bet Brian's cussing you out right now. What d'you tell him? *Sorry Brian, I've blown it, they're coming for you, but get my girl out the way so she doesn't get hurt.* Huhn? Boy, I'd love to hear what he said back." He gives a wide jack-o'-lantern smile then lets it go slack. "Well, no matter. You're too much of a dumbfuck to know what you're caught up in, aren't you? You're such a dumbfuck you're buddies with your ex's husband. How sick is that?" and he laughs. He ducks down and squints his good eye, lining up his shot. "Time to say goodbye, Mikey. Not much of a life, was it?"

Fisher can't get to his feet. Part of him means to: why not rush Lyle and die trying to live? But his legs won't work, like his brain's already shutting down in anticipation of the bullet about to come hurtling at him. All he can do is close his eyes. In the shelter of his own darkness, there's his trailer with the dawn turning the snow a delicate pink all around, and there beside it the raw wood of his unfinished house, and the tarp stretched over the stacked lumber that's waited two years and now'll never get used. He thinks, what a waste—how much did he pay for that lumber? He thinks, what a stupid thought to die with, and makes himself remember Bree when she was so small her dark hair stood up like chick feathers, and Jan was all warmth and softness, and their lives full of hope. All that's lost, and the shot rips through the air. More distant than he imagined. Not a shotgun blast. He opens his eyes to see Lyle lurching toward the window and peering out. He drags the shotgun with him, and Fisher's up and throwing himself through the space between them.

Of course Lyle sees him. He half-turns and tries to lift the gun, but it's too late. Fisher's on him and the gun clatters to the floor. Lyle cries out as the two of them fall backward over Jim's body, onto the floor, up against sacks of beans and rice under the counter. Lyle yells, "You shit," but his voice is all wrong. Fisher leans his weight across Lyle's throat. A creaking sound. Of lungs straining. He presses harder, because what's launched him across the room is the too-late realization that Bree's out there alone with Al, and he's not bright enough to wait until he's seen the cabin's empty, he's just going to kill her, and maybe just has. Fisher wants to put it right, like a movie you can wind back through, as though it'll come out any different the next time. He can't think. Can't see through the awful pinching in his head and the rush of his own breathing.

# 44

WHEN YOU HAVE to kill a man, don't look into his eyes. Don't think that his life's as miserable as your own. Don't look at his fingers scrabbling at your hands. Let your weight come down hard. Arch yourself up so that the whole of you is focused in your hands, and those hands are tight around his throat, and when he flails like a fish, let him. Killing him this way will take a few minutes. Long enough for pity to take root, if you let it. Instead think about what he's done to you. How thanks to him your friend's dead, and an innocent man, and maybe your daughter. Think how he tried to kill you too, insulted you, called you a dumbfuck when he's nothing more than a dumbfuck himself.

Don't let yourself think, this isn't who I am.

Don't let yourself think, he's just a man like me.

Don't watch the panic in his eyes. Don't let your hands go loose. Tighten your grip and repeat to yourself that if you let him go he'll seize his chance to kill you. This is self-defense. This is legally defensible homicide. For God's sake, don't let that pressure on his neck slacken. He'll feel it and jerk your hands away, and he'll suck in one breath after another with the awful sound of something almost dead coming back to life.

# 45

AT LEAST FISHER'S faster. Lyle's still heaving in lung-fuls of air, he's rolling onto his feet, but Fisher yanks the door wide and sends the shotgun wheeling out into the darkness.

Then Lyle's on his back and his good arm's around Fisher's throat. Fisher throws himself backward against the doorframe, and again, then spins around. Lyle can't hold on. He falls against the table then clutches his injured arm to his chest. He spits, "You stupid shithead. Think that's going to make any differ-ence? You're in way too deep."

Fisher's breathing hard. "I'm not like you."

"Christ, no. You're a fuck-up, a creep, a loser. Can't even save yourself, let alone your own kid. Things go bad and who's she take off with? Her step-daddy. Yeah, she must think the world of you." He lets himself down on one of the chairs, stiff as an old man. He reaches out and slaps Grisby on what's left of his cheek. It makes a flat sound. "Cannon fodder, that's all he was. That's all you are, Mikey. I don't know why you bother getting up in the morning. I wouldn't. If I was you, I'd shoot myself in the freaking head. But then, I've got the guts to do it." He smiles. And when his smile broadens, he's holding the hunting knife. "See, Mikey, got to keep your eye on the ball."

The blade gleams in the dim light. Fisher's so tired all he can think of to do is step away, but Lyle's on his feet. He has the knife held up like a candle and comes around the table with it. Fisher steps around it too, over Jim's legs, past the bed where Grisby's staring at nothing while Lyle stabs the air, saying,

"Watch it, watch the blade, Mikey, it's coming to get you."

The third time around the table, Fisher calls out, "Oh come on—for fuck's sake, this is ridiculous."

"Ring around the rosie, Mikey, come on now."

Fisher's behind the longer side of the table, but there's little room here, with the counter so close, the bags of rice and beans slumped on the floor behind him. Then Lyle lunges and the blade slices the air in front of Fisher's face, and in the second that Fisher leans back, off balance, Lyle comes scrambling around the table, fast, so fast he trips over Jim's boot.

If it hadn't been for that stumble, it might have been all over. But that moment, it's just enough. Fisher snatches a skillet off the shelf, an unwieldy thing wide as a basketball, and swings at the knife. He misses, and the skillet's so damned heavy he staggers. He lifts it again and smashes it down on Lyle's hand, and the knife goes windmilling out across the floor and vanishes beneath the bed.

Lyle leans on the back of the chair and hunches over his hand. His mouth's wide and each breath makes his head lift and fall, like someone floating on the edge of the sea.

Footsteps. On the porch. Lyle keeps his good eye on Fisher, says, "Well, well, game over." A fumbling at the doorhandle, and Lyle yells, "You forgot to knock, fuckhead."

Only, it's not Al standing in the doorway. It's Bree and she's got a twitching, scared look about her, and a gun in her hand. Not the gun Al took with him. A smaller, lighter gun. But then, Fisher thinks, Lyle and Al didn't check her pockets. After all, she's just a girl.

She says, "Keys, Dad." Her eyes look like holes someone's made by pushing their fingers into her head.

"Bree," Fisher says, "what happened? Where is he?"

The gun's got a wobble to it. Lyle must have noticed too because he steps forward. She lifts the gun. "I'll shoot to kill."

"My, my, look at you. So step-daddy didn't want to come in himself and face his old friends. How about that. He sends his step-kid instead. What a guy, huhn?" He pulls out the chair then sits with one elbow propped on the table and blows on his sore knuckles. "No guts, see. That's been the trouble all along. Soon as things got serious, good ol' Brian bailed. Not that he told us—no, he didn't have the guts for that, either."

Bree's watching. How still her face is, her mouth uneven as an old piece of wire. Fisher wonders, has she shot Al? She must have, and the thought fizzes with the crazy luck of it, Bree making it back alive, but the fizz stings too. She's shot two men. Part of her's going to die, no matter that she had no other way out.

Her eyes flick to what's left of Grisby propped on the bed, to Lyle smiling at her, to Fisher. "You're scum, the whole fucking lot of you. Just give me the keys, Dad." Her voice scratches and jitters and she holds out her hand.

"I don't have them, sweet pea. They're in the van."

Her face twitches, like he's betrayed her. She turns the gun on him. "Empty your pockets."

"I told you, darling. I don't have them. I'd give them to you. I'd give you anything, really I would." His voice fades and even to him it sounds sad and lost.

"Just look at that. And you were worried about her, Mikey. Not so worried about you, is she?" Lyle shakes his head. "What's Brian planning? A run to the border? He'll love fucking socialist Canada, oh yeah. But you can tell him he can never run far enough. There are thousands of us, and we'll find him."

"Thousands." She hurls the word out. "You morons. How many of you are there really? Nine? Ten? But oh yeah, you have big plans. Let's take out a judge, let's take over the airport, let's take over the state. All you managed was to kill one cop. A rookie. And he wasn't even on duty."

"Half the story, that's what you've got. That step-daddy of yours hasn't exactly told you what this is all about." Lyle sits back, but it must pain him because he slumps forward again with his injured arm against his chest. "But then he wouldn't, would he? Didn't want his little step-kid to know he'd ratted out his friends. Who'd respect a guy like that?"

Her lips are so pale Fisher can hardly see them. He wants to tell her—*Watch out, he's luring you in. Get out of here while you can.* But part of him's furious with her, too. After all he's done for her, even this, coming out here to save her, risking his life, and she doesn't understand any of it, not even that he's not one of the militia, that he couldn't be. Christ.

Bree juts her head forward. "Know why he wanted out? You guys were so dumb. Had to make a big deal out of everything, trying to stir things up because you wanted the feds to come in so you could shoot it out with them. Brian was in it for the long haul."

Lyle's face has stiffened. "Like hell. He's working for the feds. Did you know that? Huhn? The jerk thought he was so fucking clever, showing people around the house for sale next to the Commander's, and what d'you know but a guy buys it and moves in. Only the guy's a cop. It's a set-up, see? Next thing, this cop's walking his dog in the woods every morning, and he lets it loose so he's got an excuse to come snoop around when it runs off. Al didn't like that. Thought the guy needed a bullet between the eyes, and that's what he gave him. Bang!" He's got his left hand up with the fingers out like a gun barrel. He pretends to sight down it with his good eye, then he laughs. "Bet Brian shit his pants to find the cop on his deck. Shit his pants so hard he ran all the way out here to hide."

Bree backs closer to the door. Lyle's out of his chair and steps toward her. She tells him, "Don't move!"

"Or what? Going to shoot me?"

Fisher comes around the table, steps over Jim's legs. "Leave her." He doesn't look at Bree. He can't. Instead he tells her quickly, "Go on, get out of here. Keys are in the ignition," but he keeps his eyes on Lyle, and Lyle's so close he could touch him.

Bree's voice sounds emptied out. "Don't even think about coming after me or I'll shoot you dead." Then she tugs the door open and ducks outside, a cringing movement, like she's afraid.

That's when Lyle understands. She's gone but he launches himself after her, hissing, "Bitch, you're on your own." For a moment the shape of him fills the doorway, and he must sense it too because he yells out, "Al? Al? You out there?" Only it's too late. A shot cracks through the air, and he jerks and spins across the porch.

Fisher stumbles after him. He's bellowing, "Bree? Where are you?" Beside his head the wall splinters, and an instant later comes the sound of the shot. Al not dead. Al shooting at him. But there's no stopping now. Where the hell's Lyle? He doesn't know. Fisher blunders toward the steps as another bullet shatters the cabin window just behind him. A grating sound—the cab's side-door sliding open. A moment later comes the smack of a bullet hitting more glass, and a thin cry. Fisher throws himself across the snow. His feet slip, his whole self tilts forward until he slams into the cab.

Inside, Bree's face so stark she looks dead. But she's staring back at him and he pushes her to the side and takes the driver's seat. He twists the key in the ignition. From the cold engine comes a mournful moan. He works the gas, works it until the motor catches. Then he yanks on the stiff wheel and sends the cab bouncing and lurching in a crazy tight circle, knocking against the edge of the porch, scraping past Al's pickup, the side-door open and his bags of supplies clanging and rolling over the floor.

Jim's truck's half-blocking the driveway and there, leaning

against it, caught in the glare of the cab's headlights, stands Al. He has a gun raised, but his face is a slick mess of blood. Fisher stamps down on the gas pedal and sends the cab careening toward him. A scream of the engine as he guns it, a jolt of metal on metal, then the cab's bouncing along toward the road. In the rearview mirror, there's nothing but darkness.

※

Bree lies on the floor all the way to Sumner. She must be cold—she doesn't rouse herself to close the side-door until they've gone a good couple of miles and even then, two windows are shattered and the warmth from the vents is dragged away through them. It's another few miles before she crawls over the groceries scattered every which way and unpacks one of the sleeping bags. When Fisher looks in the mirror, all he sees is the white square of its label in the darkness. A few times he calls out, "Bree? Sweet pea?" but she doesn't say a thing.

## 46

THE MOTEL'S A miserable place. It's so late the office is locked, and only a dim light shows through the window. But Fisher knocks, and knocks harder. Eventually the dimness shifts, then a light comes on. A woman opens the door a crack. Her hair's in curlers and she holds the neck of her robe closed with one hand. When at last she lets them in, she lights a cigarette and shoves the register at Fisher like he's more trouble than he's worth.

The room's no better than he expected. Two narrow beds covered with beige nylon bedcovers. A gnarled blue carpet. A door smudged with scuff marks. A lock that rattles loosely when Fisher shakes it. He slides the chain across the door, for all the good it'll do, and hauls over a wooden chair that he jams beneath the handle. Bree's on one of the beds watching him, the sleeping bag draped around her like a shawl. One hand's in her coat pocket, but the other's still holding her gun.

"Sweetie," he says, "why don't you give me that?"

She gives a quick shake of the head.

"You aren't planning on shooting me, are you?" He says it as lightly as he can, then wishes he hadn't said it at all because when she looks up her face is heavy with misery. "Sorry," he says, but she's already looked away.

No wonder she doesn't trust him. He's an asshole. A dumbfuck.

He unzips his parka and sits down on the bed farther from the window. "You should take this one," he says. "It'll be cold over there."

"Those guys are never going to find him," she says. "He's dead, you know."

Fisher's hand's at his chin and it rasps over his stubble. He says, "Brian?"

Her eyes tighten with scorn. "Of course, Brian. Who d'you think this was all about? Who else but Major Jerkoff?"

Fisher takes a breath and stares down at the carpet between his feet. It's dotted with scorch marks from cigarettes, and worn flat where other people, hundreds of them, have sat exactly where he's sitting. "I know," he says at last. "A bullet through the head. Naked in your bathroom."

He looks up in time to see a flash of surprise cross her face.

"You had to kill him, right? I can understand that, really I can." He's talking fast now, rushing the words out before he loses her. "I took care of everything—well, me and Grisby. Wrapped Brian in a tarp and dumped him in the river. We cleaned up so good you wouldn't guess, really you wouldn't. I even packed a bag for him, you know, to make it look like he'd left town."

Her eyes look small, puzzled. Her hand sinks under the weight of the gun and comes to rest on the bedspread.

"You called, remember? You wanted me to come get you. So I did come, only it was much later. Me and Grisby. No one home so we let ourselves in." He mashes his hands together until they hurt. "Didn't find Brian until we were about to leave."

She's tipped over on herself. "I called and you didn't pick up."

"No, I didn't," he says, "and I should have. If I'd known it was you—"

She's shaking her head, but her head's down close to her knees and her short hair brushes against her jeans. Her voice is so low he barely catches what she says. "I was so afraid."

"I'd have dropped everything."

"And then when you showed up with those guys, I

thought . . ." but she doesn't say it. Instead she swallows and lifts her head. She's let go of the gun. Her hand flinches away from it, and her eyes look old. "You must've seen what they did to that cop."

He shakes his head.

"I didn't know. I came downstairs because Brian was yelling. He was on the phone in the living room, yelling like he was out of his mind. I thought Mom had called and he was yelling at her, stuff like, *You've gone too far, I want out.* Fuck. I thought she'd finally told him she was seeing someone else."

"But it wasn't your mom."

"He didn't notice me. He was saying, *I'm going to fucking kill you for this* over and over, and then I shouted, *She can't stand you any more. Let her go.* He turned round. He must've thought Mom had taken me with her to Anchorage, like he'd told her to. Only, she hadn't. She was off seeing her guy down there. Of course she found a reason to dump me at home. Said I deserved it. I can't even remember why."

"She was going to leave Brian?"

"I guess, sooner or later." She closes her eyes for a moment. "When he saw me. His face. I thought he was going to kill me. He screamed, *Get out of here* and that's when I saw him out on the deck. The light was on outside so you couldn't miss him. Only, they hadn't just shot him, they'd stapled his tongue to his chin and cut off his ears." She wrenches her head to the side and Fisher realizes, this is the way she wrenched her head away from the sight of that dead cop.

"Brian closed the curtains, like I was going to forget what I'd seen, and he kept yelling, *Get out of here.*" She opens her eyes again. "That's when I ran upstairs and called you. I could hear Brian in the living room. He put on some Zep so loud the walls were vibrating. He was yelling but not *at* anyone, just crazy stuff. He must've come upstairs, but I didn't hear him. I turned on the TV and watched a couple of shows, and the whole time, there's that dead guy on our deck." She takes a breath and it lifts her shoulders. "I didn't see the door open. Then there he was. Naked. His eyes all weird-looking and he couldn't speak right, kept slurring everything. He had a gun, and he held it to my head. I pulled away. I tried to lock myself in the bathroom, only he came after me."

Fisher sits beside her. He strokes the side of her face where the skin's so soft it's like touching air.

"He called Mom a bitch and a whore, kept going on, said I was no better. He shoved that gun against my crotch. He was so stoned he couldn't stand up without holding onto me or the wall. Christ. I shoved him and he fell. He dropped the gun and I grabbed it. All I wanted was for him to leave me alone. That's all." Her lips twitch, her eyelids too. "He said, *Shoot me. Go on.* He kept shouting it, kept on." Her hands go up to her head. Fisher has to lean close to hear her. "Know what I think now? He wanted it over with, only he didn't have the guts to kill himself, not even stoned out of his skull. And I think I knew that, right then. But, Christ, he scared me. Spit around his mouth and his eyes crazy big. So I—I—"

"Ssshhh." He tries to hold her but she's all angles, all bones, her face hidden behind her arms. "It's over now, sweet pea," he says, though he knows it's not true, that it'll never be true.

"It keeps going round in my head. Like he's inside it now."

When at last she lets herself sink against him, her breath's hot on his neck. Soon she's asleep. He slips her gun into his pocket. He eases himself out from under her to turn off the lights. He stands at the window and peers into the frozen night. No sign of Al. No sign of Lyle. Maybe they're dead. Maybe they've crawled to the pickup and are going to troll through Sumner until they spot the cab. He's parked it a couple of doors down, but really, how much is that going to help? Out here, who could save him and Bree?

I should've killed them, he thinks, should have, should have, but he turns and looks at the dark shape of his daughter curled on the bed, and he lies down as gently as he can and holds her, like he used to when she was so small he could cradle the whole of her in his arms.

# 47

WHEN SPRING COMES—AND it comes fast up here in the sub-arctic, the brightness of the day suddenly too much, the snow lumping into crystals big as rock salt all shiny with their own meltwater—the cab emerges from under the snow. It was lucky, that sudden heavy fall in January, a mighty blizzard that clogged the town for days. Lucky, because the snow coming down so fast made Fisher feel invisible when he drove the minivan back to town, and dropped Bree at a supermarket with fifty bucks for a cab home. Then he headed away at what seemed a dizzying speed along the highway north. He ditched her gun when he crossed the river—did it matter whether her shot had eventually killed Al, or whether he'd frozen to death? Not to Fisher. But he thought about it as he took the cab north. Thought about how it could matter in the bigger scheme of things.

Crazy, heading north when such a bad storm was blowing in. But what else could he do? He didn't go far. Just far enough to reach the turn-out for a gully thick with brush, a place well-known in these parts because it was choked with dumped cars and broken-down fridges. The cab almost took Fisher with it as he sent it off down the slope. For a few seconds he saw it—the happy bear on its side, the phone number, the jewelled gleam of its lights—then it was gone, and soon even the twin tracks it had scored into the snow had been rubbed out by the blizzard.

He knew the cab would be found. But that'd be months away.

And it is found, one day late in the short northern spring.


235

What's there to dispute the story he's been telling for months, that the cab was taken from him at gunpoint? That he'd been forced to drive miles out of town and had no choice but to hitch back, just when the blizzard hit, confusing everything?

The cops scarcely swallowed the story, he knows that. But they were busy searching for the nuts who'd killed their buddy, and searching for Brian Armstrong, and a few days later they had four dead guys to deal with out at Moose Lake. As for Fisher, what did he have to do with all that? His daughter was Brian Armstrong's step-daughter, but hell, what did that add up to? And when the cab melts out of the snow, it backs up what he's already told them, though they bring him in to tell it once again.

Then it's over, and Fisher's walking out of the cop station and breathing in warm air that smells of mud and rotting leaves. He drives up Airport Road with his windows down and heads toward the hills. Out here there's a shimmer of green about the birches, a sparkle of drips caught on branches where the sun hits.

He's careful on the turn toward his hill. The water down in the old dredge pond is pooled under a crust of ice. The road's slick now that the weather's warmed and he has to fight the urge to hurry. No point risking going off the edge. No point coming through so much just to drown at the bottom of his own hill, is there? Not when things are looking up. Three months of short-haul deliveries across town and he's managed not to fuck up, has made every delivery on time or close to it. Now the guy with the Anchorage run has quit and the guys with families don't want it. Fisher does. What's left of his family's down in Anchorage: Jan with her new guy, and Bree still sulking about the move. But she'll get over it.

Soon summer will be here with its long days that run into each other. Soon he'll start work on his house again. No Grisby to help him, not that Grisby was ever much help. He'll wander the aisles of the hardware store picking out what he needs, and haul it home, and it'll be nothing like the times he followed Ada around that store. She doesn't call him these days. She took Lyle dying hard. Took it hard that the cops were out at Moose Lake to untangle the unholy mess of those four corpses, and took it harder yet when the cops put the blame on Lyle. Fingerprints on the knife and the shotgun. A cold-blooded killer. Ada acted like they came up with that theory because they had something against him, just because he was part of the militia, but still, she's a little afraid of Fisher now. And so she should be—she betrayed him to Lyle, and she must sense he knows that, and could tell her things about Lyle she'd do anything not to hear.

The sun's scorching the air. Didn't old-timers hang out their laundry to let the sun bleach it clean? Fisher thinks about that as he parks on the soggy snow close to his trailer. When he gets out he hears a frantic yelping from behind the door but he doesn't climb the steps, not yet. Instead he turns toward the sun and shuts his eyes and stands there, letting it all go: the unbuilt house, his lost friend, poor Pax waiting for the ground to thaw to be buried. He thinks of his young dog who'll leap at him when he opens the door, and how next week the dog'll sit beside him in the truck all the way down to Anchorage, the two of them watching the road together, and he thinks how good that will be.

SCOTTISH BORDERS COUNCIL

INFORMATION SERVICES

# Acknowledgments

M ANY THANKS TO my wonderful agents, Howard
Morhaim and Caspian Dennis, for all their work on my
behalf. A big thank-you also to Spenser Ruppert for taking the
time to give me a glimpse into the life of an Alaskan cab driver.

NEW FICTION FROM SALT

KERRY HADLEY-PRYCE
*The Black Country* (978-1-78463-034-8)

CHRISTINA JAMES
*The Crossing* (978-1-78463-041-6)

IAN PARKINSON
*The Beginning of the End* (978-1-78463-026-3)

CHRISTOPHER PRENDERGAST
*Septembers* (978-1-907773-78-5)

MATTHEW PRITCHARD
*Broken Arrow* (978-1-78463-040-9)

JONATHAN TAYLOR
*Melissa* (978-1-78463-035-5)

GUY WARE
*The Fat of Fed Beasts* (978-1-78463-024-9)

# ALSO AVAILABLE FROM SALT

**ELIZABETH BAINES**
*Too Many Magpies* (978-1-84471-721-7)
*The Birth Machine* (978-1-907773-02-0)

**LESLEY GLAISTER**
*Little Egypt* (978-1-907773-72-3)

**ALISON MOORE**
*The Lighthouse* (978-1-907773-17-4)
*The Pre-War House and Other Stories* (978-1-907773-50-1)
*He Wants* (978-1-907773-81-5)

**ALICE THOMPSON**
*Justine* (978-1-78463-031-7)
*The Falconer* (978-1-78463-009-6)
*The Existential Detective* (978-1-78463-011-9)
*Burnt Island* (978-1-907773-48-8)